Joey
Life in Ink, Book 1
Elouise East

Publisher: Elouise East

Cover Design: Covers by Jo

Editor: Maria Vickers

Beta Readers: Emma Brown

CONTENTS

Author note

If you would like to see any potential triggers for this book and any other books I've written, please go to this link on my website: https://elouiseeast.com/triggers

1

ETHAN

E than Wright studied the men surrounding him, trying to gauge which ones were gay. Usually, he had good instincts, but sometimes, he was off his game. Tonight, it looked like there wasn't much for him to get excited about.

"No one?" Christi asked in his ear.

Ethan shook his head. "I might call it a night. I have to work early tomorrow."

"Aww, no! You can't come out just to go home early," she whined. "I need my wingman."

Ethan chuckled. "No, you don't. You have enough guys checking you out that you have your pick. Choose one and have fun." He pressed his lips to her cheek and hugged her before weaving through the crowd towards the door.

Before he could exit, though, a guy sitting at the bar caught his eye. He was of similar build to Ethan, which meant his long-sleeved T-shirt barely contained his muscles, and Ethan could see tattoos peeking out from above the collar. He was a sucker for tattoos. All in all, he looked edible. The question was, was he gay? There was no way to tell from that vantage point, so he slipped closer until he settled against the bar next to him.

Glancing down, he saw more tattoos covering his wrists and hands, and he bit his lip to contain his groan of delight. The guy turned the beer bottle in place, eyes glued to its movement. Ethan took a chance and stared at him, noting the generous beard hiding his lips in the same colour as his dark hair. His nose had a bump on the bridge, indicating it'd been broken at one point, and his eyebrows were scrunched as if he were in pain or deep in thought.

"Everything okay?" he murmured, leaning on his elbow and turning to face the man fully.

The guy blinked and peered at him for a second before he seemed to register the question. "Oh, yeah." His beard moved, and Ethan assumed he was attempting a smile. "Lot going on. Thanks."

"Can I buy you a drink?" Ethan asked.

The man opened his mouth, then closed it, the crease between his eyebrows coming back for a long second before he glanced at Ethan. "Yeah, thanks."

Ethan thumbed at his beer. "Same again?" The guy nodded, and Ethan placed the order with the bartender. He held out his hand. "I'm Ethan."

"Joey." He shook his hand, and Ethan couldn't deny the literal spark he caught from him. "Ooh, sorry. Bit of static there."

"It must be my sparkling personality." Ethan winked, and Joey chuckled and shook his head.

"So, what job could hold a candle to your *sparkling personality*?"

Ethan stood from his lean when the bartender brought their drinks and paid for them before answering. "I'm a hotel receptionist." He waved his hand. "I know, I know. It doesn't fit my look, but I enjoy it, and I'm good at it."

Joey raised his eyebrows. "I never said a word."

Ethan huffed a laugh. "Sorry. I get that all the time and thought I would cut it off before you said it."

"I can understand getting fed up with the stereotyping. The world would be a much better place if we all listened and talked instead of assuming."

Joey resumed studying his new beer, though he didn't turn the bottle this time. Ethan could sense some underlying meaning to his words, and the lost look on his face was back.

"Okay, I'm going to be forward here. I like you, and I think we could have a good time together. Maybe losing ourselves in each other for a night. Trouble is, I can't get a read on you." Ethan rested his elbow on the bar again, tilting his head and studying the enigma beside him.

Joey's eyes flicked to his and held. He worked his jaw for a moment, then nodded as if coming to a decision. "I'd love that."

"Phew! Thank fuck I didn't try to pick up a straight guy! Far too many memories of doing that, and I don't want to anymore."

Joey's smile didn't reach his eyes, but Ethan would take what he could. "Not the best thing to do."

"Nope. My place or yours?"

"Yours, if you're okay with it?" Joey stood, and Ethan guessed Joey was a couple of inches taller than him. They headed for the exit once Ethan agreed.

"Do you want to follow me, or shall I drop you back here afterwards?"

"I'll follow you. It saves you coming out again later."

Ethan got into his car and waited for Joey to climb into the monstrosity that was his own. When Joey flashed his lights, Ethan pulled out and headed for home. What had made the wave of sadness flow over Joey's face earlier? He'd love to know, but it also wasn't his place to ask. He was a one-night wonder in this guy's bleak life, and he would do whatever he could to make sure Joey had an enjoyable night. It didn't hurt that Ethan would enjoy it, too. He wanted as much fun in his life as he could cram into it because he wasn't leaving this world until he couldn't fit any more in. The world could be a dark and poisonous place, but Ethan refused to cower in it. He could shine bright enough for two people—and tonight, he would.

He parked in front of his house, and Joey pulled up on the road a few doors down. Ethan waited until Joey joined him before unlocking the door and entering.

"Welcome to my humble abode. It's not much, but it's mine, which makes it a palace." He set the keys on the hook behind the door.

"It's nice."

"It's usually bigger, but with two giants in here instead of one, it's shrunk." Ethan bit his lip to see if Joey would crack a smile, and Joey rewarded him with a flash of teeth behind the beard. "Would you like a drink?"

"I'm good." Joey's gaze pierced him, and Ethan stepped closer, sliding his hands up Joey's chest to rest on his shoulders.

"You're sure about this?" he murmured.

In answer, Joey lowered his head and joined their mouths. The scratchiness of his beard was a welcome feeling against his face, but he distractedly hoped his slightly longer-than-usual stubble was enough to reduce the chance of beard burn. If not, he'd have to moisturise the hell out of his skin... His thoughts derailed when Joey's tongue flicked against his lips, requesting entry, and Ethan's focus narrowed on where they touched.

Joey slid his arms around his waist, holding him tightly but with a tremble. Was it need or something else? Ethan slipped his hands around Joey's neck and deepened the kiss, wanting him to forget whatever troubled him. Their groins rubbed together, and Ethan moaned into the kiss, enjoying the feel and wanting more.

He broke away from the kiss and stepped backwards, not letting go of Joey, which meant he had to move with him. Luckily, he knew the layout of his house, and he got them to the stairs, where he had no choice but to pull away.

"The stairs are a bugger. They're far too steep," he explained while panting. He climbed the steps as quickly as he could and turned right into the main bedroom. He spun and grabbed Joey as soon as he closed the door behind him.

Their mouths clashed, and they tore at each other's clothes. He needed to feel the warmth of Joey's skin against his own. When they were down to their briefs, Ethan pulled his mouth free, though Joey suckled on his skin.

"How do you like it?"

Joey licked over the area and lifted his head. "I prefer to top, if that's okay?"

"I love to bottom." He grinned, his eyes locking onto the canvas of tattooed art in front of him. "Are you into anything else?" He glanced up when there was no answer.

Joey studied him for a long moment before nodding slightly. "I'm a Dom."

Ethan groaned and dropped his head back. "I hoped you were. Thank fuck."

"Safe word?" Joey asked, scraping his teeth against his jaw.

"Coconut."

"Hard limits?"

Ethan blinked, trying to concentrate. "Whipping, fisting. Anything else is fair game. You?"

"No ropes."

"Don't have any." Ethan gasped when Joey latched on to his nipple.

Ethan's cock was so hard he was sure he'd blow at the first touch, but he couldn't help grinding against Joey's hardness. Joey grasped his thighs and lifted him—which was quite a feat and showed how much he worked out—before depositing him on the bed and crawling over him again. Their mouths met as their bodies thrust, reaching for the ultimate goal. Joey slid his thumbs into Ethan's briefs and slid them over his dick and down his legs, repeating the action with his own. When he lowered himself back over Ethan, he gripped Ethan's wrists and held them over his head while their cocks slid and dripped and rubbed against each other.

"Fuck!" Ethan moaned. "Please! Inside me!"

Joey lifted Ethan's leg around his back, and Ethan whimpered when he settled a smack against his ass. "Pardon?"

Ethan opened his mouth, then hesitated when he met Joey's gaze. "Please, sir!"

"Much better." Joey dropped a kiss on his lips. "Condom? Lube?"

Ethan glanced at his bedside table. "Top drawer."

Joey's grip tightened on his wrists. "Stay."

"Yes, sir."

Ethan bit his lip against the noises that wanted to escape as Joey disappeared for all of ten seconds—he knew it was ten seconds because he counted—and returned with the essentials. Joey remained on his knees, and Ethan splayed his legs, pulling them as wide as he could, hoping to entice Joey to hurry the fuck up.

Joey squirted the lube on his fingers and tested the limits of Ethan's restraint while he prepared him. Despite Ethan's mumbled requests for him to go faster, Joey took his time, which Ethan was truly grateful for when Joey rested the head of his cock against his entrance and pushed forward. Even with Ethan being prepared and bearing down, the head was like a fucking boulder being shoved up his ass. The pressure relented, and Ethan glanced at Joey, who slapped his hip.

"Up and over. Show me that ass."

Ethan scrambled to his hands and knees, and Joey slid his cock between his cheeks, nudging the head against his pucker several times. Then he pushed forward, and Ethan bore down until the head popped past his ring. Ethan panted, and Joey froze, running his hands up and down his back and sides, calming him.

JOEY

It took him a minute or two before the pain receded, but then he nudged back, wanting more. Joey complied, slowly thrusting and withdrawing in small increments. Ethan lost track of how long they danced before their hips met. Now, all the way in, Joey leaned forward, bracketing Ethan with his arms and kissing his back and shoulders. Ethan turned his face to the side, and they kissed. Their tongues met and explored while Ethan relaxed into the feeling.

He exhaled. "Fuck, sir. You're huge."

Joey chuckled, the sound vibrating through Ethan's body. "I am. I would say sorry—"

"Don't you fucking dare!" Ethan spat. "Sir," he added.

He could feel Joey's smile against his shoulder. "Are you ready?"

"To be split in half? Of course. I'm always ready."

The heat against his back disappeared, only to bloom on his ass cheek when Joey's hand met his skin, and he bit his lip as the warmth spread to his cock. Joey withdrew slowly, his shaft igniting the nerve endings in Ethan's channel. Ethan groaned and hung his head, his fingers clawing into the bed with some idea of holding onto his sanity. Joey paused, then slid back in just as slowly, sending waves of pleasure crashing over Ethan. When he did it again, this time stopping almost fully withdrawn, he slapped and soothed Ethan's ass alternately before sliding deep once more.

Ethan dropped his head to the bed, putting his hands against the headboard to stop him from banging his head with every slam of Joey's hips against his own. He couldn't even reach for his cock to stroke it—not that he thought he needed to. If he had any inkling of his own body, he would believe he'd come hands-free if Joey kept up the pace.

"Hands behind your back," Joey growled, and Ethan could do no more than obey. His body wasn't his own. It was Joey's to command.

7

Joey gripped his wrists in one hand and pounded into him, the slap of their skin loud, and Ethan had a brief moment to wonder about what the neighbours would think; then he didn't care because Joey let go of his wrists and lifted Ethan's body upright. He was sitting on Joey's dick.

Their mouths met in a frantic need, and Ethan wanted to wrap his hand around his cock, but he'd not been told he could. Joey's hips circled as they kissed, and Ethan moaned, gripping Joey's muscular thighs. Joey's hand tightened on Ethan's neck while his other encircled Ethan's shaft.

All it took was three strokes, and Ethan tensed, then flew over the edge, gasping into Joey's mouth while his brain went on hiatus. When the contractions ended, he slumped in Joey's arms.

"That was fucking beautiful. My turn." Joey groaned. He kept his hold on Ethan, circling his hips faster and harder, then tucked his face into his neck and held himself still and deep as he growled his release.

"Holy fuck!" Ethan said, not wanting to move from their position but knowing the bubble that surrounded them would pop soon.

Joey kissed up the column of his neck and along his jaw until he met his mouth. Their tongues danced as Joey moved them, pulling free from Ethan's body. Ethan winced but gasped when Joey's fingers filled him. He was tender, but Joey massaged him from the inside, rubbing his fingers along his channel. Ethan trembled, his mouth gaping, while Joey worked him over. Joey pecked a kiss on his lips and withdrew completely. Ethan dropped to the bed, exhausted, letting his limbs fall wherever.

"Holy schmoly," he mumbled.

"Where's your bathroom?" Joey asked.

Ethan dragged his arm up the bed and pointed at another door. The toilet flushed, and the water ran before Joey returned, the bed dipping by Ethan's hip.

"Let me clean you," Joey murmured.

"Mmm," was all he could manage.

A warm flannel wiped across his stomach, groin and ass. Then Joey pulled the covers from beneath him, and Ethan half-heartedly rolled to his side to make it easier. When the covers fell over him, he snuggled down.

"Ethan, you need to drink," Joey said.

Ethan blinked repeatedly, then gave up and reached for the drink with his eyes closed.

"Let me help."

An arm came around his back and lifted him. He lolled back against him, and Joey held the bottle to his lips. Ethan curved his mouth around the opening and sipped the cool liquid until he'd had enough. He rubbed his cheek against Joey's chest.

"Thank you."

"You're welcome. I'll leave this on the bedside table." Joey pressed a kiss to his forehead. "Thank you for a wonderful night."

Ethan sank back into bed, smiling, and when his alarm woke him the next day, Joey was gone.

He knew the way things were supposed to be. No one stayed over uninvited, but Ethan wouldn't have kicked him out of bed. At least until he had to go to work. He groaned and rubbed both hands over his face. He didn't want to work now. He wanted to stay in dreamland and remember what a magnificent night he'd experienced. Would he ever see Joey again? It was unlikely, as he'd never seen him before. Joey was probably just passing through.

Ethan climbed from bed and stood under the shower spray, thoughts of Joey not far from his mind as he went through his usual routine. After he'd dressed and had breakfast, he locked his house and got in his car. He'd never had a problem brushing thoughts of one-nighters from his mind before, but Joey wouldn't leave.

He turned the radio up as loud as he could stand, tapping his fingers to the beat and singing the odd bar, and pretended he wasn't thinking about the man. Even when he passed the club they had met at the previous evening and saw Joey's car in the car park, he thought he had imagined it. He continued driving but slowed down, finally turning down a side road and going back the way he'd come. He pulled into the club's car park and stopped a distance away.

Why was Joey's car here? The club wouldn't open until that evening, and there was nothing around here, not even houses. Ethan's mind conjured the sadness in Joey's expression, and he couldn't leave without checking on him.

Decision made, he switched off the engine and climbed out, wandering closer and closer. There was no movement, and no one sat in the front seats. He peered into the back seat and frowned. A mountain of fabric lay haphazardly, but a tuft of brown hair against pale skin nestled among it.

He gently knocked against the window, not wanting to scare whoever it was. The head popped up, and grey slate eyes peered at him, the crease between Joey's eyebrows more defined.

Why was Joey sleeping in his car?

2

JOEY

Joey Reynolds didn't intend for anyone to see him sleeping in his car, which was why he'd chosen a darkened corner of the car park. Unfortunately, he must've overslept because he'd planned to be on the road before dawn.

He stared at Ethan, who stared back. He sighed and looked away. Pushing the covers aside, he rubbed his hand over his face and head, slipped on his shoes and climbed out of the car.

"Morning," he said.

Ethan blinked at him. "It's too early for this conversation without caffeine in my bloodstream." He shook his head. "Get yourself organised and meet me at The Cliff End Hotel." He started to walk away. "Don't leave me hanging, Joey," he called over his shoulder.

Ethan climbed into his car and drove away, and Joey stood there wondering what the hell had just happened.

He did as Ethan ordered, though. He found some public toilets, got washed and changed in not the cleanest of amenities he'd ever seen, and checked the route to the hotel Ethan had mentioned. The man had been dressed in a suit, tie and waistcoat, and Joey could imagine him standing at the reception desk in a swanky hotel. He fit in perfectly. Just like Joey would've if he'd been in his old life.

He parked in the hotel car park and stood staring across the landscape. It had a magnificent view of the ocean, the waves crashing against the pier and the cliffs. He'd never planned on stopping at Whitby for longer than a few hours, but when he'd driven by the club, he realised how much he needed a breather, even for one night. And what Ethan had offered, Joey couldn't resist.

Inhaling the salty, cold air, he aimed for the entrance, hoping Ethan was there. He didn't want to be in public for too long in case anyone looked at him too closely. He could hide some things—like his neck tattoos—but he couldn't do much about his actual facial features. He was miles away from London, though, so he hoped it was far enough.

When he stepped inside, the white walls and dark furniture immediately took him back to the many hotels he'd visited prior. It was probably a four-star hotel—he hadn't paid attention to the information on the door—but what drew his focus was Ethan's melodious voice. Ethan spoke to a woman who had a baby on her hip and a large suitcase at her feet. She appeared tired and wrung out, but his tone was calm and comforting as he checked her out of her room. The click of the computer keyboards and mouse merged with the gentle music playing, and Joey relaxed in the familiar surroundings.

Joey stayed back while Ethan dealt with the people waiting. Ethan leaned in to speak to a colleague, who nodded, and then grabbed Joey's attention.

"This way."

Joey followed Ethan to an almost empty restaurant and pointed to a table while he carried on to the coffee machine. Joey sat, staring out of the large—and if he wasn't mistaken, tinted—windows offering a similar view to the car park. He could see Whitby Abbey in the distance and the lighthouse at the end of the pier. It brought back memories of when his parents had brought him there as a child. It wasn't often by any stretch, but he remembered at least two visits.

"I wasn't sure how you took your coffee," Ethan said, setting a cup in front of him with packets of sugar and milk.

"Thanks." He added a splash of milk and stirred it before sipping and almost burning his mouth. He covered it by rubbing his lips together.

"So," Ethan said, his hands around his cup. "Do you have no place to go?"

Joey sighed. He wasn't getting out of this without some answers. "Yes and no." Ethan raised his eyebrows, his jaw tense, so Joey continued, "I have a home in London, but I needed to...get away." He glanced out of the window. "I got into my car and drove. No destination in mind. Just stopping when I needed to sleep or eat."

"What brought you here?"

Joey gazed at Ethan and shrugged. "No idea. I've been here before," he said, echoing his earlier thoughts, "but it was years ago."

"Are you planning on staying a while?"

He stared at his cup and shrugged again. "I honestly don't know what I'm doing, Ethan," he whispered. "I just know I can't go back. Not yet."

Ethan remained quiet for a moment, and when Joey glanced at him, his forehead was furrowed as he stared out of the window. Joey let him have the silence, undoubtedly trying to figure out what was going on. He jumped when Ethan started talking.

"Answer me one more question." Joey nodded. "Are you wanted by the police?"

Joey shook his head. "I promise I'm not. I'm just..." He sighed, not wanting to go into what was happening in his life that made him want to run away from it all.

"Not ready. I get it." Ethan sipped his coffee, holding it in both hands with his elbows on the table. "If you found a place to stay, would you stop running?"

Joey considered his question. If he could guarantee no one would find out who he was, he would be happy to stay, and not only because Ethan was here. He liked how relaxed he'd felt breathing in the sea air. "If I could keep below the radar, yes." Ethan narrowed his eyes. "I promise it's nothing to do with the police. It's more to do with...the media." He had to give Ethan something.

"The media?" He waved his hand almost immediately. "Don't answer that. Do you need a job?"

"I'm fine for money."

"You have three choices, as I see it. You can get a room here, and I'll book it under my name so no one knows it's you. You can find a guest house somewhere and do the same thing. Or you can stay with me. I have a second bedroom in my palace."

Joey grinned at the mention of his palace. Despite the house being small, it had a big personality, just like its owner. "I won't put you out like that, and I won't stay here. It's too close to where I've been before. If you can recommend a guest house that can keep quiet, I'd be willing to try."

Ethan grimaced. "Unfortunately, most of the places around here are gossip mills. Everyone knows everyone in the hotel business. Whitby has famous people visiting all the time, and I'm going to assume you're famous enough to be noticed in certain circles, so it might not be your best option." He drained his cup. "I don't mind you staying with me, especially if you can cook." He winked.

Joey chuckled. "I actually can."

Ethan rested a hand on his chest. "Oh, be still my heart. I'd consider marrying someone for less."

"Honestly, I don't want to intrude in your space—"

"It's fine. Do you want to head over there now, or do you want to wait until I finish my shift? I finish at two o'clock."

Joey rubbed a hand over his beard. "I'll wait. I won't be there without you. It's not right."

Ethan stood. "Okay, well, you know where I live. I'll be home around two-thirty." He smiled. "I'll see you later." Joey nodded, and Ethan headed away, then stopped and faced him. "I know you said you have money, but are you any good at handyman jobs?"

Joey frowned at the change of subject. "I get by doing my own."

"Do you fancy some busy work?"

"Like what?"

Ethan stepped closer again. "Our usual handyman is off sick, and everyone is busy. We have some lightbulbs that need changing, a leaky pipe in one bathroom, stuff like that."

Joey chuckled. "I can try. That's all I can promise."

Ethan grinned. "It's better than what I can do." He tilted his head in the direction they'd originally come from. "Let me introduce you to my manager." He paused. "What's your surname? If you can give it to me."

Joey licked his lips. "Use Joey Rendall."

"Pseudonym. Got it."

Joey followed Ethan out of the restaurant and into the foyer. Ethan stopped briefly to let the other receptionist know where they were going and then pointed down the hall to a room at the end. Ethan knocked.

"Come in."

The woman sitting behind the desk was in her fifties if he was to guess. She had black hair streaked with grey, black glasses and wore a suit similar to what everyone else wore.

"Ethan! What can I help you with?" She frowned at Joey.

"Meredith. This is Joey Rendall. He's a friend of mine who's staying with me for a little while. He's offered his limited handyman services if you'd like them."

She narrowed her eyes. "How limited?"

Joey smiled. "I can do basic things that any house would need, but nothing major."

Meredith rubbed her forehead. "If you're sure, I'll take you up on that. We're seriously in need of someone who can help around here, even if it's just a few minor things."

Ethan clapped him on the shoulder. "I'll leave you with Meredith. He'll need to finish with me at two o'clock today."

Meredith nodded. "Understood."

Ethan disappeared, and Joey settled into a chair opposite the manager. She narrowed her eyes again.

"Are you legit?"

"On the up and up. No arrests or jail time. Not wanted by the police."

Meredith sighed. "That's all I can ask, really." She grabbed a list from an immense pile of paper on her desk, making Joey think it would all topple over, and handed it to him. "This is the list we have so far—that we know of. If you can try to fix what you can, leave what you can't, and add to the list anything else you find that you can't fix yourself."

"Okay."

"As for wages, I can offer just above minimum wage if that suits you?" She named an amount.

He opened his mouth to decline being paid but then realised how suspicious that might look. "Perfect. Thanks."

"Brilliant. Get Ethan to show you where everything is, and I'll have a contract ready for you before you leave today."

"Thank you."

"No, thank you," she said with a smile. "You're saving us at the moment."

Joey found Ethan back at his post at reception, and he showed him the handyman's closet, as Ethan called it.

"Sorry for throwing you into it. It might help to keep you off the radar if you're working and aren't around many people." Ethan grabbed a baseball cap and shoved it on Joey's head. "Even better." He chuckled.

Joey raised his eyebrows but hid his smile as he readjusted the cap. "It's fine. May as well keep busy."

He headed for the first job on the list, which was changing the lightbulbs in the corridors of the third floor. He carried the ladder with him, smiling at those people whose gazes he met but trying to keep his head down as much as possible.

By the time Ethan found him and told him it was nearly finishing time, Joey had lost himself in the mundane but occasionally physically demanding work. He'd enjoyed every moment.

"You ready to go?" Ethan asked.

"I'll just put these back, then yes." Joey carried the stuff to the closet, locking it up. "Oh, I need to see Meredith again. She wanted me to sign a contract."

Ethan nodded and led the way down the hall. "Yes, it would seem rather weird if you didn't want to be paid."

"Exactly what I thought." He planned to give the money to Ethan as rent and for any food or whatever else Joey might need to use or borrow.

Meredith had the contract waiting, and within seconds, they were out of the hotel and heading for their respective cars. Joey sat behind his steering wheel and realised he'd never felt so relaxed. At least, not since... He brushed that aside. He couldn't think about that now.

Following Ethan again, he tried to decide what he could make Ethan for dinner that night. He made a mean curry, or he could make lasagne. He'd have to see what Ethan wanted and go to the supermarket if he didn't have what Joey needed. It was a little unnerving how quickly things had snowballed since he'd met the guy, not even twenty-four hours ago. Had it really been less than a day?

He was able to find parking closer than he had the night before, probably because people were out at work. He grabbed a bag from the boot but left everything else where it was.

"Is that all you're bringing?" Ethan asked, opening the door.

"At the moment. If I need anything else, I'll get it later." He put the bag near the stairs, out of the way, and asked, "What would you like me to make for dinner?"

Ethan chuckled. "I was only joking about cooking for me. You don't need to."

"I don't mind. I like to do it to relax, especially after a long day doing..." He stopped himself.

Ethan stepped in front of him. "Look, I know you're hiding something, and it's absolutely fine. I have no issue with it. But know that I can keep a secret if I need to. If you want someone to confide in, I'm here. You don't have to watch your words with me."

Joey sighed and rubbed a hand over his head. "It's not that I don't trust you. If you've not recognised me by now, you probably won't, but it's still too...raw to talk about."

Ethan rested his hand on Joey's chest. "Okay. Offer will always be there."

"Thanks."

"As for dinner," Ethan continued, "anything." He waved his hand towards the kitchen. "Whatever I've got is yours to use."

Joey leaned down and placed a kiss on Ethan's cheek. "Thank you for everything."

Ethan smirked. "You're welcome. Now, I'm going for a shower. Feel free to join me—oh, I mean, shower after me." He winked and sauntered to the stairs.

Joey wanted to follow him, but he refused, not wanting to mess up their new friendship. He was beginning to like it there. Checking the fridge told him Ethan liked meat and fruit but not much else, and unless he'd already eaten them all, he wasn't a vegetable fan. There was some chicken, which he could use to make stir-fry, but he'd need to grab some peppers and onions. And maybe some tortillas. Ethan was also nearly out of milk, so Joey made a list, and when Ethan came back from his shower, all pink and toasty, Joey said he needed to go to the supermarket.

"Let me go. You stay here and have a breather. It won't take me long," Ethan said.

Joey offered him some money, but Ethan refused, and Joey set a note to tally whatever Ethan spent on him so he could pay it back later.

While Ethan was gone, he familiarised himself with the kitchen and where everything was, then settled on the sofa and rested his head back. He knew he needed to call his mum and let her know he was doing okay, but he didn't want to ruin the even keel he was on. He had people who counted on him, even those who worked for him, but he'd left Ani in charge, and she knew what she was doing. If she had a problem she couldn't solve, she would call him, and he'd answer.

The lock clicked, and he sat upright, expecting to see Ethan, but a woman came in.

"Hey, babe! I didn't see your car, but that doesn't mean you're not here!" She shut the door and then stopped, her bright green eyes boring into him. "Who are you? And where's Ethan?"

He held up his hands. "He's at the supermarket."

She pointed a sharp nail in his direction. "And who are *you*?"

"His new lodger."

She put a hand on her hip and pursed her lips. "This house is barely big enough for one giant, let alone two. Who are you really?"

At that moment, the door opened, and Ethan returned. "Oh, hey, Christi." He glanced between them. "This is Joey. Joey, this is my best friend, Christi." He pushed the door closed with his ass, and Joey jumped up to grab the bags from him. "I bought a bit more than I went out for."

He'd say. Definitely more than the peppers, onion, milk and tortillas he'd put on the list. Carrying the bags to the kitchen, he left the two friends to argue not so silently in the living room while he put away what Ethan had bought, which included crisps, more fruit, vegetables he was sure were just for him, and some milk, plus other snack food.

"Okay, then," Ethan said, smiling brightly. "I thought you had work this afternoon?"

Christi tucked her dyed blonde hair behind her ears and rolled her eyes. "Two appointments cancelled at the last minute. I have to go back at four o'clock for my final appointment, but I wasn't waiting around just to get harassed again. I thought I'd harass you instead."

Ethan chuckled, flicking the kettle on. "Leave Di alone, and she'll leave you alone."

"She started it!"

"And you can finish it and have a happy work environment again." Ethan glanced at Joey. "Christi is a beautician, but her arch nemesis is trying to take her clients." He looked at Christi again. "You know your clients are loyal."

Christi stared at Joey. "Please tell me you're straight?" she asked instead of responding to Ethan's words.

Joey cleared his throat. "Sorry, no."

She huffed. "Ethan, why are all the big ones gay?" she whined.

Ethan snorted. "I promise, not all big guys are gay, but we are. Sorry, hun."

"Are you a model?" She tilted her head. "You look like you could be."

Joey ducked his head a bit, trying to stop her from examining him too closely. "No. Just a normal guy." He helped Ethan with the drinks.

"I love these tattoos." She stepped closer.

"Oh, Christi. Didn't you want to show me those pictures on your phone? The different patterns you wanted my opinion on?"

"Yes! I'd almost forgotten. Let's sit down so I can show you without spilling my tea down me." She sauntered off.

Ethan stopped in front of him. "You owe me big time for this. I hate listening to her drone on about these designs, but I'm doing it for you."

Joey didn't think. He dropped his head and kissed Ethan on the lips. "Whatever you want in return."

"Whatever is a big word," Ethan cautioned.

"Whatever," Joey stated again.

He leaned back against the counter and blew out a breath. Should he stay, or should he hightail it with the next dawn?

3

ETHAN

E than's alarm woke him the next morning with its usual incessant beeping. So annoying, but that was the point. He also charged the thing on top of his chest of drawers across the room, so he had to get out of bed to turn it off. It's the only way he would get up in the morning.

Bleary-eyed, he stumbled into the bathroom and under the shower, letting the shock of the initial freezing spray wake him up before the warmth could send him back to sleep again. He washed, dried, brushed his teeth and dressed in his uniform before descending the stairs, pausing when he heard sounds from the kitchen. It took him far too long to calm his racing heart and to remember he'd invited Joey to stay with him.

Entering the kitchen, Joey stood at the counter, pouring beans on top of toast on two plates. Ethan didn't eat that early in the morning, but he hadn't told Joey that, and he refused to deny him.

"Morning," he said.

"Morning," Joey replied, a hint of a smile on his lips. "I've made coffee as well."

Ethan frowned. "I don't have any coffee."

Joey put the pan back on the hob. "I went for a jog this morning and bought a few things. You mentioned not having had caffeine yesterday, so I thought I'd make you some. And breakfast." Joey frowned. "I hope that's okay?"

Ethan blinked. "Yes. That's...fine."

Joey handed him a plate and some cutlery, and Ethan settled at the small dining table. His new friend brought their mugs over to them before going back for his own plate.

"You don't have to cook for me," Ethan said. "I was only joking."

"I don't mind. I'm usually up early, anyway. But today...more so."

Ethan cut up his toast and paused. "You didn't sleep well?"

Joey sighed. "I haven't for a while. It'll get better." He glanced at Ethan. "You're not an early bird, I take it?"

"God, no. Whoever invented time should have the early hours of a day shoved up their ass until it hits their throat."

Joey laughed. "Quite a visual."

Ethan shrugged and finished his mouthful. "I have a way with words."

"That you do."

They finished their breakfast in silence, and Ethan carried their used dishes to the kitchen, leaving them in the sink. "I'll clean them when we get back," he murmured. "I'll drive."

Joey nodded, and they headed for the door. As they passed the hook where Ethan kept his keys, he grabbed the spare key to the house and handed it to Joey.

"In case you need to get in when I'm not here."

Joey shook his head. "I don't want to be here when you're not here."

Ethan glared at him. "I trust you, Joey. Mother help me, but I do. You need this for any time that I won't be home, for whatever reason that might be. Take it."

Joey sighed and curled his hand around the key. "Okay, thanks."

They parted ways when they reached the hotel, Joey going for the handyman's closet, Ethan to the reception desk to relieve the night receptionist.

"Hey, Thomas. How were things?" Ethan asked, squeezing the man's shoulder.

"Morning. All good. No issues except for the couple in room 406. They called down a couple of times to say their TV kept cutting out. I took them through the usual, but in the end, they said they'd go to bed and not watch it. Might be something we need someone to look at."

Ethan pressed a few keys on the computer. "They're checking out today, and no one is scheduled to book into that room. It'll give Joey the chance to have a look at it."

"Joey?" Thomas asked, collecting his jacket.

"Our stand-in handyman for a bit," Ethan explained. "He's a friend of mine."

Thomas nodded and yawned. "Right, I'm off."

"Have a good sleep." Ethan smiled, focusing on the computer and starting up his morning checklist.

He worked through nearly all the morning paperwork before Charly arrived. The manager believed that having staggered start times worked best for the hotel rush times, so there were always two receptionists working at the hotel except between midnight and eight in the morning.

"Who's this new handyman I've heard about?" Charly asked, smirking at Ethan. "I've been told he's your tattooed best friend. You kept that quiet."

Ethan snorted. "He's a friend, not my best friend. But yes, he's tattooed."

"Where's he from? Why haven't you told us about him? Is he single? Is he straight?" Charly popped off a dozen questions Ethan refused to answer. "You're no fun."

"It's nunya beeswax," he said.

Charly frowned. "What?"

Ethan grinned. "It's *nunya beeswax*. None of your business."

Charly huffed but couldn't respond because their first guests arrived to check out. From then on, time flew. He saw Joey a couple of times, once when he found him to compare a list of empty rooms to Joey's list of repairs, in case he could do anything before the rooms were occupied again. He found him again at the end of their shift and drove them towards home.

"I'm having dinner at my parents' house tonight. Would you like to come?"

Joey shook his head. "You don't need me hanging on. I'll be fine on my own."

"I'd like you to come. I think you'll like them. Especially Dad. You can compare tattoos." Ethan chuckled.

"No, it's okay. I'll be fine."

Ethan sighed. "I know you will, Joey. I'd still like you to come. I like your company."

Joey stayed quiet until Ethan parked outside the house. "Why can't I say no to you?" Joey whispered.

"You say no plenty," Ethan said. "I just don't enjoy taking that as your final answer." He smirked at Joey and climbed out of the car. "Dinner is at five o'clock, so I'm going to shower and decompress first."

"Decompress?"

"Yoga," Ethan explained. "How else can I keep this giant body limber?"

Joey licked his lips, his gaze travelling down Ethan's body and back up again, making a wave of heat consume Ethan. "It obviously works."

Ethan rested his hand on his cocked hip. "Want to join me?"

Joey shook his head slowly. "I can guarantee I wouldn't be able to do any of it. Jogging and weights are about my limits."

"You could just watch."

Ethan winked and climbed the stairs, dressing in some leggings and a vest, before descending the stairs again. He grabbed a glass of water and found Joey in the living room. Ethan hid his smirk and ignored the man, setting up his usual video. It would take him an hour, but by the end, he would be relaxed and ready for anything.

He ignored Joey and rolled out his mat, settling down with crossed legs before he hit play. Closing his eyes, he followed the instructions. He could probably do it all from memory by now, but he enjoyed listening to it.

An hour later, he was sweaty but as relaxed as he ever was. He opened his eyes from his final pose and blinked a few times to reorientate himself. When he sat upright, Joey stared at him, his face red, his breathing shallow.

"You should've joined in," Ethan said, sipping his water.

"I think you did just fine on your own." Joey's voice was like gravel, and a shiver worked down Ethan's spine.

"Maybe next time." He rose, rolling up his mat and storing it next to the TV. "We'll be leaving in about half an hour."

Joey nodded, licking his lips, but didn't say anything. Ethan readjusted himself as he climbed the stairs again, the heat in Joey's eyes searing him even though he couldn't see him. He stripped and climbed into the shower, letting it warm up first this time. Unable to help himself, he encircled his cock straight away, needing to get the release out of his system. He pressed a hand against the cool tiles, bowed his head and closed his eyes. He brought up an image of him doing "downward dog"—an inverted V shape, which basically meant his ass was up in the air—and Joey sliding into him, gripping his hips to ensure he didn't fall. The blood would rush to Ethan's head as well as his cock while Joey pounded into him.

Ethan's hand pumped faster, twisting a little at the head, and he gasped as tingles flowed down his spine and into his groin. With every thrust of Joey's hips, he would yank Ethan back to stop him from overbalancing, sending Joey's dick right into Ethan's prostate.

He growled his release beneath the spray, stroking until he hissed at the sensitivity and let go. Leaning a shoulder against the cold tiled wall, he waited until his breathing returned to normal before finishing his shower. He wrapped a towel around his waist and wiped a hand over the steam-covered mirror. His eyes sparkled with a need that no amount of jacking off would appease. He needed the real thing, but he refused to take advantage of the fact that Joey was staying with him. Joey might not want more than that one night, anyway.

He descended the stairs to silence and wondered if Joey had run off instead of wanting to have dinner with his parents. Ethan wouldn't blame him. It wasn't like they were in a relationship, so there was no need for it, but Ethan didn't want Joey wallowing in whatever hell he was living in. If Ethan could distract him, he would.

Though why he felt the need to, he had no idea.

He found Joey in the kitchen, staring out into the garden, two travel mugs beside him on the counter. "Joey?"

Joey gazed at him, eyes sad, and Ethan wanted to wrap his arms around him and protect him from the world. But he didn't have a clue what he would be protecting him from.

"Ready?" he asked instead.

Joey nodded and picked up the mugs. "I made coffee for the journey."

"Thanks."

For once in his life, Ethan didn't know what to say as they drove. He always had some quirky words to knife through the quiet, but not this time. But it wasn't uncomfortable. When he pulled up outside his parents' house, Joey broke the silence.

"Anything I need to know about them?"

Ethan exhaled. "They won't invade your privacy. They may ask questions, but they'll respect it, without question, if you don't answer. Their names are Bridget and Alan, both are retired, and they hate that I don't live with them anymore."

Joey huffed a laugh like Ethan wanted him to, and they climbed out of the car. Ethan had sent a message to his mum earlier to warn her of an additional guest and to ask her not to pry too much. He knocked on the door and opened it, calling, "Mum! Dad! We're here."

Joey closed the door behind them and stood, tense and alert, as Ethan's mother came bustling into the hallway.

"Sweetheart!" She hugged him, and he kissed her cheek.

"Hi, Mum." He pulled back. "This is Joey."

Bridget shook his hand and smiled. "Nice to meet you, Joey. I'm glad you could join us for dinner."

"Thanks for having me."

"I'm just about to dish up. Go wash up, and it'll be ready."

Ethan led the way to the small downstairs bathroom, letting Joey wash his hands first. "I promise, they're harmless," he whispered. Joey didn't relax. Had he made a mistake in asking?

They settled down at the table, side by side, and Joey stood again to shake his father's hand.

"We don't stand on ceremony here. Tuck in," his dad said.

They hadn't even picked up their cutlery before his mother said, "So, Joey, what do you do?"

Joey froze for a second, then smiled. "I'm a tattoo artist."

Ethan stared at his plate, tucking that titbit of information away for later. His dad, however, perked up. "You are? How fantastic! I have a few tattoos myself. Got them when I was a hot-headed twenty-something, but I still like them now."

Joey smiled. "I'm glad you do. There are far too many people who regret them."

Alan nodded. "I can imagine most of those are the ones who chose their designs unwisely." He chuckled, and Joey joined in. Alan nudged Bridget. "Do you remember me telling you Richard

28

had his wife's name tattooed on him?" Bridget nodded. "He's trying to get it removed now they've got divorced." He snorted. "Even more expensive than the tattoo itself."

Alan asked Joey about the tattoos he did, and it seemed to be a topic Joey didn't mind talking about. Until his father asked whether Joey worked for himself or owned a business.

Joey hesitated before answering. "I have my own business in London."

His mother seemed to hear the reluctance in his answer, and she focused on Ethan. "How's Christi doing with that woman at work?"

Ethan smiled at her, trying to thank her with his expression and not his words. "She's struggling. I keep telling her if she'd stopped antagonising the woman, she'd stop trying to take her clients, but she won't listen. Hopefully, it won't matter soon. She nearly has enough for her deposit."

"That's good. I can't believe she's nearly there. She's done so well."

Ethan nodded. "She has. With all the problems she'd encountered at that salon, I didn't expect her to stick it out."

Bridget laughed. "She's stubborn if nothing else."

"That she is."

The conversation continued, but Joey remained mainly silent unless a question was asked of him. Ethan's parents kept the questions to mundane topics that didn't ask for personal information, and Ethan watched Joey slowly relax throughout dinner. Ethan helped his mother clear the dishes when they'd finished, leaving Joey and Alan talking about tattoos again.

"He seems nice, sweetie."

"He is," he said, filling the dishwasher.

"How long have you known him?"

"A few days," he hedged.

He could feel her eyes boring into him, so he stood and leaned back against the counter. "I don't know him that well, Mum. But there's something about him... Something happened, and he won't talk about it, so I'm going to help distract him until he can deal with it." He shrugged.

"And when he goes back to London," she murmured, and he could see the worry on her face.

"Then he goes back, hopefully, strong enough to deal with it."

Bridget stepped closer, cupping his cheek. "You are such a generous soul, Ethan. Just be careful with this..." She tapped the left side of his chest.

Ethan nodded. He would do everything he could to protect himself—and his heart—during the time Joey was with him. He knew Joey wouldn't stay there forever, and London wasn't exactly down the road. It was two hundred and fifty miles away. A good six-hour journey if he didn't take any breaks. Not that he'd checked or anything.

They said goodbye to his parents, and Ethan drove them back towards the centre of town. "Would you like to go out for a drink? We could call Christi and Kole to join us."

"Kole?" Joey asked.

"My other friend. He's a tour guide and works weird hours."

"I don't know..."

Ethan shrugged. "It's okay. We can stay home."

Joey stared out of the window for a while before sighing. "Okay, but can we go somewhere quiet and less likely for me to be noticed?"

"We can go back to the pub we met at. You must've chosen that one for a reason." He asked without asking, or at least tried to.

Joey nodded. "It seemed out of the way. Not too busy."

"We can do that. Do you need to go home for anything first?" Joey shook his head. "Okay, then. Let's go. I'll call Christi and Kole when we get there."

Within the hour, they settled at a booth and downed their second round of drinks. Christi and Kole had joined them shortly after they'd arrived, and Kole had gushed over Joey until Ethan had levelled a look at him. Ethan sat beside Joey, keeping people away from him until he blanched.

He glanced at Joey and licked his lips. "Am I cockblocking you? Because I can stop. I just thought you wanted some space."

Joey shook his head. "Nah, I'm not interested in them."

Their gazes met and held, and a frisson of heat pooled in Ethan's stomach, sinking lower and lower until his cock pressed against his zip. Would they end up in Ethan's bed again? Ethan could only hope because their first night was imprinted in his brain, and he wanted more of it. They'd barely scratched the surface of what Joey could do to dominate Ethan, and Ethan wanted to know. Desperately. However, he wouldn't admit it because he didn't want Joey to feel pressured.

But the thought of Joey's cock spearing him open again was almost more than he could bear. He swallowed hard.

"I'll just keep...doing it then."

He tore his eyes away and tried to keep his breathing even while he regained some control of his body. He could ruin everything if he jumped Joey the minute they got home, but he might not have a choice. His body had a mind of its own sometimes.

4

JOEY

Joey had promised himself he wouldn't touch Ethan again. He didn't want to throw his help back in his face by assuming he could touch him, have him. But he wasn't sure he could keep that promise. His cock was pressing against his jeans, and he could do nothing to ease the pressure. So, he kept drinking, although he alternated it with water—he didn't want to be *drunk* drunk. Just a little tipsy. He'd make sure to sober up before they left.

His phone buzzed against his thigh where it lay snug in his pocket, but he ignored it, as he had been doing for the past few days. He wasn't sure why he hadn't turned it off completely if he wasn't going to answer anyone, but there was always that little niggle in the back of his head that he needed to keep it on—just in case. He made sure to check the names of those who'd rung and messaged him, but he didn't listen to or read messages unless they were from Ani. Most of his family and friends knew they could send a message through her if they couldn't contact him—it had been that way for years.

"What about you, Joey?"

Joey blinked at Kole. "Sorry. I missed that."

"Would you like to come on a ghost tour? I have a few spaces left on the tour tomorrow, and Ethan here is too scared."

Ethan pursed his lips and glared at Kole. "I'm not scared, and you know it. I hate it when people jump out at you. I'm sure my heart can't take much more."

Kole snorted. "If that's not a textbook definition of scared, I don't know what is."

"I'll come. What time is it?" Joey said, dragging Kole's attention back to him and giving Ethan a break.

"Nine o'clock. At night, naturally."

"I'll be there."

Ethan huffed and said, "I suppose I could join in."

Kole lifted his glass towards them. "A toast to epic ghost adventures."

Joey clinked their glasses together and hid his smile by taking a drink. Ethan didn't look happy, and Joey made a note to ask him about it. It seemed like it was more than just because people jumped out at him.

They stayed for a couple of hours longer until Ethan yawned. "I'm done for. Gotta get some sleep."

They bid goodnight to Ethan's friends and headed out to the car.

"Do you want me to drive?" Joey asked, laughing when Ethan held out the keys without a word. "Will I end up pouring you into bed, too?" His voice tripped on the last word when the double meaning hit him. "I didn't mean…" He hadn't meant that, but now that he had the idea in his head, he couldn't stop it from running circles around his brain.

Ethan snorted. "In the unlikely event that I fall asleep in the car, yes, you will." He paused while they climbed into the car. "I've never been able to sleep in cars. Even as a child."

Joey started the car and clicked his seatbelt into place. Once he'd pulled out of the car park, he said, "I have no trouble sleeping anywhere if I'm tired enough." He hesitated. "Under normal circumstances, anyway."

Ethan didn't say anything, and the quiet extended the entire trip. Had Joey said something to upset him? If he had, he had no idea what it could be. When the front door closed behind them, Ethan faced him.

"I have no idea what you're going through, Joey, but if you need anything, let me know."

Joey needed something, but he couldn't voice it. It felt like he'd be taking advantage of Ethan's hospitality and expecting something he had no right to expect. So, he nodded and stared at the man who had helped him with barely any questions asked.

Ethan's lips curled at one side, and he stepped closer. "Or you could just stare at me like that. I can take a hint."

His hands touched Joey's chest, and Joey's restraint snapped. He banded his arms around Ethan's back while his mouth attacked. He crushed Ethan to him as he plundered and explored, using all his air supply until he dragged his mouth away to breathe. Ethan's gasping inhales tugged at Joey's cock, hardening it even more at the noises he made. He stepped forward, herding Ethan towards the stairs, but once they got there, Joey didn't make a move to climb them. Instead, he pushed Ethan to sit on a step and towered over him until he leaned back.

"Take my cock out," he ordered.

Ethan's hands trailed down his chest to his jeans, unfastened the buttons and dragged the material away from Joey's body, allowing his cock to strain upwards once free. Ethan wrapped a hand around his length, and Joey hissed but pulled away.

"I didn't say to touch." Joey rested his hands on either side of Ethan's head. "Take your cock out."

He watched the bob of Ethan's Adam's apple as he did what Joey told him. Heat washed over him as the shaft appeared, red and swollen and reaching for Ethan's stomach. Joey moved one of Ethan's legs to rest on a step, then repeated it with his other leg, spreading him wide enough for Joey to press between them. And when he did, they both gasped when their cocks slid against each other.

"Hands above your head." Joey waited until Ethan complied, one of his hands gripping hold of Joey's wrist still pinned by his head. Then Joey wrapped his free hand around both their shafts and held still. "You want this?" Ethan nodded, and Joey raised his eyebrows.

"Yes, sir."

"I want to hear everything. Understood?"

"Yes, sir." Ethan's nostrils flared, and his pupils dilated.

Joey stroked from base to tip, and Ethan's trembling exhale set Joey's blood on fire. Ethan's fingernails dug into Joey's skin, and he enjoyed the bite of pain. He stared into Ethan's eyes as he tortured them both with his hand. He thrust his hips as well, nudging the head of his cock against the underside of Ethan's, and the sounds Ethan made were music to his ears.

"God, I'm so close already," Ethan said, biting his lip, his chest heaving.

"You can come whenever you want to. But I want to hear it all."

Ethan closed his eyes and moaned, his hips moving in time with Joey's hands. He studied Ethan's expressions and body language, noting everything. What made him moan. What made him gasp. What had him trembling so forcefully that he couldn't help but grip Joey's arm harder. By the time Joey's release sparked down his spine towards his cock, Ethan's eyes rolled back in his head, and his teeth latched onto his wrist as his dick spurted over Joey's hand. The sights, sounds and feel of it sent Joey following, and afterwards, he rested his knees on the step between Ethan's thighs, lowering his head to Ethan's shoulder.

"Oh, fuck! I'm so sorry!" Ethan said, and Joey lifted his head, frowning.

"Why?"

Ethan stared at Joey's wrist, and Joey followed his gaze and then grinned. He had a perfect set of teeth marks around his wrist and no broken skin, but the indents were complete.

"I didn't mean to!"

Joey lifted his come-covered hand and turned Ethan's face to his. "It's fine, but as penance..." He held up his hand to Ethan's mouth, and Ethan's eyes darkened again before he licked Joey's hand clean, a hum leaving him as he did.

When he was clean, he lifted off Ethan and held out a hand. Ethan winced when he moved.

"Are you okay?" Joey asked.

"Yeah. Maybe no sex on the stairs anymore." Ethan gasped when Joey spun him around and lifted the back of his shirt.

There was a red line blooming across his back from where he had rested against the stairs. "Fuck, I'm sorry. I never thought."

Ethan waved a hand. "I'm good. I doubt it'll bruise because it's not like you were pounding me into it. Anyway, it's the least I deserve after marking you."

Joey's heart somersaulted at the words, but he tamped down on the words he wanted to admit—that he wouldn't mind having his mark on him always—and chuckled. "I didn't feel a thing." He rotated his wrist. "It doesn't hurt."

"Even so. That wasn't very...nice of me."

"Hot, though."

Ethan's lopsided grin appeared again, even as he turned to climb the stairs. "A little. It's time for bed."

Joey stared at his ass as he climbed but made no move to follow him. Ethan paused at the top, frowning down at him.

"Are you not coming?"

Joey smirked. "I thought I just had." Ethan rolled his eyes. "Not yet. I'm not tired."

Ethan narrowed his eyes. "Okay. Wake me if you need anything."

Joey nodded, and Ethan disappeared into his room. Joey's fingers traced over the teeth marks gently, not wanting them to disappear too quickly. Then, pushed by an urge he couldn't explain—or didn't want to—he raced out to his car and grabbed his box. Despite the risk of leaving such expensive items in his car, he hadn't wanted to bring them into Ethan's house. Not because he didn't trust Ethan but because he hadn't wanted to explain.

Now, though, he couldn't resist. He set the box on the dining room table and cleared a space, going through his usual motions of checking his tools and disinfecting everything he needed. Then, he settled on a chair and prepared his skin. The marks were already disappearing, so he had to be quick. Hoping Ethan was already asleep, he switched on his tattoo machine, the low-level vibration settling something inside Joey he hadn't realised had been unsettled.

Thankful that the marks were on his left wrist, he carefully traced them with the needle, inking them permanently onto his skin to carry with him for the rest of his days. It didn't take him long, and soon, the two sets of semi-circles were completed. He couldn't understand why he felt the need to keep them with him, but no matter. It was too late now.

He cleaned himself and his equipment and packed it all away again, taking the box back out to the car. Once he'd locked the front door behind him, he climbed the stairs and headed to the spare room. He didn't want to wake Ethan, and he hadn't even been given permission to join him, anyway.

As he lay staring at the ceiling, he remembered his phone and finally checked for messages. There were several from his family, as he'd expected, but only one from Ani.

ANI: *Everything is fine. People are asking after you, but nothing urgent. I do have some news. The funeral is on Friday. Eleven o'clock. Let me know if you need anything.*

Joey's breathing stalled, and he stared at the words until they blurred. Then he closed his eyes and let the tears overflow down his temples and into his hair.

It was too soon. He couldn't do it. Not yet.

He rolled over and buried his face in the pillow, praying sleep would come.

And it must have because a knock on his door woke him.

"Joey? Are you in there?"

"Yes," he croaked, clearing his throat before repeating his answer in a louder voice.

"Oh, good. I'll be heading to work in half an hour if you want to come with me. You don't have to, though. You can work whatever hours you want, according to Meredith."

"I'll be ready."

"Okay."

Silence descended, but Joey didn't hear Ethan move away for several long seconds. When he did, Joey flopped back onto the bed and sighed. He was exhausted. He rubbed his face and climbed out of bed, frowning when he saw his phone wasn't on the bedside table. Then he remembered and fumbled around in his sheets until he found it. No more messages graced his screen, which was a blessing, but it was still early.

When he was decent enough—with his wrist covered by a long-sleeved shirt—he descended the stairs and met Ethan in the kitchen. Ethan's eyebrows rose when he glanced at him, but he said nothing, which Joey was grateful for.

"Do you want anything to eat or drink before we go?"

Joey shook his head. "I'm good."

Ethan didn't look like he believed him but didn't argue. "Okay. Let's go."

The day went quickly because Joey kept himself busy. This time, though, when Ethan finished his shift, Joey opted to stay longer. He wasn't sure he could keep everything pushed down if he had some downtime. Too many thoughts crowding in his head, and he needed them to stay away, which would only happen if he kept himself busy.

"Are you sure?"

Joey nodded, fighting with the lightbulb that didn't want to come out. "Yeah, I'm good. I can get a taxi or something."

"Just call me when you're done, and I'll fetch you."

"You don't—"

"I know. But call me anyway."

Ethan's expression told him he needed to listen, and for once, it didn't pull Joey's dominant side to the front. Instead, all he wanted to do was go home with Ethan and relax in his arms for several hours. Which was exactly why he didn't do it.

Joey stayed for another three hours, and as he put away the tools in the closet, someone cornered him.

"Hello, Joey," David said.

Joey had experienced a few brief conversations with the assistant manager, but he couldn't get a read on him. As always, he tried to keep his interactions with anyone as quick as possible.

"Hey. Anything wrong?"

David smiled. "Not at all. I just wanted to check in. How are you doing with the list?"

Joey pulled it from the shelf he'd left it on and handed it over. "Not bad. There are several things I can't do, but I'm making progress on the little things."

David glanced over it and handed it back. "Good, good. I'm glad to have something nice to look at for a change."

David murmured the words as he walked away, but not quiet enough for Joey not to hear them. He narrowed his gaze at David's back. There was something about him that screamed smarmy and oily, but Joey couldn't figure it out. He'd try to stay clear as much as possible.

"Ethan, what are you doing back?" he heard David say.

"Just picking up Joey."

Joey closed his eyes as his body ached to get closer to the voice he wanted to hear every minute of the day. He resisted for as long as possible—which was barely a few seconds—then headed their way, frowning more as the conversation continued between Ethan and David.

"—didn't know you were friends."

"Yes, David. We are friends. I'm the one who brought him to Meredith."

"Oh, really? I didn't know that." Joey rounded the corner in time to see David lay a hand on Ethan's arm and lean closer. "He's nice to look at, isn't he?"

Joey's eyes narrowed on the contact between the two men, and his heart raced. His nostrils flared as he tried to regulate his breathing, but he calmed when Ethan met his gaze.

"Ah, there you are," Ethan said, moving closer, causing David to drop his hand. "I thought you were going to start living here."

Joey couldn't stop himself, even though he knew it was wrong. He grabbed Ethan's arm and dragged him closer, sealing his lips over Ethan's and holding his head in place while he ravaged his mouth. He wasn't a caveman. He wasn't. But he couldn't help himself. Ethan didn't fight him, just slid his arms around Joey's waist and kissed him back. That, more than anything, helped settle Joey, and he pulled back, resting their foreheads together.

"Sorry," he whispered.

Ethan smiled. "It's okay. David's an asshole."

"Regardless, sorry."

Ethan kissed him chastely and pulled away, threading their fingers together. Louder, he said, "Are you all finished?"

"Yeah."

"Let's go home, then."

Joey liked the sound of *home*. Even though his home was much further away than Ethan's house, the idea of Ethan's being home was more enticing.

They wandered past David and out into the salt-scented air, neither taking any notice of the man. Joey inhaled a lungful and exhaled, gazing out across the landscape.

"It never gets old," Ethan said. Joey glanced at him. "The smell or the view. I love it here."

"You never wanted to move?"

Ethan shook his head. "No. I don't think I ever will."

Joey swallowed down the denial because he had no right to argue with him. Just because Joey was getting all emotionally involved didn't mean Ethan was.

"I can see why," he made himself say.

Ethan pointed to the bench across the road. "I sometimes come and sit there when there's a storm. I can watch the waves crash into the pier without getting caught in it. It's beautiful."

Joey wanted what he could hear in Ethan's voice, though he couldn't identify it. Longing? Wistfulness? He didn't know. But he liked the sound of it. He liked the idea that it could wash away his sadness, his loss. Maybe even those emotions he didn't want to truly acknowledge, like anger and resentment. Because what man wanted to admit he was angry and resented the friend who'd left Joey with no sign of what he'd been suffering through?

He inhaled and held it for as long as he could, pushing those thoughts and feelings down once more. When he exhaled, it was shaky, but he was able to smile at Ethan, who'd given him a worried look.

"Shall we get some dinner before the tour?" Joey asked.

5

ETHAN

E than wished with everything he had in him that Joey would open up to him. He had no right to ask it of him, though, which was the only reason he'd kept quiet. But he could see whenever Joey was in pain, and it hurt Ethan, too. Whatever had brought Joey to Whitby and had him sleeping in his car weighed heavily on the man.

As they walked down the street towards Kole's meeting point for the ghost tour, Ethan pushed down his need to pry. But when Joey pointed to something in the distance, Ethan was distracted by the plastic wrapped around his wrist. Ethan grabbed his hand and pulled him to a stop.

"Oh, god! Did I hurt you that badly?"

Joey tried to pull his hand away. "No. I'm fine. I..." He sighed and stopped fighting, letting Ethan look over where his teeth had gouged into Joey's skin.

Ethan frowned. He couldn't see anything at first, then his eyes focused on the black lines where his teeth marks would've been. He glanced up at Joey, frowning.

Joey sighed and looked away, then refocused on Ethan again. "I wanted to keep the reminder with me," he whispered and dropped his gaze to his wrist.

Ethan licked his lips and stared at the tattooed marks of his teeth. Something warm unfurled inside him, but he couldn't get his hopes up. Not until he knew more about the man who had fallen into his life when Ethan had least expected it.

"When did you get that done? Did you go out after I went to bed?"

Joey shifted and gritted his teeth. "No. I...did it myself."

Ethan stared at him. "You what?"

"I mentioned I'm a tattoo artist. It's what I do," he murmured, looking away again. "That's the business I mentioned. I own a shop, but I can do simple tattoos on myself, too."

Ethan couldn't decide what he felt about that admission, but he was glad to learn something more about him. His stomach flipped with the image that entered his mind. The image of Joey tattooing Ethan somewhere no one but he could see. He being Joey. He gazed at the tattoo again and raised Joey's wrist to his lips, gently kissing the covered skin.

"It looks good on you," he said, his voice hoarse.

He didn't let go of Joey's hand as they continued on their way. Instead, he threaded his fingers through Joey's thicker ones and stepped closer, resting his head against his shoulder. They didn't say anything, which Ethan was glad about because he wasn't sure what he could say. He couldn't explain how he was feeling because he didn't understand it himself. It was too soon to feel anything heavy. At least that's what he kept telling his heart. It didn't seem to want to listen, though. Luckily, they arrived at the Whalebone Arch, the first stop on the ghost tour.

"Welcome to the Ravenwood Whitby Ghost Tour," Kole said a few minutes later. "I'm your host, Kole, and I promise you stories, scares and sass for the next hour and a half." He grinned, ruining the effect his makeup—a half skeleton—and outfit had on his guests. His cloak wouldn't have been out of place with Dracula, and his suit was perfect for a wedding—or a funeral.

Ethan wasn't scared about the stories themselves, as he'd mentioned to them the previous night. It was the people who sometimes jumped out at them during those stories that scared the shit out of him. Having actors dressed up like ghosts and goblins while roaming the darkened streets of Whitby could easily give the least scared person a run for their money.

Kole began his first story, a tale he'd told Ethan before, and Ethan tuned out, more interested in studying Joey. His...friend seemed engrossed in the words tumbling from Kole's mouth, a small lift to the corners of Joey's mouth whenever he laughed at something Kole said. But even though his outward appearance showed humour and happiness, his eyes showed the truth. His eyes were filled with a pain Ethan wanted to soothe, but he didn't know how he could help when he had no idea what Joey was dealing with.

"Arrrr!"

Ethan screeched as a man dressed as a pirate jumped out from a shadowed doorway. Instinctively, his fist rose to protect himself for a split second before everything else came back to him.

"Holy fuck, Kole!" he said as his heart rate calmed. Ethan swiped a hand over his forehead while the other guests chuckled.

"You weren't the only one," Joey said when they started walking again. "There were at least four others who screamed."

Ethan shook his head and sighed. "I knew this was a bad idea."

Joey slid his arm around Ethan's shoulders. "I'll protect you from the big bad."

Ethan poked a finger into Joey's side, causing him to laugh and squirm away before settling back against him. "Are you enjoying it?"

Joey smiled and nodded. "I love the stories. I can imagine them being turned into films. Elliott would love—" He stopped, and Ethan glanced at him, waiting for him to finish, but he didn't.

Patience was something Ethan had plenty of, but he wanted to know *everything* about Joey. More than he should. More than he needed to.

Before long, they crossed the Swing Bridge and wandered through the alleyways to the base of the 199 Steps.

"And this is the end of the first part of the tour. For those who are not joining us for the last stretch, I thank you for your company and hope you join me again soon." Kole spoke to a few people while others departed.

"Are we continuing?" Joey asked.

Ethan shrugged. "We might as well. It's a long way to climb, though." He smirked, side-eyeing Joey.

"I'm up for it."

Ethan nodded. "Okay, but don't say I didn't warn you."

Seven minutes later, they reached the last step, Ethan resting his hands on his knees as he panted to regain the air his lungs so needed. Joey wasn't faring much better, and Ethan snorted.

"Told you."

"Fuck, man. I didn't realise how steep they were. And when you said climb, I didn't think you meant at a speed close to jogging. Bloody hell." Joey put his hands on his hips and exhaled heavily, staring out across the view.

Ethan tried for a laugh, but it came out as more of a snort. "Welcome to Whitby."

Kole came over to them, a smile on his face. "What did you think?"

Joey clapped his shoulder. "It was great. Loved the sound effects."

Kole's chest puffed up, and Ethan bit back a chuckle. "I'm glad you liked it."

"How long have you been doing this?"

"Four years now. Originally, it was a side job, but when I saw how much potential it had, I went full time." He rocked his head. "Well, as full-time as this can get. It pays the bills if nothing else."

Joey held up his hands. "No shade from me. If you enjoy your job, then you're where you should be, as far as I'm concerned."

"Do you fancy a drink?" Kole asked Ethan.

Ethan shook his head. "I need my beauty sleep."

Kole scoffed but turned to Joey. "You?"

Joey hesitated, then said, "No, sorry. Not tonight."

Kole blew a raspberry. "Party poopers. Okay, fine. I'll drink for the both of you." He dragged Ethan into a hug and did the same for Joey before waving and starting his jog down the steps. Kole was used to the damn steps because he climbed them almost every night.

"You could've gone with him if you wanted to," Ethan said, though he didn't like the idea of it. He didn't own Joey, so he couldn't keep him by his side forever, as much as he seemed to want to.

"I'm not in the mood, to be honest." Joey sighed, sliding his hands into his jeans pockets and facing the view again.

He didn't say anything for a long while, but Ethan didn't want to interrupt whatever musings he was having. The view can have that kind of effect on people, especially on a night like that where the moon was bright in the clear sky, the sea calm and the surroundings quiet.

"I own Life in Ink in London. We do tattoos for people from all walks of life, often travelling to wherever the person who wants work done is. It could be two miles down the road or two thousand miles on a plane."

Ethan was gobsmacked. He hadn't heard of the business, but he knew about tattoo artists who travelled because they'd had them stay at the hotel before, and he'd also heard about them through the gossip mills.

"Busy then," Ethan finally said.

Joey glanced over his shoulder. "Extremely."

"Where's your favourite place you've visited?"

Joey turned back to the landscape spread out before them, and Ethan stepped close enough for their arms to touch.

"Italy. Absolutely stunning. My retirement plan." Joey smirked.

"Sounds lovely. I've never been out of this country." Ethan hummed. "Okay, yes, I have. But not since I was a teenager. My parents took us to France for a week every year during the summer. I stopped going when I finished school. Since then, I've not really wanted to go anywhere." Not until now.

"France is nice, too."

"Where's the furthest you've had to travel for someone?" Ethan shivered, the sea air finally making itself known.

"California."

Ethan gaped at him. "Seriously?" Joey nodded. "Don't they have tattoo artists in America?" Ethan bit his lip. "Sorry, no offence intended. I know you're great at your job."

"How do you know?"

Ethan waved to Joey's wrist. "You must be to be able to get those marks so well done on yourself."

Joey chuckled. "It doesn't take much to be able to tattoo."

"You're being modest. You have to be an artist to be able to tattoo." Joey nodded. "Why don't we head home?" Ethan murmured when Joey said nothing further.

"Race you to the bottom?" Joey said.

"No chance." Ethan snorted. "I'd fall and break my neck." Joey stared at him, and Ethan could see his face paling even in the weak light. He reached out and gripped Joey's biceps. "What's wrong?"

Joey licked his lips and opened his mouth, but no words came out. Instead, he panted as if he couldn't get enough air, and Ethan settled him on the top step and pushed his head between his knees, keeping his hand on Joey's nape and stroking his skin. What the hell? It must've been something Ethan said because there was nothing else around them. He thought back over his words. *I'd fall and break my neck.* Ethan frowned. Had something similar happened to someone Joey knew? Had Ethan inadvertently brought up the pain that Joey had been fighting hard to keep down?

"It's okay, Joey. I'm here. I'm here." He kept murmuring words over and over until Joey lifted his head.

"I'm sorry," Joey whispered.

"You don't need to be sorry. How are you feeling?"

"Tired."

"I can imagine. Are you ready to head down? We can get a taxi home when we get to the bottom."

Joey inhaled and stood slowly. Ethan stayed beside him and held onto him to make sure he was steady. He didn't want Joey falling down the steps and hurting himself. Threading his fingers through Joey's, he took them down the first few steps, Joey tightening his hold on Ethan's hand more than he expected. There was a noticeable shake to it, which made Ethan hold tighter, too.

Ethan wanted—no, needed to know what was going on. He hated that Joey was streaked with pain at every turn. Even when he seemed to have fun, there was a telltale sign he was somewhere else in his mind. He couldn't ask, though. All he could do was be here for when Joey wanted to open up. *If* he wanted to open up.

When they reached the base of the steps, Joey seemed to relax. Not completely, but enough for their hands to loosen their steel grip on each other. They didn't let go completely. Ethan led Joey to where the taxis usually waited for customers coming from the pubs. It didn't take long to find one or get home, and once they were locked inside his house, Ethan stopped in front of Joey.

"How are you?"

"Feeling stupid."

Ethan cupped his jaw. "Never feel stupid about that. Panic attacks happen. It's not my first rodeo."

Joey turned away, rubbing a hand over his face and head, leaving his arms over his head for a long moment. Just as suddenly, he turned back. "It's mine."

Ethan frowned. "What's yours?" he said, having lost track of the conversation.

"I've never had a panic attack before."

"Not everyone does. And some people go all their lives having them every day." He moved closer. "Whatever you're dealing with, Joey, there's someone who can help. I promise you." Joey stared at him, but Ethan knew his answer. He could see it in his eyes. He wasn't ready yet. Ethan held out his hand. "Let's go to bed."

Ethan spent a long time undressing Joey, showering him with affection as best he knew how, and when they settled into bed with Ethan as the big spoon for once, his heart broke all over again for the man he barely knew. How long would Joey stay around before his demons caught up with him? How long did Ethan have to hold him? Those types of questions kept Ethan awake most of the night, watching over Joey as he restlessly tossed and turned.

When Joey finally roused around five o'clock in the morning, Ethan was exhausted, but he was happy that Joey's eyes were a little clearer.

"Morning," he said.

"Hey," Joey rumbled in his sleep-drenched voice, rolling closer to Ethan. He rested his head on Ethan's pillow so they were only inches apart. "Thank you for yesterday."

"No problem." As he looked into Joey's slate-coloured eyes, he was again reminded of how much he didn't know about him. And how much he didn't care that he didn't know much about him. He should care. He should worry about having a complete stranger in his house. He should be concerned about introducing him to his friends and family.

But he didn't.

There was something about the connection between him and Joey that he couldn't explain, but he didn't want to lose it. He didn't want to push the man away and lose what they could have. What he was beginning to believe was their potential. Yes, Joey lived in London and had a business there. It wasn't like he could leave it behind... Only he had done, hadn't he? At this moment, his business was still running from what Ethan believed, and yet Joey was here. Could they figure out a way to make a relationship work between them? Would Ethan be willing to leave everything behind if they made a go of a relationship?

He wasn't sure, and that, more than anything else, kept him from announcing what thoughts were running rampant through his brain.

"Fancy watching a movie in bed? I don't have to be at work until later today?" he asked instead.

Joey lifted up and reached across to the drawer in the bedside table. The drawer slid open, and Joey grabbed something, but Ethan was too busy staring at his chest, which was warm and covered with some amazing ink. He still hadn't the chance to trace every line with his tongue.

And he wouldn't that day either if those handcuffs were any clue to Joey's plans.

"How about we do something else first?"

Ethan slid his arms up Joey's arms to his shoulders, then let go and laid them on the pillow above him.

"I'm sure the movie will be there when we're done."

Joey clicked his tongue. "I don't know. This may take a while."

He straddled Ethan's chest, bringing his impressively erect cock to the forefront of Ethan's vision and attention. His mouth watered, but he couldn't do anything until Joey said he could. He also couldn't keep his eyes away from that magnificent dick.

The cool leather wrapped around Ethan's wrists as Joey fastened the cuffs. When he finished, he slid the key into Ethan's hand.

"Hold tight to that."

Ethan gaped. "You can put it on the bedside table. I might let go and lose it."

Joey stared at him with a look that both set fire to his groin and had him curling into a figurative submissive ball.

"Yes, sir." He tightened his hold around the key. He had a spare, but he couldn't remember if it was in the bedside drawer or not.

"Open."

Joey didn't need to explain. Ethan opened his mouth, and Joey rested the head of his cock on Ethan's lower lip. Ethan wanted to lick it, but he stayed still, eyes fixed on Joey, awaiting orders. Joey's mouth curved.

"Good. Lick."

Ethan did, almost groaning with the taste that exploded over his tongue. He always loved the slightly musky taste and smell of his partners, especially if they'd just woken up. Sleep musk, he called it. The name might catch on one day.

His eyelids fluttered closed as his tongue lapped and licked and laved the head. Then Joey slid further inside, and Ethan moaned. He tugged on the cuffs, wanting to touch Joey, wanting to pull him closer, but he couldn't. He could've lifted his head, but where was the fun in that?

Joey slid deeper and deeper until he touched the back of Ethan's throat. Ethan had been expecting it, so he didn't gag, and he loved it. Being held in place with the cuffs while Joey gave him enough cock to stop his breathing was everything he ever imagined it could be.

Maybe he enjoyed breath play a little more than he realised.

6

JOEY

Watching the dilation of Ethan's eyes was a wonder Joey would never tire of. He focused fully on the man, wanting to push away any encroaching thoughts about what had happened the previous evening. Despite Joey's size, Ethan didn't gag, which was a heady experience. Tears brimmed along his eyelashes, spilling over whenever he blinked, but Ethan kept steady while Joey used his mouth for his pleasure.

"Fuck! You're so good. Taking what I'm giving you like you were born for it," he murmured as he thrust and withdrew into the warm cavern. With gritted teeth, he pulled himself free and shuffled down Ethan's body until they were face-to-face again. Joey wiped away Ethan's tears. "Fucking perfect."

Ethan's nostrils flared as he regained his breathing, only for Joey to take it again with a hard and deep kiss. Joey closed his eyes, concentrating on the feel of Ethan's tongue against his, battling for a dominance Ethan wouldn't win. The cuffs rattled against the bed, and Joey softened the kiss, gently pulling back.

"Ready for more?"

Ethan groaned and rolled his hips against Joey's body. "Yes, please."

Joey wasted no time, prepping him as quickly as he could so Ethan would only feel pleasure when Joey entered. He rolled on a condom and slicked it, resting his cock against Ethan's entrance. Meeting Ethan's gaze, he pressed forward ever so slowly, keeping eye contact the entire time. Ethan's mouth gaped as Joey slid deeper. From the corner of his eye, he watched the flush cover Ethan's chest and wanted to press his lips there to see if it was as warm as it looked.

Fully seated, he paused for a few seconds before withdrawing and sliding deep again. He did it a few times, then picked up his speed. Pleasure tingled down his spine, pooling in his groin. He stopped and panted, Ethan contracting around him even before his orgasm found him. Joey hooked his arms under Ethan's legs and leaned down, resting his hands on the bed beside Ethan's chest.

"You look fucking amazing like this."

"Please, Sir! Please! I'm so close!" Sweat dripped down Ethan's temples into his hairline, and he bit his bottom lip, writhing beneath Joey.

Joey didn't reply. He held Ethan steady, withdrew and slammed back in, drawing a litany of chanted words from Ethan's mouth. Joey pounded into him, chasing the ultimate pleasure. The slap of skin on skin, the words falling from Ethan and the sight before him sent Joey soaring faster than he'd ever come before. He kept his rhythm even as his mind blanked and Ethan contracted around him, finding his own release. Finally, he held himself deep and groaned through the last twitches of his orgasm before panting against Ethan's chest. He released Ethan's legs but, otherwise, kept his position, pressing his lips against Ethan's sweat-slicked skin.

"Sorry," he said. "I usually last longer than that." Any other time, he would've felt bad about it, but he knew Ethan had climaxed, so that was the main thing.

"Sorry? Jeez. If you do any better, I'll probably not survive it."

The cuffs rattled, and Joey lifted his head. Wincing, he pulled free from Ethan's channel and threw the condom into the bin by the bed. He reached up and pried open Ethan's hand, where it had clutched at the key so tightly it had left an imprint in his palm. Joey unlocked the cuffs and massaged Ethan's wrists to get the blood flowing again.

"Ah, pins and needles." Ethan groaned, flexing his fingers.

"Sorry. Maybe you were in that position too long."

Ethan shook his head, even as he grimaced. "No. It was perfect."

"Let me get a cloth."

Joey rose from the bed and wet a flannel in the bathroom, returning to clean Ethan's stomach, cock and hole. The pucker twitched and made Joey want another go at it, but he didn't want to push Ethan too hard.

"Thanks," Ethan said once Joey finished cleaning him. "Get back in here so we can watch that movie."

"Let me grab some food for you first," Joey said, slipping on some boxers. "I'll even bring you a coffee."

"Don't become even more perfect. I might not let you go."

Ethan met his gaze, and something sparked between them, but Joey didn't answer. Instead, he strode for the kitchen, trying to push down the butterflies in his stomach at the words. This was a stopgap only. He couldn't put down roots here. He had a life. Though he didn't feel the urge to go back as harshly as he had before.

And that was a problem he would eventually have to face.

Two days later, Joey knelt by a socket while he swapped it out for a new, unbroken one. He'd done it many times in the tattoo shop, so it wasn't a hardship to do it here. It didn't hurt that he was in earshot of Ethan, whose voice was like a balm to his hurts.

Listening to Ethan was the excuse he gave himself for not paying attention to his surroundings. From one minute to the next, he went from screwing the socket back in place to hearing a squeal and being surrounded by three women who were all talking over one another.

"Oh, my god! It's you! I can't believe you're here! I never thought I'd see you in person! Oh, my god! Is it really you? You're amazing! You have so much talent! I can't believe you get to work with all those celebrities! Oh, my god! Oh, my god!"

Joey couldn't differentiate which woman said what, but his heart hammered in his chest, and his mouth went dry. He'd let his guard down, and now he'd have to leave. He tried to extricate himself from the woman, but they were tugging on his sleeves and had their hands on his chest as they spoke. His brain threw images at him, and he lost track of what was the present and what was the past. Memories of him laughing on a night out, drinking with friends, smiling for photographs with his clients, crying with his head in his hands, sobbing through the pain of his loss.

Until a voice blasted through it all.

"Excuse me, ladies. I think it's time for you to head to your rooms, don't you?" Ethan said.

"But we just—"

"You just got overexcited and need to rest now." Ethan's voice was firm, and the women stepped back, shocked. "Please head over to the reception desk, and my colleague will see that you are checked in quickly. Just over there." He pointed towards the desk and herded the women off. They kept looking back but followed his lead. Ethan turned back to him and rested his hand on his biceps. "Come with me."

Joey couldn't do anything else. Lethargy claimed his body, and he stumbled next to Ethan, who kept a grip on him. They entered the staff room, where they took their breaks, and Ethan led him to a chair in the corner.

"Sit. I'll get you a drink."

Joey stared at his shaking hands, clenching them into fists and spreading them again repeatedly. His breath heaved in and out of his chest, and he tried to slow it down, but his heart had no qualms about continuing to pound hard enough to jump out of his chest. He ran his fingers through his hair, clenching at the strands and resting his elbows on his knees. What the fuck was he going to do? He had to get out of there before the media turned up because there was no way those women were going to keep quiet about his whereabouts. All he needed was for one post on social media to mention seeing him, and everyone would be here quicker than Concorde used to fly.

"Here you go," Ethan said, plucking Joey from his circling thoughts. He knelt in front of Joey and held out a glass of water.

Joey's hands shook as he took it, but Ethan cradled his hands around the glass, helping him to drink a few sips. The liquid was icy enough going down his throat that it settled him a little. His heart rate decreased, as did his breathing.

"Sorry," he said.

"You need to stop apologising."

Joey glanced up at Ethan, who had taken the glass once Joey had enough and set it on the table near them. "I have a lot to apologise for. This especially." He waved in the approximate direction of the hotel foyer.

Ethan laid a hand on Joey's arm and squeezed. "You have nothing to apologise for."

Joey snorted. "I have *everything* to apologise for. Except maybe bringing business to the hotel once my whereabouts are made public."

Ethan raised his eyebrows but didn't comment. He had every right to ask. "Let's go home, and we can figure out what's going on from there."

Joey shook his head. "You have to work. I'll be fine. I'll—"

"Do as you're told, for once." Ethan's expression brooked no argument, and Joey found his mouth twitching up into a smile.

"Yes, sir."

Ethan nodded. "Stay here for a moment, and I'll speak with Meredith." He handed Joey the glass, which he took with now steady hands, and said, "Drink it all. I'll be back in a minute."

Joey blew out his breath once Ethan had closed the door behind him. There was no "figuring out" what he should do because there was only one option. He needed to leave before he brought more scrutiny to Ethan than the man deserved. The journalists were no joke to deal with, especially when they found a worthwhile story.

And Joey's story was worthwhile in that he'd gone "missing" for far too long.

"I hear we have a celebrity in the house."

Joey jerked his head up, having not heard the door open, and stared at David. Of all the people he hadn't wanted to see, that man was at the top of the list. There was something about him that Joey didn't like, and he was the last on the list of those he wanted to find out about what happened. Luck wasn't in his favour that day, it seemed.

"They got it wrong."

David's mouth quirked. "Really? How unfortunate." He stepped closer, and though still half a room away, it was too close for Joey's comfort. "They seemed very clear that you were someone worth noting. If you're hoping to keep your head down, it seems like it hasn't worked."

Jocy stood. "I'm not who they think I am."

"Okay." David nodded slowly. "They seem adamant, though."

Joey strode to the sink and placed the glass inside. He couldn't wash it. He needed to get out of there. David was reaching for an answer Joey refused to give him. When he reached the door, his hand clasped around the handle, David spoke again.

"Gossip is a funny thing. It can take the most innocent of statements and tweak and fold and twist until it becomes something completely different. Be careful, Mr Reynolds."

Joey didn't look back, not wanting to see if David's face revealed the truth of the threat he'd just made. It hadn't slipped his notice that David used his real name, not the pseudonym he'd given Meredith. Ethan strode towards him as he exited, eyebrows raised.

"Everything okay?"

Joey shook his head and headed for the exit, not caring if Ethan followed or not. He pulled his hat further down on his head and hunched his shoulders, shoving his hands into his pockets. Ethan's car unlocked as he reached it, and he slid inside without a word. Ethan slipped in beside him and started the engine. He didn't hesitate and drove straight home.

Staring out of the window, Joey worked through everything he had to grab from the house before he could leave. He needed to give Ethan an explanation, too. It was the least he could do, especially if journalists were going to be bugging him because someone told him of their connection. He had a feeling David wouldn't be as quiet as people expected him to be.

When the front door of his current sanctuary closed behind them, Joey faced Ethan. "I have some explaining to do."

"You don't need to explain anything you don't want to."

Joey snorted and shook his head. "Yeah, I do. I've drawn you into this, which means you need to know what might come your way."

Ethan blinked at him. "Okay." He sighed. "I think we need coffee for this." He slipped past Joey and disappeared.

Joey waited a few minutes before following and settling into a chair at the table. He had no idea where to start with his story. He wasn't even sure if he could voice some of it. But Ethan deserved the truth. His life might be irrevocably changed by hiding Joey away from prying eyes.

A mug appeared in front of him, the scent of coffee relaxing his shoulders. "Thanks," he said.

Ethan sat opposite him and sipped the steaming brew, seemingly uncaring of scalding his mouth. "So…"

Joey wrapped both hands around the piping hot mug and let the heat warm him as far as it could reach. "My real name is Joey Reynolds. I own a tattoo business in London called Life in Ink. That's the truth. What I neglected to say was that we tattoo celebrities regularly. My business comprises four artists, including myself, who often travel across the country to meet with celebrities to tattoo them." He licked his lips. "As you can imagine, I'm in the public eye a lot. It's no secret what I do or for whom, except for the NDAs I've signed, stopping me from sharing certain information I see or hear. That means, when something happens, it becomes public knowledge quickly." He scraped his lower teeth over his upper lip, unsure if he could continue.

"I'm assuming something big happened. You don't need to tell me."

Ethan's simple acceptance of Joey's words had his shoulders unwinding further. "I do. I need to tell someone. I need to tell *you*." He glanced up, becoming ensnared in Ethan's gaze. "You've given me so much. Even things I can't explain. I owe you everything. Instead, I'm bringing chaos down on you."

"Pfft. Chaos is good for the soul." Ethan winked at him, making Joey chuckle, half-hearted though it was.

He blew out a breath, squaring his shoulders to take the weight of the pain he would feel once the words started flowing.

"Elliott Kennedy." He glanced up to see if the name registered with Ethan, but his expression stayed the same. "My best friend." He huffed a laugh. "Always getting into trouble, ever since we met in high school. High on life. Loved without question. Fearless."

Joey swallowed, nostrils flaring as he tried to take in enough oxygen. "We'd been at a party. A fairly high-profile one. Elliott was tipsy, the same as me, but not overly drunk. He disappeared for a while, as he usually did when he was on the prowl for a partner, but eventually, he made his way back to me. We called a taxi and headed home. I dropped Elliott off first, then the taxi took me to my place."

Joey inhaled, trying to stop the wave of emotion threatening to close his throat. His eyes burned, and he breathed through it all, pushing everything back.

"I visited him the next day because he'd asked me to tattoo him. I knew he'd be hungover, so I didn't go over until after lunch, taking some food and coffee with me to perk him up." His stomach roiled. "I let myself in as I always did. When he didn't answer when I called his name, I went searching. I found him..." He exhaled. "I found him hanging from the bannister."

Images flashed through his head, taking him through the scene over and over, still trying to figure out why Elliott had done it. It made no sense. Joey had seen nothing to advertise that Elliott had felt depressed or worthless or anything like that. It had come as a complete shock to him. He'd spent more hours than he wanted to admit trying to figure out what he'd missed. What had happened to make Elliott desperate enough to end things? Joey had yet to find the answer. And that was something that hurt more than anything else. How could Joey trust himself when he couldn't see that his best friend was in such pain?

"It wasn't your fault, Joey," Ethan said, reaching across the table to cover Joey's hands with his own. "Sometimes, you can't see inside of someone, no matter how close you are to them. Some people are good at hiding."

"He was my best friend, Ethan. How could I not see it?" A drop of water hit his hand, his tears no longer held back.

"It's not your fault." The words wouldn't penetrate Joey's pain, though he understood Ethan was trying to help. "What made you come here?" Ethan asked.

"After I called the police and made a statement, people flocked to the shop, trying to get news and photos. It was a circus. I couldn't deal with it. So I ran. Just up and left. Kept driving and stopping to sleep in my car, then driving again. I only answered messages from Ani, the assistant manager of my shop. I've not spoken to anyone else since, except for the police, and that was only once."

"I can understand you needing to hide. That would've been overwhelming," Ethan said.

Joey inhaled and met Ethan's gaze. "I can't stay any longer. I have to leave."

7

ETHAN

E than swallowed down the lump that had stuck in his throat at Joey's words. He'd always known Joey wouldn't be there forever, but he'd hoped he had more time.

"If you believe you need to go…" Ethan said.

"If I don't, you're going to end up on the front page of the newspaper, spread across social media, plus wherever else people decide to put your picture up. They won't leave you alone. Just as they don't leave me alone."

"They don't know you're here," Ethan countered.

"And how long do you think those women will keep quiet? They'll tell people where they saw me, then David will corroborate it, and then they'll find out about you, and it won't take long for them to realise where you live. If I know the media as well as I think I do, they'll be camping outside within two hours."

Joey gritted his teeth and shook his head, but Ethan focused on his words.

"What was that about David?"

Joey scoffed. "He knows who I am. He called me by my real name as I left today as if he'd known all along." The crease between Joey's eyebrows deepened. "He implied he would speak with the media and twist the truth of what happened here."

"Fucking asshole," Ethan murmured. He'd never liked the man, and this proved his reticence was well-founded. "I'd like you to stay," he said finally.

Joey lifted his head, staring right into Ethan's eyes. "I want to, but I can't put you through that. It's not fair after everything you've done for me."

"Isn't that my decision?"

Joey lowered his head to rest on his crossed arms, and Ethan sat quietly, letting him work through his thoughts. He pulled his phone from his pocket and searched for "Joey Reynolds." He wasn't looking for more information than what Joey had given him, but he wanted to see if anything mentioned where Joey was. As he scrolled through the results, only checking for glaringly obvious headlines, Joey's phone rang.

Joey banged his head against his arms three times, then grabbed his phone and stared at it. "And so the circus begins." He lay it face down on the table and wrapped his hands around his mug, which must've gone cold by now.

Ethan put his phone down, too. "I can't see any news about you being here yet."

"It won't take long."

Ethan raised his eyebrows and met Joey's gaze. "What do you *want* to do, Joey?"

"It doesn't matter what I want. I signed up for this when I started taking on celebrity clients and then allowed it to continue when I employed more artists. My opinion no longer matters."

"It matters to me."

Joey's eyes widened, and Ethan's mouth curled at having shocked him. "I like you a lot, Ethan. If I had a choice, I'd stay. At least for a little while longer."

Ethan rose and knelt beside Joey. "Then stay a little while longer because I like you a lot, too," he murmured, staring up at him.

Joey cupped Ethan's cheek, and Ethan closed his eyes as he nuzzled against Joey's palm. He didn't want Joey to leave, that much he knew, but could he deal with the repercussions of

Joey staying? Mainly the media attention. Ethan had spent his life under the radar, quietly plodding through his days, hoping, though never expecting, to find what he believed he had with Joey. Life with Joey would come with additional interest, and could he cope with life in the spotlight? Having never had the experience of such a thing, Ethan couldn't answer, though he wanted to think he could manage.

"Ethan..." Joey sighed.

Ethan dropped his head and stood, grabbing their cups with a small smile. "It's okay. I understand." He refilled the kettle and started a new drink. "Do you want another cup?"

"No, thanks. Ethan—"

"Look, I get it. Okay. I know you can't stay here. I'm not going to throw a tantrum because you're making the best decision for you. If you need to leave, as much as I don't want you to, you need to leave. End of."

Ethan finished making his drink and cradled the mug in both hands despite it scalding his palms. He needed something to focus on as his heart broke. He leaned back against the counter and stared out of the small window in his kitchen, blinking rapidly as his thoughts highlighted how deep he'd already fallen. *Holy fuck!*

The mug was lifted out of his hands, and his attention snapped to Joey as he stepped in front of him. Joey slid his hands across Ethan's jaw, and Ethan's eyelids fluttered.

"You're not one to throw a tantrum, I know. But you're also not one to let your feelings stop other people from doing what they want to do." Joey's eyes transfixed Ethan as his voice lowered to a rumble. "I don't want to leave because I'll be leaving behind the one person who understands me. I've let no one else as close as you've burrowed inside me. And *that* is why I'm leaving. You don't deserve your life being turned upside down by me. You deserve a life of freedom, the chance to make mistakes that won't be publicised for the world to see, the opportunity to love without giving up the anonymity. If you're with me, you'll get none of that." Joey's mouth came closer, and his voice lowered further, breathing across Ethan's skin. "I care about you too much to allow you to forfeit everything for me when I don't deserve it," he whispered.

Joey brushed his lips across Ethan's, and Ethan automatically opened for him. The spell Joey had cast over him had him lightheaded with need. Ethan grasped at Joey's back, gripping handfuls of his T-shirt as Joey slowly explored Ethan's warm cavern, their mouths never sealing completely. Ethan's chest lifted and dropped in sharp movements as he sucked air in and breathed it out in between the licks and nips Joey gave him.

Finally, Joey sealed their mouths, and Ethan's knees gave out. Joey tightened his hold, sliding one hand behind Ethan's back to support him while his other hand slid into Ethan's hair. A hint of coffee remained on Joey's tongue as they tangled, taking everything the other gave.

Joey's hands skimmed over Ethan's clothed body to squeeze his ass, and Ethan groaned, bucking forward. Joey responded by grabbing Ethan's thighs and lifting him to sit on the counter. It made Ethan taller than Joey, and he lowered his head to join their mouths again. He couldn't get enough, needed more.

"Joey," he breathed, his head dropping back against the wall cupboards while Joey fumbled with the button and zip of Ethan's trousers.

One second, the cool air bathed his cock; the next, Joey's mouth surrounded him with wet heat. Ethan's hand rested against the back of Joey's head as his tongue did amazing things to his dick.

"Fuck!" He gasped, the fire-like sensations bombarding him. He couldn't buck his hips, precariously positioned as he was, but he could encourage with his words. "Yes, Joey! Fuck, yes. That's so good."

His free hand gripped Joey's shoulder while Joey swallowed around Ethan's tip. Ethan licked his lips and opened his eyes, peering down at Joey a second before something caught his eye. He glanced at the window and cursed, pushing at Joey.

"What the fuck!" Ethan shouted, covering his groin when Joey stood.

Joey glanced over his shoulder, swore and raced to the back door, flinging it open and disappearing, though Ethan heard his words. "Get your ass back here, or you'll find yourself in jail!" he shouted at the person who had been either taking photos or filming them through Ethan's back window.

Ethan jumped off the counter and shoved his dick back in his trousers. When he was decent, he stepped into his back garden. Joey was in a standoff with a young-ish man with dark hair and eyes, though his mouth was curled in what Ethan thought looked like satisfaction.

"If any of those photos or videos, whatever you were taking, find their way online, you will be arrested for trespassing," Joey said.

"It's a free alley," the man said, waving his hand towards the alley that ran the length of the back of the houses.

"Yes, that alley might be," Ethan said, "but my back garden is not a public right of way."

"I want to watch you delete them," Joey said. "Now!" he added when the man shook his head.

The man huffed. "It's just a fucking job, man." He brought his camera up, and Joey stepped closer, watching as the man did something—hopefully deleting those photos. Then he stepped back to Ethan's side.

"What's your name?"

JOEY

"Devlin Cooper, Whitby Chronicles. Nice to meet you." The man had the audacity to hold out his hand with a smile.

Ethan and Joey ignored the outstretched hand, and Devlin huffed again. "Who told you where I was?" Joey asked.

Devlin shrugged. "An anonymous tip to the paper. The moment it came through, my editor told me to check it out."

"So you thought gaining unlawful entry into someone's back garden was the way to do it?" Ethan said.

"Hey, man. I need this job. I need something to keep it, especially with how things are now."

"Not at the expense of our privacy," Joey said.

Devlin laughed loudly. "Privacy? You're a celebrity in your own right, Mr Reynolds. You forfeited your privacy years ago, I'm afraid to say."

Joey glanced at Ethan as if to say, "I told you so," but Ethan was having none of it. "But I didn't. You have no right."

"No one plays by the rules anymore, man. Get a life." Devlin turned and exited the garden, stopping in the alley and facing them again. Ethan heard the click of the camera, and Devlin held up his hands. "Can't say I can't keep that one."

"Get lost, Mr Cooper," Joey said, closing and locking the back gate.

"Fucki—"

Joey held up a finger to his mouth and gestured for them to go back inside. Once the back door was locked behind them, he said, "Sorry, you can talk now. You never know whether they're within hearing distance."

"Fucking asshole was all I was going to say," Ethan said, lowering the blind in his kitchen to hide them from anyone else who might have the same idea.

Joey sighed. "I'm sorry about that, but this is what I meant, Ethan. This is just the start. I could almost guarantee at least one person is waiting out in front of the house for one of us."

Ethan settled into a chair and leaned his elbows on his knees, linking his fingers. "It was a shock, I'll admit. But I stand by my words, Joey. If you want to stay, you're more than welcome to."

Joey crouched in front of him. "I want to, but I can't."

Ethan wanted to fall into his arms, but he refrained, tensing his muscles lest they ignore his brain and follow his heart. He nodded slowly. "Do you need any help with anything before you go?" Joey shook his head. "Where are you going?"

Joey stood and scrubbed his hands over his head. "I guess it's time to face the music."

"You're going home." It wasn't a question. Ethan swallowed hard and stood. "I'll let Meredith know you won't be back."

"Thank you. Please tell her I'm sorry for leaving so suddenly."

"She'll understand." Ethan would, too. Eventually. Right now, though, everything hurt, and it had nothing to do with blue balls. He inhaled and smiled. "Take care driving home. It's a long journey. Make sure you rest along the way."

Joey faced him, and Ethan's heart tried to claw its way out of his chest. How could he have fallen so hard and so fast? He didn't want to imagine his days without Joey in them, even though it had only been a short time ago that his life had been empty. Was that what happened when people met the one they wanted to spend their life with, but they weren't allowed? A vast emptiness spread out in front of them. Ethan wasn't sure he wanted it. Unfortunately, he didn't have a say in it.

Joey reached for him, but Ethan stepped back, a band crushing his chest. Joey gritted his teeth and nodded. "Thank you, Ethan. For everything. I will never forget you or your generosity."

Ethan made himself smile. "Just pay it forward. That's what I always say."

Joey stared at him for a second longer and then headed for the front door. Ethan went with him. Before he opened it, Joey said, "Stay behind the door in case there are photographers. They won't get you in the photos, then."

Ethan did, and Joey gave him one last look, yanked the door open and stepped through to calls of his name. Joey dragged the door closed again, and he was gone.

Ethan wasn't sure how long he stood staring at the door, but it was long enough that his knees started complaining. He sank onto the sofa, transferring his gaze to the floor instead. His mind was surprisingly blank, and he breathed. Well, he did until his inhales became choppy, and hot tears splashed down his cheeks. His eyes burned, his throat swelled up, and his nose ran. He grabbed a cushion to his chest and lay down on the sofa, curling himself up.

The cavern in his chest yawned wide and empty as he contemplated his future. He would never again find what he had with Joey.

"Why are there photographers outside?"

Though he hadn't heard Christi come in, the voice didn't even shock him, but he couldn't answer. His throat ached with the need to scream, but he couldn't.

"Ethan? What's wrong?" Christi crouched in front of him, making him blink, more tears trickling over his lashes. "What happened?" She placed a hand on his shoulder, and it must've been the spark to the kindling because a sob tore through his scratchy throat.

He tightened his grip on the cushion and burrowed his face into the sofa to muffle his cries. The more he cried, the more he hurt, and the more he hurt, the more he cried. He could hear Christi mumbling, but not exactly what she said. His ears were focused on his pain.

He must've fallen asleep at some point because the ache in his throat woke him, and a soft light was on, and the curtains had been closed. Ethan pushed himself upright and sighed at the aches in his body. The sofa was not comfortable for sleeping, even at the best of times. And this definitely wasn't the best of times. He rubbed his hands over his face, wiping away the dried tears and crusty sleep, and breathed deeply.

It was done. Joey was gone, and Ethan would continue as he had been. The pain would lessen, but he needed to give it time. It was a grieving process, after all.

"Ethan?" Christi whispered, and he glanced over to the door of the dining room.

"Sorry about that," he croaked. He cleared his throat and winced.

"Why don't we have a drink? See if we can get that throat of yours working again," she said with a small smile.

Ethan stood, holding onto the arm of the sofa when his legs threatened not to hold him. Following Christi into the dining room, he settled into a chair, and she placed a mug in front of him. She sat across from him, cradling her mug, and smiled at him, careful though it was.

"Do you want to talk about it?" she asked.

Ethan stared at the small bubbles on top of his drink, watching as they popped and disappeared as if they'd never been. Just like Joey. Ethan swallowed hard. "Joey's gone home."

Christi raised her brown eyebrows—her having not dyed them when she'd dyed her hair blonde—and licked her lips. "Wasn't that the plan?" she asked hesitantly.

Ethan nodded slowly, refocusing on his drink. "Someone recognised him, and it brought the journalists out."

"So I see." She glanced to where she would've been able to see them had the walls of the house not been there. "He couldn't have been that famous. I didn't recognise him."

Ethan huffed a laugh. "Not hugely, but in his circle, he is. His name is Joey Reynolds. He's a tattoo artist for celebrities."

"Hoo-boy. No wonder there are so many photographers out there."

"What?" Ethan glanced at her. "They're still here?" She nodded. "But he's gone?"

"I don't think it's him they want to talk to at the moment."

Ethan dropped his head into his hands. "They were supposed to leave when he did," he mumbled.

"It looks like you might be a celebrity for the next few days," Christi said. "Maybe you should talk to them and get it over with."

"No." Ethan shook his head to confirm his denial. "Joey's been through enough. He doesn't need me talking about our time together on top of that."

Christi sipped her drink. "What are you going to do?"

"Ignore them. They might follow me and photograph me, but they won't get any words from me other than 'fuck off.' And that'll be me being polite." Ethan gulped his coffee, the heat soothing the ache in his throat. After his bout of crying, his sinuses complained bitterly, the pressure around his eyes and nose immense, but it would ease eventually. What he needed was more sleep. To fall into a dreamless state where nothing could touch him for a few hours.

"What time did he leave?" Christi asked, her question prodding the pain in his chest and setting it afire once more.

"Around three o'clock, give or take." Ethan glanced at his watch. "Jeez. It's nine o'clock. I've lost far too many hours." He gulped the last of his drink. "Thank you, Christi. You didn't have to stay."

"Of course I did. You're my best friend."

Ethan yawned. "I need to sleep more. Are you okay with those vultures out there, or do you want to stay over?"

"I'll be fine. They'll get nothing from me."

He said goodbye and got ready for bed. Sinking into the mattress made him groan as his body conformed to it, easing some aches he'd achieved with his sofa snooze. He lay on his back, staring at the ceiling, then reached for the pillow Joey had used while he'd been there. Ethan inhaled, closing his eyes as Joey's scent filled his lungs. Ethan's eyes burned, but he held back the tears. He placed the pillow back in place and rolled to his side, burrowing his nose into the edge of Joey's pillow. He didn't want the scent to disappear too quickly, and if Ethan hugged it, his own scent would replace it sooner than he wanted.

He fell asleep to the scent of Joey in his nose, hoping that when he woke, it would all have been a bad dream.

Instead, he was abruptly pulled from a dream by someone screaming his name.

8

JOEY

"Joey! JOEY! Why are you here? Who is Ethan to you? Why were you working at The Cliff End Hotel? Joey! Why haven't you been home? Do you feel guilty about what happened to Elliott? Was it your fault?"

Joey swallowed down his responses to the half a dozen reporters shouting questions his way, even though he wanted to smack them about with how evil their questions could be. Yes, Joey did feel guilty about what happened to Elliott, but he wasn't going to admit that to them. Vultures.

He pressed the car key, unlocking the doors, and climbed inside. He slammed them closed, muffling the questions being thrown at him, and locked them for good measure. Starting the engine, he carefully pulled out of the space and drove down Ethan's street. The photographers ran alongside him for a short distance, then stopped. They wouldn't be able to keep up with him without a car.

He hoped they would leave Ethan alone, but he knew better than that. They would stay around his house until he made an appearance. If being by Ethan's side wouldn't have made things worse, he would've stayed.

As he worked his way through the windy streets of Whitby, then the hills and valleys of the Yorkshire Moors, his focus remained on the man he'd left behind. Just before he reached the junction to join the motorway, he pulled into a lay-by. After putting the handbrake on, he gripped the steering wheel, glaring at the road ahead of him. He smacked the palm of his hand on the wheel, squeezed it tight, and then smacked it again. There wasn't much more he could do to release the fury inside him.

Those reporters had a lot to answer for. If those women—or David—hadn't recognised him, he would still be holidaying in Ethan's arms.

He exhaled and rested his head back. But wasn't that the problem? His *holidaying* thought showed exactly what he hadn't wanted to see. This wasn't Joey's normal life. He'd taken a break from reality and ended up living the dream with Ethan. A dream that could never become real life because Ethan didn't deserve to be thrown into his celebrity lifestyle. Ethan deserved to be worshipped from afar with nothing bad ever touching him.

Joey closed his eyes, picturing Ethan's face. Other than one photo on his phone of them both, his memories were all he had. But that photo of them lounging in bed, both sleep and sex mussed, was something he would never delete.

He inhaled and exhaled, then checked around him before pulling out. He had a long journey ahead of him, but the least he could do was let Ani know he was on his way.

"Call Ani," he told the car, and his phone rang through the speakers.

"Joey?"

"Hey, Ani," he breathed.

"Are you okay? I wasn't expecting to hear from you."

"Have you seen the news?"

Ani was quiet for a moment, and Joey assumed she was checking the sites. "Ah, they found you." A woman of few words, though they were always on point.

"It won't take them long to find me." He sighed. "I'm on my way home."

"You are?" She sounded hopeful.

"It's time."

"I'm glad."

Joey wasn't so sure he was, but he didn't comment. "It's going to take me a good few hours to get there. Can you keep it quiet for now?"

"Of course."

"I'm sure the vultures will hover around again soon. If they're not already."

"Have you spoken to anyone else?"

"No, and I don't plan to. Not yet."

Ani sighed. "I'm glad you'll be back for the funeral."

Joey didn't reply, not wanting to think about it. "I'll call you when I'm close."

He hung up after saying goodbye and focused on the road. He didn't put any music on to distract him. Instead, he let the images of the past week flow through him. He couldn't believe it had been such a short time. There was no way he could ever repay Ethan enough for what he'd given him in those few days together. But he would still try. Once he'd got himself sorted, he would make it up to Ethan. He didn't know how, but he'd try his hardest.

Seven hours later, he drove through the familiar streets of London towards home—a place he'd not seen for three weeks. He'd stopped for an hour at a service station, buying a drink to tide him over for the rest of the journey and hiding in his car in case anyone recognised him again. And if he'd spent most of that time staring at Ethan's number on his phone screen, no one needed to know.

He wasn't sure whether the reporters would be there, as it was closing in on eleven o'clock at night, but he wouldn't put it past them. After all, the city that never sleeps has nothing on celebrity life.

Holding his breath, he rounded the corner to Life in Ink and exhaled when no one waited outside. The shop itself was on the ground and first floor of a four-storey building. The upper two floors belonged to him. Well, the entire building did, but the top two floors were his haven. No one was allowed inside without his express permission.

Parking next to his designated spot, in which his own car sat, he let the engine idle while he settled his nerves. The slightly rough noise of the engine would most likely annoy his neighbours, so after a few minutes, he switched it off. The silence within the car would break the moment he opened the car door, and the sounds from the businesses around him would infiltrate his bubble.

Before he did that, he checked his phone. He'd received no messages or calls from Ethan when he stopped at the services, and he shouldn't expect any, but he couldn't stop the hope from flaring inside him. But no messages lit his screen.

He sighed, shoved the phone back into his pocket and opened the door, the streetlamp above casting shadows. As expected, laughter and merriment from the surrounding bars filled the air. Despite the chill of the evening, some patrons of those businesses appeared to be making use of the outdoor areas. Most of the time, it didn't bother him because he was busy working or not even present. That night, it grated on him, though it shouldn't. They were entitled to be happy. It wasn't their fault that Joey had suffered a loss that tore at the fabric of his life.

No, that was Joey's fault. For not seeing that Elliott was in pain. For not checking on him sooner that day. For not making sure he was okay after the previous evening.

"Joey?" a soft voice said.

He glanced up. Ani stood a few feet away. Her green hair was ear-length on one side and shaved on the other, and tattoos peeked out from beneath her vest top, along her arms and up her chest and neck. Any other day, Joey would tease her about her pint size, but he didn't feel particularly humorous that night.

"Hey," he said.

Ani wasn't a touchy-feely person due to problems she had in her past, so she surprised him when she wrapped her arms around his waist.

"I'm glad you're back." She stepped away, slipping her fingers into the back pockets of her jeans, which were undoubtedly black, though he couldn't see for definite in the streetlight. "I've locked everything up for the night. I didn't think you'd want an audience for your arrival."

He hadn't. "Thanks." He opened the back passenger car door and pulled his bag free—the one he hadn't left at Ethan's house when he departed without taking anything he had brought with him. It hadn't been much, but he didn't need any of it. "I'm going up. Thank you for taking care of Joelle." He hadn't realised how much just saying the name would hurt his chest.

"She's been fine. Wouldn't come down to the shop, though."

"Thanks, Ani. Sorry for leaving all this for you."

Ani shook her head. "You don't need to be sorry, Joey. You needed space. I get it. We all get it."

He tried for a smile and stepped around her to the metal staircase leading up his part of the building. He could reach it by going through the tattoo shop as well, but this was closer. As he reached the top, Ani called his name again.

"Call me if you need anything."

Joey waved a hand and unlocked the door to his apartment. He held his breath again as he stepped over the threshold, waiting for the pain of the memories to tear through him. It took him several seconds to close the door behind him, setting the triple lock into place so people couldn't get in from the outside. Then he leaned back against the door and stared at the open-plan layout of the home he'd lived in for close to ten years—the first two of which Elliott had lived there with him.

It still held the markings of his best friend. The scratch along the laminate flooring where he'd decided to move the sofa by himself instead of asking for help, not realising until too late that there was a small but mighty stone caught underneath one of the wooden feet. The dent in the corner of the counter in the kitchen where he'd dropped a heavy-based pan as he'd tried to lift it onto the shelf. The faded rectangle by the window where he'd put up a picture he had taken to his new home two years later. Joey had left his own marks, too, but Elliott's were too close to the surface.

A soft miaow sounded, and Joey dropped his gaze to the floor, smiling as Joelle pushed her head against his calf.

"Hey, sweetheart," he murmured, sliding to sit on the floor. He picked her up, brushing his cheek against her fur. "I'm sorry I was gone so long."

Joelle bumped her head against the underside of his chin. She'd always done the same greeting, even when she was a kitten.

More memories invaded. He and Elliott going to a friend's house because they'd had a litter of kittens, and Elliott wanted to play with them. Neither had expected to go home with one, but Ryan could be persuasive when he wanted to be. Elliott's apartment didn't allow pets, but Joey didn't mind having her at his. When the kittens were old enough to leave, Joey and Elliott had gone to pick her up, arguing for the entire journey about a name for her. In the end, Elliott had crossed his arms over his chest and grumbled, "Might as well call her Joelle. Then she'll belong to both of us."

At first, Joey hadn't understood what he'd meant until he'd explained that by mixing Joey and Ell—which was what Joey called him sometimes—they would get Joelle. The name had stuck. And now it was one more reminder of what Elliott had left behind.

"What are we going to do without him, Joelle?"

Joelle miaowed and rested against him as if trying to comfort him. He didn't move for a long time. It was only when his ass went numb that he realised how cold he was. Ani had turned the heating down to the bare minimum. Enough to keep Joelle from freezing, but not enough to keep a human from becoming a block of ice.

Joey moved to stand, and Joelle jumped off his lap. He stumbled a bit before reaching for the wall to steady himself. Wandering to the wall where the thermostat lived, he twisted it higher, hearing it click on. It would take a while, but he could manage for now.

Heading back for his bag, he kept his gaze lowered, not wanting more images to surface, but he glimpsed a photograph on the side table. It was of him and Elliott decked out in rainbows from when they'd joined a Pride parade several years ago. It was Joey's favourite photo of them because they both looked so happy.

He pulled his gaze away, grabbed his bag and aimed for the stairs. There were two bedrooms, both with en suite bathrooms on the floor above his living area. When he entered his, there was a slight musty smell from the windows not being opened for a week, so even though it was chilly, he cracked them wide. He dropped his bag onto the floor and sat on the bed.

It was strange to be home. Although he'd only been gone for a short period, in the grand scheme of things, anyway, the place felt like it was waiting for something. Joey shook his head and dropped onto his back, staring at the ceiling, lit only by the shine from the streetlights through his open curtains. Usually, he'd shut them, but he couldn't bring himself to.

He slid his phone out of his pocket, pausing before unlocking it. He rolled to his stomach when he saw a message, though he hesitated to check who it was. It might be his parents, a friend or a colleague, but he wished it was Ethan, and he wasn't sure he could take the blow if it wasn't.

Clicking on it was the hardest thing he'd had to do in a while.

ETHAN: *Please let me know when you get home. I want to know you're safe. x*

Joey exhaled, his entire body releasing the tension he hadn't realised he'd been holding. His shoulders and legs ached, his head pounded, and even his ass hurt. But with that one message, Ethan had helped more than he could know.

JOEY: *I'm home. I'm safe. Thank you for everything, and I'm sorry for leaving you to deal with the reporters by yourself. x*

That was the message he decided on after writing and deleting several versions of the same "Are you okay?" type question. Ethan would be okay. He had to be. Because Joey couldn't live with himself if Ethan wasn't. He hadn't meant to blast into Ethan's life and mess it all up. He'd intended to stay alone, moping for as long as he could get away with it. But then Ethan leaned an elbow beside him in that pub that day, and everything changed.

Now, it was all going back to the way it was before. Joey would hook up with random individuals, sleep alone, work too much and play too little. Especially now that Elliott wasn't there to drag him out with him.

ETHAN: *I'm glad. Don't be sorry. I wouldn't change a minute. x*

Neither would Joey. He wished he'd come without celebrity acquaintances. That he lived quietly and out of the spotlight. No one deserved to be thrown into that lifestyle, especially if they hadn't been prepared for it beforehand. That was why he'd left

Ethan. The reporters might bother him for a few days, but then they'd leave for fresh news.

JOEY: *Me neither. x*

Another message came through, but this time, it was from his mother. He ignored it, needing to escape real life for one more night. He closed the windows and curtains, curled up beneath his covers, fully dressed, and held the phone by his face as if he could see or touch Ethan just by holding the device.

Joelle jumped onto his bed and settled onto the pillow beside him, as she always did, and Joey closed his eyes. He brought forward images of his time with Ethan, wanting to remember every minute, every scent, every taste. Hoping that the memories would help him sleep enough to get through the following day, and the day after, and the day after that, too, because the days were going to get harder before they got easier.

As he remembered the feeling of Ethan in his arms, he relaxed further, drifting towards sleep, though not fully asleep. It was the best he could hope for without Ethan beside him. The man had helped him to sleep all night for several nights in a row. A feat that hadn't happened since Elliott... No, he wouldn't go there. He refocused back on Ethan.

Was he ever going to see him again? They were from two different worlds. It seemed impossible that they could find anything more than what they had, but maybe. One day, when Joey was a better person, he might find his way back to Ethan. And maybe Ethan will have found someone new to live his life with, but that would be okay because Ethan would be happy. That's all Joey wanted for him.

9

ETHAN

Every time Ethan fell asleep, his dreams woke him. Joey shouted for him, reaching for him, but Ethan couldn't grab hold, and Joey moved further and further away. With every scream of his name, it woke something inside him, and Ethan jerked himself awake, sweat coating his skin and the covers tangled around him. By the time his alarm went off for him to go to work, he was as exhausted as if he hadn't had any sleep at all.

He wished he understood what the dreams meant, but he couldn't interpret them. Was it his subconscious telling him something, or was it just hopeful thinking?

Ethan stood behind the reception desk and took a breath before the next wave of checkouts bombarded them. It always happened between nine-thirty and ten o'clock in the morning. The hotel had a policy requiring guests to check out by ten o'clock, and most guests waited until the last minute. He was glad it was busy because it kept him distracted from his thoughts. From Joey.

He had never been someone who clung to the other person in the relationship; he was strong enough to stand on his own two feet. But something about Joey had knocked Ethan for six—to use the old cliché.

Smiling at the older couple heading towards him, he pushed other thoughts aside.

"Mr and Mrs Geller. I hope you've had a wonderful time this week."

The Gellers stayed at the hotel every six months for a week to have time away from their rather large brood. They had a large bed-and-breakfast-style house, which they'd turned into a foster home. They had been looking after children for more years than Ethan had been alive, and he loved them dearly. They often said that the only reason they were still able to look after so many children was because of those breaks they took; otherwise, they would be drained and of no use to anyone.

"It's been great, as always, dear," Mrs Geller said with a smile. "Just what the doctor ordered."

Ethan chuckled. "Back to the chaos again for you."

Mr Geller groaned. "Roger has his birthday next week, so we'll be baking all week, I'm sure."

Ethan checked them out while they chatted about their kids and what their plans were for the next few weeks. The Gellers were taking all seven children abroad on holiday that summer, and Ethan didn't envy them. He wasn't sure if he wanted kids or not, but he wasn't completely opposed.

"Well, have a fantastic time, and make sure you bring lots of photos when you next visit us. I want to see that sunshine," Ethan said.

"Will do."

Ethan focused on the computer to ensure he had completed all he needed to and closed the form.

"I hear Joey has gone back to where he came from."

Ethan tensed and clenched his jaw, still annoyed at David for being part of the reason Joey had left. "He had work to do." He continued to focus on the screen, pretending to look at things as if he was busy.

"Didn't stop him from coming here. He didn't do too bad of a job while he was wasting his time with us," David said, leaning a hip beside where Ethan stood.

Ethan refused to be baited.

"Ah well, he's already onto his next lay, according to the news. You're well shot of him."

David disappeared as quickly as he appeared, but those parting words hurt more than Ethan wanted to admit. He wasn't naïve. He knew Joey had another life in London and that his time in Whitby was just a stopgap, but Ethan had hoped it meant more. He shook his head when his phone buzzed, and he pulled it from his pocket, glancing around to make sure David wasn't peering over his shoulder.

CHRISTI: Let's go to Neon tonight. You need to get out.

Ethan stared at the message. He wasn't sure going to the place he'd met Joey at was the best idea, but was staying at home any better? David's words came back to him, and his fingers hovered over his phone screen.

ETHAN: I'm there. What time?

He might regret it, but dancing with someone might help him to get over the feelings that had been growing inside him since he'd met and got to know Joey.

CHRISTI: Fab! Seven o'clock. See you there as I'm working until six.

Ethan replied to say he'd be there; he hoped he wasn't making a mistake. Already, he could feel the churning in his stomach, but he couldn't live his life in stasis. He'd never fallen so hard and fast for anyone before, but he needed to let Joey go. Joey had another life in London, one that Ethan had no part in, and he needed to remember that.

Eight hours later, after a brief cat nap, which ended the same way his previous night had, he entered the Neon Lounge, holding his breath as he passed the bar and letting it out slowly while he searched for Christi. She waved from across the room, and he made his way through the already-heaving crowd. He still stood by his assessment that Thursday was becoming the new Friday of the working week people.

"Hey! I got you a vodka and orange. I wasn't sure how hard you were going to hit it tonight," Christi said, pushing the glass towards him.

Ethan picked it up and downed half of it in one go, wincing when the strength of the drink hit him.

"Okay. Duly noted. Sloshed is the aim tonight." Christi snorted and sipped whatever her cocktail was. "How was work?"

Ethan rolled his eyes and settled onto the stool beside her. "Busy, which was good. How're things with Di?"

Christi huffed and put her drink on the table slightly harder than needed. "She purposefully double-booked me yesterday!"

He let Christi go on about her arch nemesis—though, as Ethan had always said, if she just stopped baiting her, it would all end—letting her distract him enough to cope until a guy approached him. He was roughly Ethan's height but had wider shoulders. His hair was to his shoulders and had been dyed blond. Basically, he reminded Ethan of a surfer. Christi fell silent beside him.

"Hey, I'm Addy. Would you like to dance?"

Ethan opened his mouth to decline, then thought better of it. "Sure." He downed the rest of his drink and glanced at Christi. "You okay for a few minutes?"

Christi nodded. "Kole will be here soon."

Ethan stood and gestured to the dance floor. "After you."

He followed Addy to the couples that were already moving to the beat and slid his arm around Addy's waist when they faced each other. Addy fitted his body to Ethan's, and they caught the beat immediately. Ethan lost himself in the music, sometimes wrapped around Addy, sometimes dancing in front of him. They stopped briefly to get another drink, which Ethan threw back and then returned to the floor.

He wasn't sure how long they danced, but he was soaked with sweat when he began to tire. Addy stared at him, faces close, and Ethan knew what he was going to do. It was in his eyes, and Ethan didn't know what his response would be. His mind was whirling, even as he stared into Addy's eyes. As his head lowered. As his breath flowed across his mouth.

Ethan swallowed hard and turned his face, and Addy's kiss met his cheek. Ethan closed his eyes and tightened his hold on the man. "I'm sorry," he whispered in his ear.

Addy pulled back with a small smile. "It's okay. I can tell when someone is trying to forget. I thought I might be able to help."

"You have." Ethan sighed. "But I need to go."

He kissed Addy's cheek and stepped back. He hesitated for a second longer and then turned to their table. Christi and Kole were in a conversation with a man and a woman who had joined them. Ethan grabbed his jacket and touched Christi's shoulder.

"I'm going. Have a good night. You, too, Kole."

"But what about..." Christi waved her hand towards the dance floor, and Ethan smiled.

"Good night."

He escaped from the building as quickly as he could and stopped, hands on hips, head dropped back, and stared at the stars as he breathed in the cool night air. What was he doing? He couldn't put his life on hold because of one man who was unlikely to be returning.

How was Joey coping with being back? From what Joey had told him, the funeral was the following day. Would he make it through?

Ethan sighed, cursing himself because he wanted to be there for him. He wanted to hold his hand, slide his arm around his waist to hold him up on one of the toughest days of his life. Burying his best friend—or any person—was not something Ethan would wish on anyone. But Joey didn't deserve this. Especially as he was the one to find Elliott.

He wandered down the street towards home, not wanting to get a taxi yet, and pulled out his phone. He stared at Joey's number. Would it make things worse to hear his voice? Would he make things worse for Joey?

Ethan sighed and shoved the phone into his pocket again. Joey had left and had a lot of things going on. He didn't need Ethan butting in and making it worse.

He'd only walked ten more steps when he pulled the phone out again and hit call before he could reconsider. As the ringing sounded in his ear, he closed his eyes and shook his head. What was he doing?

"Ethan?"

The moment he heard Joey's voice, Ethan's entire body released its tension, and he had to lean against a nearby wall to stop from sinking to the ground.

"Ethan?" Joey asked again. "Are you okay?"

"Yes," he whispered and then cleared his throat. "Sorry. I didn't mean to interrupt. I don't know..." He couldn't finish the sentence because he didn't want Joey to think he couldn't cope without him. He didn't want to think he couldn't cope without Joey, especially as Ethan was fiercely independent and decisive in his own right.

"You're not interrupting. I'm just feeding Joelle."

Ethan frowned and straightened. "You have company. Sorry. I'll go."

"No! There's no one here."

Ethan squeezed his eyes closed, confused. "Joelle?" he reminded him.

Joey's deep chuckle filtered through the line. "Joelle is my cat."

"You have a cat?" He didn't mean for his voice to sound so surprised.

"I do." Joey sighed. "Elliott and I picked her out. She was both of ours."

"What does she look like?" Ethan headed home once more, a lightness in his steps now he had Joey's voice in his ear.

"She's a British Longhair. A deep grey fluff ball is what she is," Joey crooned. "Aren't you? Yes, you are."

Ethan's smile widened. "She sounds beautiful. You'll have to send me a picture."

"Hold on."

There was a bit of noise and then silence, and Ethan glanced at his phone; they were still connected. He put it back to his ear.

"Okay. I've sent you a photo," Joey said suddenly.

Ethan pulled the phone away from his ear again. He clicked on the photo Joey had sent, and his heart pounded when a gorgeous grey cat appeared. Ethan had to keep his eyes on the cat, but it was difficult because Joey had the cat cuddled up to his face, and the man's eye colour stood out—it was the same colour as the cat.

"She's gorgeous."

"She is."

They fell into silence, and the cool air bit into Ethan's skin, but he didn't care. As much as he could deny being wound up in someone enough that he struggled to function, it was startlingly obvious to him now that it was the case. In the few short days they'd had together, Ethan had fallen hard. But where did that leave him now? He had always been stubborn and insisted on standing on his own, but somewhere along the line, those days had changed things. Changed him.

"Are you okay, Ethan?" Joey asked.

"I should be asking you that." He crossed the road.

"I'm fine. I'm not looking forward to tomorrow, but it'll be what it'll be. I can't change things."

Ethan's heart broke for him. "I wish I could be there to help you through it." The moment he said it, he wished he could call it back. Joey didn't need that from him. He needed him to give him—

"I wish you were here, too." The words were so softly spoken that Ethan hadn't been sure they were truly said until Joey continued. "I'm sorry I left how I did. Have they left you alone?"

Ethan allowed the change of subject. "They have, for the most part. I still have people visiting the hotel and asking me questions, but I think they're mainly fans rather than reporters."

"I'm sorry."

"You don't need to be. I wish they'd leave you alone," he admitted, crossing another road and finally reaching his street.

"It's how they earn their money. I can't begrudge them it, but yeah, I wish they would, too."

"How bad will it be tomorrow?" He reached his door and slipped into his house, grateful for the warmth emanating from it.

Joey was quiet for a moment. "Bad enough that I'll want to hide away from the world for a week or two. Unfortunately, I won't be able to."

"Why not?"

"I have clients to tattoo. I've already rearranged them once. I can't do it again without it affecting my business. And it's not just me I have to think about anymore. The artists rely on me as much as I rely on them."

Ethan nodded, though Joey couldn't see him, and slipped off his coat. "I'm sure they'll find some other news soon."

"It'll die down once the funeral is done, and there's no more light shining on the situation."

"I don't know if I would ever get used to that level of scrutiny," Ethan said, settling on the sofa. Joey was silent, and Ethan replayed his words and grimaced. "I mean, I would if needed, but it's really hard on you, isn't it?" He hadn't wanted Joey to think he wasn't capable of the pressure of being in the spotlight. Though why, he wasn't sure. It wasn't like they were going to be a couple, was it?

"It takes some compartmentalising, that's for sure."

"Do you get a break from it at all? I mean, I know you don't always have celebrity clients, so does that mean the reporters leave you alone sometimes?"

Joey sighed. "Sometimes, yes. We each travel a lot, but there's always one artist who remains in London when everyone else is away. When we're travelling, there's less commotion during the actual journey, but it's worse when we get to wherever we're going. We try to keep our calendar secret, but somehow, it always gets out. Some celebrities tell everyone for the exposure. Some reporters probably pay for someone to tell them. Regardless, we're always caught in the media trap." He snorted. "I probably shouldn't complain since this is my livelihood."

"It's okay to be bitter about it, even if you do have to rely on them sometimes."

They lapsed into silence again, and Ethan knew he had to let him go, but he didn't want to. For that reason alone, he did.

"I'll let you go. No doubt you have things to do. Call me if you need anything, okay?" Ethan said. "Anything at all."

"Thanks." Joey paused. "Take care, Ethan."

Pulling the phone away from his ear and ending the call was difficult, but he managed it. He stared at the dark TV screen while his brain revisited all the things he'd experienced with Joey. It needed to stop, but Joey had been the first person to make him feel every inch the submissive he wanted to be, and those memories reminded him of how it felt. He hated losing it, but he hated losing Joey even more.

Ethan closed his eyes and shook his head, sighing. He reached for the remote and flicked through the offerings until something caught his eye enough for him to set it playing. There would be no sleep for him tonight because he couldn't go through Joey's shouts and screams again. Not when there was nothing he could do about seeing him in the near future.

Ethan frowned. Could he visit Joey? What would be the point when the end would be the same result? He'd still be leaving Joey in London while he returned to Whitby. It wasn't an insurmountable distance, but it would put a strain on any relationship they tried. And then there was the media to think about. If he was seen with Joey too much, they would start hounding Ethan, too. Would it be worth it to spend time with Joey?

Ethan didn't have to think about that answer because it was a resounding yes. But if they started something, one of them would have to give something up eventually, and Ethan understood it would probably be him.

Could he give up his life in Whitby for Joey? It was all Ethan had ever known; he'd never lived anywhere else. He'd never wanted to live anywhere else. But could he?

It wasn't a decision he could take lightly, and certainly not one he could decide upon while still slightly inebriated, although he hadn't drunk so much that he didn't know what he was doing. It stood to reason, though, that he shouldn't be making split-second decisions when his emotions were bubbling at the surface. He'd set them aside for another day.

Ethan grabbed his phone when it beeped and stared at the words.

JOEY: *I'll always need you, Ethan.* x

10

JOEY

J oey stood beneath the spray of the shower, head lowered, concentrating on the feel of the water hitting his neck and back rather than on the hours that were to come. He'd not slept at all, so the shower was for more reasons than freshening up. He needed to stay awake.

He pressed his palms into the cool tiles, ignoring the churning of his stomach, and focused on Ethan. He'd found it was the only way to get through the hours. It had only been two days since he'd seen the man, but it was two days too many as far as Joey was concerned. He'd told Ethan it was for the best—and it was—but Joey needed him. More than he had ever needed anyone before, including Elliott.

And there his thoughts went again.

Joey switched off the shower, dried off and dressed in his black suit, not even checking his reflection in the mirror because he knew what it would show. Joelle wound through his legs, mewling as if she knew what that day would entail, and if Joey could've brought her with him for the comfort she unknowingly gave, he would have.

He drank a glass of water, needing a drink but not taking the chance of having coffee—as much as he needed the caffeine hit. He placed the glass in the dishwasher as the doorbell rang. Straightening, he exhaled and smoothed a hand down the front of his jacket as he opened the door to Ani.

"Are you ready?" she asked. She was dressed in similar black attire, though she'd opted for a white shirt instead of the black shirt Joey had chosen.

Joey nodded, tucked his phone into his pocket and locked the door behind them. They descended the stairs and headed for Ani's car. She had insisted on driving him, and Joey hadn't argued. He doubted he would've got to the church in one piece.

The radio was on low for the journey, and Joey kept his eyes on the passing scenery. Everyone was going about their day as if Joey's life wasn't unravelling. That day, everything was ending, and he could feel it. This would make everything real. He couldn't pretend Elliott was away on holiday when they were burying him instead.

A pressure weighed on his chest, and Joey breathed through it silently, willing it away. He wouldn't ever be able to find out why Elliott had done it. There was no one alive who could know, except if he believed in psychics, and that twisted Joey up even more. The why. If he could understand that, maybe he could find the peace that he hoped Elliott had found. If that had been his only way out, Joey had to believe he was now at peace. He had to be.

Ani parked the car in the church car park and climbed out, leaving Joey to follow. He stared at his fingers for a moment, bracing himself for the barrage of people he was about to see, and then climbed out of the car.

Cameras flashed as they strode for the doors of the church, where people milled around, waiting for the... Joey exhaled. He waited off to one side with Ani while other people chatted. Some of them Joey knew, others he didn't, but he didn't interact with anyone. Not even Elliott's parents when they arrived, looking distraught. He couldn't unless he wanted to lose it.

Too soon, the hearse arrived, and Joey stared at the coffin inside, surrounded by flowers. Elliott would've hated that because he had never been a flower person. Joey couldn't keep his eyes from the coffin as the pallbearers pulled it from the hearse and lifted it to their shoulders. As they fell into step, heading for the church, everyone followed. Ani led him to a pew, but Joey couldn't keep his eyes from the coffin now he'd seen it. Imagining Elliott lying inside.

He didn't listen to the service. He stood for the hymns but didn't sing. His entire body was numb, which was better than feeling the pain he had before. Elliott's parents had asked him to say a few words, but he'd declined, knowing he wouldn't get through it. He had so much he could say about his best friend, but his throat would close up, and nothing would come out. Of that, he was certain.

As the coffin was carried out again, the attendees followed, spilling out onto the path. The sun shone through the clouds as if Elliott was telling them he was there, but no one seemed to pay mind to the weather. Joey was attuned to it because it had been something of a hobby for Elliott.

Ani led him to the car, ignoring the reporters, and they followed the procession to the cemetery before climbing out and walking towards Elliott's last resting place. Joey slowed to a stop, staring at the gathering. A knot formed in his stomach, and he was grateful they'd hired security to stop the media from coming onto the grounds.

"I'm going to go to wait by the trees," he murmured, squinting into the distance.

"Are you sure?" Ani asked. He was grateful she didn't press.

Joey nodded and wandered towards the bench beneath the weeping willow. He leaned back against the bark and watched the burial in the distance. He could only see the backs of the people, which he was grateful for. He didn't want his final memory of Elliott to be him being lowered into the ground. He wanted to keep the memory of him looking peaceful in the coffin as if he was asleep. It beat the other image burnt into his mind.

His gaze wandered across the surprisingly pleasant view. He'd visited cemeteries before, but he couldn't remember them being so peaceful. Creepy, yes, but not peaceful. The calls of the birds, the distant rush of water, and the whisper of the wind blowing through the trees drew some tension from him. The hum of the priest's unidentifiable words mixed gently with the sounds, soothing him.

His gaze passed over the stone arch entrance and carried on. It flicked back again, and Joey blinked several times before his heart began racing. He stared as the unexpected angel in disguise strode towards him.

"Ethan," Joey whispered, gasping for air.

Ethan slid his arms around Joey, and Joey collapsed into him, tears streaming down his face.

"It's okay. I'm here. I'm not going anywhere," Ethan crooned, stroking Joey's hair while he cradled him.

Joey hadn't realised how much he'd needed Ethan until he was there. He grasped hold of Ethan's arm, burying his face against his chest, and let himself go. He wasn't sure how long had passed, but he eventually became aware of Ethan's heartbeat against his ear, and he wiped at his face, sitting upright.

"Sorry about that," he murmured.

"You don't need to be sorry. It's what I'm here for."

Joey stared into Ethan's eyes, seeing the sorrow and uncertainty in them. He threaded their fingers together. "What are you doing here?" Ethan had already said why, but Joey needed more.

Ethan sighed and looked away into the distance. Joey was sure he wasn't going to answer, but Ethan turned back and smiled. "You needed me. It doesn't matter what happens from here on out, but you needed me, and I'm here."

Joey's heart skipped a hopeful beat. "For how long?"

Ethan shrugged. "Until we decide what we want or two weeks, whichever is sooner." The corner of his mouth curved up, and his eyebrows rose. "I still have to go back to work, but Meredith has given me two weeks off."

Joey closed his eyes and exhaled. "Thank you."

"You don't need to thank me for this." Ethan glanced behind Joey and straightened, though he didn't let go of Joey's hand.

Joey glanced over his shoulder to where Ani approached. She studied Ethan and then focused on their joined hands before peering at Joey.

"Everything okay?" she asked.

Joey sniffed and cleared his throat. "Ani, I'd like you to meet Ethan. Ethan, this is my shop manager, Ani. I don't know where I'd be without her."

"You'd be swallowed whole by the weight of admin," she joked, holding her left hand out to Ethan, presumably so he didn't have to let go of Joey's hand.

Ethan chuckled and shook hands. "I know that weight. It's not pleasant. You must be a heavyweight champion to take all of what I'm sure he throws at you."

Ani grinned. "He tries his hardest to break me, but I pull through every time."

Joey's tension eased as they joked back and forth despite it being at his expense.

"They're going to the hotel now. Are you joining them?" Ani asked him.

Joey glanced over to the gravesite, watching the people disperse in groups. He shook his head. "I don't see that I'm needed, so no. I'm going home." He peered at Ethan. "Are you coming?"

Ethan nodded. "If that's okay?"

"More than."

"I'll head over to the hotel then, just to keep up appearances. Are you okay getting home?" Ani asked.

Joey opened his mouth, but Ethan beat him to an answer. "I have my car. We're good."

Ani nodded and squeezed Joey's shoulder before waving and striding down the path towards the stone arch.

"Did the reporters catch you on your way in?" Joey asked.

Ethan nodded. "It doesn't matter. I don't mind."

"We need to talk, don't we?"

"We do, but let's get you through today first."

Joey slid his hand across Ethan's cheek and to his nape, pulling him forward for a kiss. The moment their lips connected, tingles started everywhere, and it was all he could do to stop them from going too far in such an inappropriate place. It had been far too long since he'd touched Ethan. He rested his forehead against Ethan's and licked his lips, getting every taste of him he could.

"Let's go back to yours," Ethan said. "I bet you haven't eaten today."

Joey shook his head. "I've not had much of anything if I'm honest."

"Then let me look after you."

"You don't—"

"I want to do this, Joey. I *need* to. You're hurting, and I need to help."

Joey pulled Ethan into a hug and then stood, tugging Ethan to stand. "Lead the way."

"No. Side by side."

Joey's nostrils flared as he tried to contain his emotions, not wanting to be a mess when the reporters photographed them when they left.

"This is a beautiful place," Ethan said.

"It is." Joey glanced around as they wandered towards the entrance. "Elliott would've loved it. I didn't even know this place existed." The closer they got to the entrance, the tenser Joey became. "Are you sure you're ready for this? We can go our separate ways and meet up at the house instead."

Ethan pulled them to a stop just before they exited. "I will do whichever you want to. I don't want to hide, but if it would make your life more difficult, then yes, we can. Is there a wake?"

"There is, but I'm not going."

Joey wrapped his arms around Ethan and closed his eyes, soaking in his amazing strength. Joey was the Dom of this relationship, but it seemed Ethan had taken over the role for the moment. He pulled back, threading their fingers once more.

"Let's go. As one."

Ethan smiled and nodded. "As one."

Joey and Ethan exited the cemetery to a gentle hum of conversation until the reporters saw them, and then they were bombarded by flashes and questions and swarmed. Luckily, the security company had left a couple of guards for them, and they helped clear a path to Ethan's car.

"Is Ethan your boyfriend?"

"Are you moving in together?"

"Are you leaving London?"

"What would Elliott think of your relationship?"

Joey sighed, knowing he would eventually have to make a statement about what happened but refusing to do so that day. They could wait a little longer. He climbed into Ethan's car and slammed the door on the questions. He nodded and smiled at the guard, and then Ethan drove away.

"You'll have to direct me, I'm afraid. I don't know London at all," Ethan said with a soft chuckle.

"It can be confusing, but I will tell you where to go." He explained the next couple of turns and then said, "When did you get here?"

Ethan's nose crinkled. "About an hour before I found you. I got stuck in traffic; otherwise, I would've been here a couple of hours before."

"That's the joy of motorways, isn't it?" Joey chuckled. "Thank you."

Ethan smiled across at him but didn't say anything, and Joey transferred his attention to directing him. When they made it to Life in Ink and parked behind the shop, Joey was exhausted. Now that everything was done, he could barely get his body to move. Ethan helped him from the car and up the stairs, and Joey unlocked the door and locked it behind them again. Within seconds, Joelle twined through his legs, and he braced himself, as always, so he didn't fall over.

"And this must be Joelle," Ethan murmured, crouching low and holding out his hand for Joelle to bump her head against. She could be stubborn sometimes, but she easily transferred her attention to Ethan once she was satisfied he meant no harm to her.

Joey slipped into the kitchen to replenish her water and food and felt the moment Ethan joined him, even though his back was to the entrance. When he turned, Ethan leaned against the counter with his arms crossed and a small smile playing across his face.

"What?" Joey asked.

"I missed you."

Joey placed the bowls on the floor and stepped closer to Ethan. "I missed you, too."

Ethan slipped his arms around Joey's waist and stared at him, his hazel eyes taking on an indecipherable sheen. Joey skimmed his fingertips across Ethan's cheekbones and down his jaw, following them with his gaze, reacquainting himself with the man who had come to mean so much to him in such a short time.

"How did we get here?" he murmured.

Ethan didn't pretend he didn't know what Joey was asking. "Fate. Destiny. Serendipity. There are so many names to call it. And as much as I hate what you've been through, it brought you to me. I wouldn't wish what happened to anyone, and I wish with everything inside me Elliott was still here, but I don't know if we would've met had this not happened."

Joey understood what his meaning was and didn't get upset. "As my mother always says, I wouldn't be where I am today without going through what I've been through."

"Smart woman." Ethan pecked a kiss on his lips. "Come on. Time for food and a nap."

Ethan pulled away and went to the fridge, dragging some items from it. Joey didn't interrupt, allowing Ethan to look after him like Joey knew he wanted. Ethan made a ham salad sandwich, cut it into two and placed it on a plate, pausing to rub his finger against the dent in the corner of the counter, his lips curving. He poured two small glasses of apple juice and handed one to Joey before carrying the plate and the second glass to the sofa. Joey followed and settled into a cushion. Ethan passed him the plate and took his drink from him.

"Eat. Then we can nap." Ethan stifled a yawn and laughed. "Even thinking about a nap is making me tired."

"I'm not surprised. You've been driving for hours." Joey took a bite and groaned. Having not eaten anything that day, it was the best-tasting food he'd ever eaten.

Ethan waved him off. "It's only six hours normally. But yes, I didn't sleep at all last night, so I'm flagging now."

Joey finished his sandwich quickly, wanting to get Ethan into bed—in the non-sexual way—before they both collapsed from exhaustion. Joey took the plate and glasses to the kitchen and led the way to his bedroom.

"Do you want to freshen up?"

Ethan groaned. "Yes, please."

Joey chuckled and pointed to the en suite. "Have at it."

While Ethan scrubbed the grime from his journey from his skin, Joey stripped down to his boxers and grabbed some pyjama bottoms in case Ethan didn't have anything with him. When Ethan came into the room with a towel around his waist, his hair dripping onto his chest, Joey's mouth dried.

"Oh, great, thanks," he said when Joey held out the pyjamas. "I forgot to get my bag from the car." Ethan dropped the towel and pulled on the pyjamas, then picked up the towel again. "Where do you want this?"

"Just in there will do." Joey pointed to the washing basket.

Ethan threw it in and climbed into the bed beside Joey. Joey slid down onto his back, and Ethan snuggled into his side. The rest of the tension Joey had been holding released, and he closed his eyes at how perfect Ethan felt in his arms.

"Sleep, Joey. We'll talk and figure stuff out later."

Joey pressed his lips to Ethan's forehead. "Okay. I—" He cleared his throat. "Sleep well."

That hadn't been what he was about to say. Could he have fallen in love with Ethan already? How was that possible? Joey kept his eyes closed, and although he was tired, he waited until Ethan had relaxed into sleep before allowing himself to follow. When they woke, they would have plenty to discuss and decide upon, but for the moment, he would content himself by holding Ethan in his arms again.

He wasn't sure where they would go from there, but Ethan had driven all this way to support him, so he refused to give him less than his undivided attention while they figured themselves out. He wasn't sure he could find what he had with Ethan anywhere else; therefore, he had to try.

11

ETHAN

than woke with the heat of someone at his back, and he
smiled. He'd recognise Joey's soft snores anywhere. It took
him a couple of minutes to get his bearings, especially when he
opened his eyes and didn't recognise the bedside table. Then, the
memories of that day and the previous night came back to him.

After receiving the message from Joey saying that he always
needed him, Ethan had stared at the words for hours, pressing
to light his screen every time it went dark. He'd not known what
to do. Then something had clicked in his brain, and he'd jumped
up, racing around to fill a bag and sending a message to Meredith
to apologise for taking off with no notice. Surprisingly, she had
replied almost instantly, saying it was okay and to take his time.
He'd thrown his bag into the car and set off with barely a thought
further than getting to Joey.

When he'd neared London, he'd had second thoughts. Would
Joey truly want him there? Ethan had stopped at a service station
to fill up the car with petrol and to try to find where Joey lived. He
knew the name of Joey's tattoo shop, which was easy enough to
find, but he didn't know where he lived. If Joey had mentioned it,
Ethan couldn't remember. But he found an obituary about Elliott,
which led him to the church and cemetery. It was pure chance
he had been there at the right time.

Joey had looked distraught, though with a slight sense of
peacefulness, as if he'd realised Elliott was in a good place now.

But there were so many questions surrounding Elliott's decision to end his life. Joey had been left with so much uncertainty, and Ethan wanted to help, but he didn't know how.

One thing he did know was how to reassure Joey that he wasn't going anywhere. At least not yet. And despite the act he was about to perform, their relationship wasn't solely about sex. Or about the Dom/sub lifestyle. It was a way to show each other how they felt without saying the words because Ethan had plenty of feelings bubbling at the surface, and it wouldn't take long for them to burst free.

Carefully, he extricated himself from Joey's arms without waking him—a feat in itself, but he assumed Joey was exhausted enough to sleep deeply. Ethan slid down the bed, keeping the covers from being disturbed as much as possible. Despite it being darker beneath the covers, he could still see the intricate black and coloured designs on Joey's body. The black swirls on his upper thighs appeared to be directing him to where he wanted to be.

He took hold of Joey's softened cock and licked his lips before sucking at the head and swiping his tongue across the tip. Making sure to get it nice and wet, he sucked more and more into his mouth, wanting Joey deep in his throat before he woke. Joey's dick responded as expected, growing harder with Ethan's ministrations. The head peeped out from behind the foreskin, something Ethan loved to watch, and he tasted the precome that was escaping.

Joey breathed a moan, his hips twitching, but he still sounded asleep. Ethan continued, licking stripes up his cock, teasing the nerves and catching more precome. Then he sank down on the shaft, wrapping his hand around the part at the base he couldn't swallow. Breathing through his nose, he swallowed around the tip, and Joey bucked, his hand coming to rest against Ethan's head.

"Ethan..." Joey groaned. "Fuck."

Not being able to see Joey's expression was torture. He loved watching him, but the sounds he was making were enough to send fire licking through Ethan's blood. He pushed at Joey's upper leg, and Joey lifted it to give Ethan more room. Ethan took advantage of that, and with his free hand, he slid his finger back to Joey's pucker, pressing but not entering. He pulled off, gasping for air as he stroked to keep Joey moving towards his climax. Then he swallowed him down again, massaging more firmly against his entrance. Ethan bobbed his head up and down, Joey using the hand on his head as a guide, and Ethan felt it when Joey hit the edge. His thigh muscles tensed, his grip tightened, and he groaned. Ethan filled his throat with Joey's cock and swallowed.

"Ethan!" Joey shouted as he fell over the cliff and into his orgasm.

Ethan worked him through his release, stroking, sucking, fingering until Joey collapsed onto his back, his legs sinking to the bed. Ethan pulled off, breathing as heavily as Joey was and climbed up Joey's body to peek his head out of the top of the covers. Joey's gaze was already on him as he emerged, and Ethan smiled.

"Hello," he said.

Joey raised his eyebrows, and Ethan chuckled. "That's one way to wake up." Joey's voice was hoarse. From sleep or his orgasm, Ethan didn't know, but it didn't matter either.

"Only the best for you."

Joey cupped Ethan's jaw with his hands, brushing his thumbs over his cheeks. "Thank you for being here," he whispered.

"You're welcome."

Joey sighed. "We have things to sort out, don't we?"

"There's no rush, Joey. You've had a draining day already. We don't need to do this now."

"Wouldn't it be better to get it sorted? Then, we can either say goodbye or start now, depending on what we decide."

It would be, but Ethan wasn't sure he was ready if the conversation went in the direction he didn't want it to go. On his drive down, he'd already been through the options he could see, and he'd decided that if he had to, he would move to London to be with Joey. It wasn't his first choice, but he didn't have a business like Joey did. Joey couldn't just up and leave without considering a lot more things than Ethan had to.

"I suppose."

Joey traced his lips, the soft sensation leaving prickles along the route, and Ethan could barely contain his need to scrape his teeth over it to rid himself of the tickle.

"Come on. Let's shower, and we can talk while I make some food."

Joey kissed him chastely and climbed from the bed, striding for the en suite without a backward glance. He didn't need to, after all. Ethan would follow him wherever he went.

He stood, heading for the bathroom, when he heard a soft mewl at the door. "Joey, should I let Joelle in?"

Joey popped his head out of the doorway. "No, leave her for now. She's just asking for food because she's heard us moving around. I'll get her something when we're done." He crooked a finger at Ethan.

The shower was a mutually beneficial arrangement, and Ethan's knees were weak when Joey finally switched the water off.

"Do you want to borrow these until you grab your bag?" Joey asked, holding out joggers and a T-shirt.

"Thanks. I'll grab my bag once I'm dressed."

They dressed in silence, though their gazes roamed each other's bodies despite how many times they'd orgasmed in the shower. Ethan didn't think he had another one in him. While Joey disappeared into the kitchen area, Ethan left to grab his bag. It was the only one he'd brought with him, and to be honest, he couldn't guarantee what he'd put in there. As he grabbed it from the backseat, he heard shouting and glanced towards the road. The car park was behind the shop and apartment, but there was an alley from the road to allow cars entry. Several people stood on the path at the entrance to the alley, pointing and shouting towards him, although he couldn't hear what they said. He nearly went closer when there was a flash of light. He blinked and realised they were reporters.

He blew out a breath, locked his car and ran back up the steps to the apartment. The car park was private property, and the reporters would be breaking the law should they come into it, which he was glad about. Some reporters probably wouldn't care, but those seemed to be hesitant. For now, at least.

He didn't mention it to Joey when he entered the house. He just put his bag next to the door and headed into the kitchen to see if he could help with anything.

"No, I've got it." He nodded to the counter where a glass of apple juice and a cup of tea sat. "I made you those to keep you going until the food is ready."

"Thanks." He sipped the tea, closing his eyes and enjoying the warmth. He knew what was coming.

"What do you want from this, Ethan?" Joey's back was to him, so he couldn't see Joey's expression.

"Is this a good day to have this conversation?" Ethan said instead of answering.

Joey glanced over his shoulder. "If I'm going to lose you, I may as well grieve two losses at the same time."

Ethan dropped onto a bar stool and closed his eyes. "I'm scared to lay it all out there in case it's too much."

"You're not scared of anything," Joey countered. "Except ghost tours."

Ethan smiled and swallowed. "I'm scared of losing you."

"Tell me what you want, Ethan. Please. Be as blunt as you need to be."

Ethan took another sip of his tea, fortifying himself for laying himself bare. This could backfire spectacularly.

"I want to be with you. I don't care about the media. I don't care if I have to move. I don't care if I'm making a mistake. I want you. Whatever I need to do to have you."

Joey moved the pan off the burner and switched it off before facing Ethan. He kept his hands on the counter behind him as he stared across the space at him. Ethan worried he had put too much on Joey until the sheen in Joey's eyes spilt over and ran down his cheeks.

"Truly?"

Ethan nodded. He couldn't speak.

"I want you, too. I—" Joey sniffed and blew out a breath before meeting his gaze again. "I'm falling in love with you, Ethan."

Emotion bubbled up inside Ethan, and he inhaled shakily, trying to calm his racing heart. "I'm falling for you, too," he whispered.

Joey closed the distance between them, and his lips were on Ethan's, almost sealing a deal they hadn't yet made. Ethan didn't mind, his brain misfiring as the admission sank deep inside him. When they pulled apart, they stared at each other.

"Now that's out of the way, we need to talk about logistics. But we can do that over food. I made French toast."

"Sounds like a plan," Ethan answered, trying not to sound like he'd stepped off Whitby's West Cliff and streamed towards the ocean, only to stop a few inches short.

Joey kissed him again, then returned to the stove, plating the food. Ethan carried his drinks to the dining table and went back for Joey's. They settled at a ninety-degree angle to each other, able to see the other person but able to look away if they needed a minute. Ethan's stomach had so many butterflies filling it that he wasn't sure he would be able to eat. But as they sat, knees bumping, Joey smiled, and Ethan's nerves reduced a little.

"I'll make a proper dinner for us later, but this will tide us over for a short time."

"It smells delicious. It's been a while since I've had it." Ethan took a bite and hummed. "It tastes a lot better than I remember my version being."

Joey chuckled. "A few added ingredients make it taste divine. In my opinion, of course."

Ethan snorted, taking a sip of his apple juice. They ate in silence for a few minutes, then Joey rested his cheek on his fist, his elbow on the table and stared at Ethan. "You said you were willing to move. What if you didn't have to?"

Ethan frowned and wiped a crumb from the corner of his mouth. "I don't see how. You have a business to run."

"A business I can run from anywhere as long as I have someone in the building during opening hours. I travel for business. I don't have to be in one place all the time. I could use Whitby as my home base."

"But don't a lot of your clients live or work in London? You'd be travelling a lot more than if you lived here."

Joey nodded. "I would. But I'm willing to. Can you see yourself living in this city?"

Ethan inhaled. "Not really. But I would. There are plenty of jobs I could find here."

"You love Whitby."

"I do. It's in my blood. But I can still visit."

Joey frowned, the crease between his eyebrows deepening. "I could change how I work. Not take as many London clients or get them to come to me."

"Would those clients be happy about that, though? I don't want you to lose business over something that's easily changed." Ethan would love to stay in Whitby, but he would live in London without hesitation if it meant he could stay with Joey.

Joey clicked his tongue. "Let's speak with Ani and get her opinion on the best way to do this. She won't decide for us, but she might have some more ideas or insight we can use to make the decision easier."

Ethan nodded. "Sounds good."

"The media will be a problem. It'll never completely die down. There will always be someone who takes a picture of you in random places or in positions that could be twisted to seem like something else. You've probably seen the type of story in the news about celebrities who appear drunk when, in fact, they only had their picture taken as their eyes were closing. Or you could be photographed coming out of the supermarket, carrying a chocolate bar and then everyone who is everyone has an opinion about your weight. It's horrible, but it's true. Everything you do will be scrutinised to see if it could be used to sell a story, whether or not that story is true."

Ethan nodded. "I can imagine it's awful, but I'll manage. I might need some talking down occasionally, but I'll be fine."

Joey threaded his fingers through Ethan's, squeezing tightly. "There will also be celebrity events. Parties and premieres, you name it, I've had an invitation for it. Some I will have to go to. I need to show my face occasionally, but you don't have to attend with me if you don't want to."

"Rub shoulders with celebrities? Sign me up," Ethan joked. "Truthfully, though, that scares the hell out of me, but I'd still attend with you." He shook his head. "You are a celebrity yourself, you know?"

Joey raised his eyebrows, his mouth twitching. "Not on their scale, I'm not. Some people know who I am if they've been to me for tattoos or if they're interested in a celebrity's life and know everything about them. But mainly, I'm below even a Z-lister."

"I bet you'd be surprised how well-known you are." Ethan cocked his head. "Have you ever tried searching for your name?"

Joey chuckled. "No."

Ethan pulled his phone free and typed into the search with one hand. The immediate results were several pictures of Joey, some of the tattoo designs, and a link to his shop. Ethan turned the phone towards him, showing him the results.

"See."

"That proves nothing."

"It proves that you're more well-known than you think."

Joey sighed. "Is that a game-changer?"

Ethan shook his head, grinning. "Nope."

"I'll introduce you to some artists in a bit. There are at least two downstairs today. Maybe more. It depends on what was in the diary."

Joelle miaowed and twined between Ethan's legs under the table, and he chuckled. "She's finally come out to see me," he said, scooting his chair back. The moment he did, Joelle jumped onto his lap, and he stroked her soft fur. He glanced at Joey, a small smile playing around Joey's mouth as he watched the cat. "Has she been fed?"

Joey snorted. "Yes, though she would deny it if she could. If I didn't feed her the second I came out of the bedroom, I wouldn't hear the end of it. I remember one time, I had a phone call just as I'd left the room, and I needed to answer it because it was a client. As I was talking, Joelle wound between my legs, almost tripping me, and mewling as if I were torturing her. In the end, my client asked if everything was okay, and I had to explain about my cat needing to be fed as if she were the queen of the house. Luckily, the client was a nice one, instead of one who looked down on us peasants."

Ethan cooed at the gorgeous cat. "You aren't like that, are you?"

"She truly is."

Ethan held Joelle to his chest and smiled at Joey. "So, we're going to speak to Ani about location. I'm okay with the media thing. I'll attend events with you if I can. It depends on the job situation. Anything else?"

"You need to meet my parents."

Ethan's heart skipped a beat, and he stopped breathing for a few seconds before resuming, as if the thought had already crossed his mind and he was okay with it. It hadn't, and he wasn't. Well, he was, but he was nervous. Now, he understood how Joey felt about going to Ethan's parents' house for dinner.

"Okay."

"I'll call them and sort out a day we can go."

"Okay."

His voice sounded high-pitched even to his own ears, and a smile slowly spread across Joey's face. "It'll be fine."

"Okay." This time, his voice did crack, and he hid his face in Joelle's fur, Joey's laughter in his ears.

Joey's phone rang, and he apologised as he glanced at the screen and answered it. "Hi, Ani." Ethan watched the emotions play across Joey's face as the low hum of Ani's words filtered into Joey's ear. Ethan couldn't hear it, but he could see the anger cross Joey's face. "Who?" he said, his voice hard. "Give him my number. I want to talk to him… I'll be kind. Possibly… If he had anything to do with it…" Joey sighed and gritted his teeth. "Okay. Get him to call me. I want to know what happened that night." He ended the call and stared at the screen, even as it went dark.

"Is everything okay?"

"A man just called the shop saying he was with Elliott the night he died."

12

JOEY

Joey inhaled. "Apparently, they hooked up at the party, but the guy lost track of Elliott afterwards. I want to hear it all, and preferably without the police present. He'll be more likely to answer truthfully around me."

"Is that a good idea? Not getting the police involved, I mean," Ethan said, setting Joelle back on the floor.

Joey pushed his plate aside. "I will tell them, but I want to talk to him first." He stood, unable to stay still and strode the length of the apartment and back several times, checking his phone at the end of every stretch.

Ethan didn't say anything else, and Joey was grateful. It wasn't the best idea to talk to this guy before the police, but he needed to know whatever he knew, and if they went to the police first, he might never find out the truth. This guy might not even know, but at least he spent some time with Elliott. He might have some information into Elliott's state of mind because Joey sure as fuck didn't.

He slid his fingers into his hair and closed his elbows around his head. How did he not see what Elliott was going through? Even now, when he thought back over their interactions in the last few months, Joey couldn't see anything amiss. Had Elliott been suffering in silence? Joey hated the idea that he had been. He'd thought they were close enough to tell each other everything, and in some ways, it burnt that Elliott couldn't talk to him about whatever had been bothering him.

Joey checked his phone again. "Why isn't he calling?"

Ethan came over to him. "Maybe he got caught up in something. Didn't you want to introduce me to your staff?"

Joey gritted his teeth and exhaled through his nose, his shoulders slumping. "Yeah, I did."

"Come on, then. You've got your phone with you, so you can answer when he calls."

Joey stared at Ethan and dropped his head down for a brief press of their lips. "Thank you."

Ethan raised his eyebrows. "For what?"

"Talking me down. If you haven't noticed yet, I can be a dog after a bone. Or a tattoo artist after a client."

Ethan threw his head back and laughed, his mouth curving into his trademark lopsided grin. "I like that. I'll have to remember to use that analogy in the future."

Joey slid his arm around Ethan's shoulders and led him towards the door. "We'll go around the front. I don't want to scare anyone by appearing out of the blue when they're not expecting us."

Ethan's hesitation was clear. "Um, there were reporters outside when I went to get my bag."

Joey nodded. "That doesn't surprise me. Are you okay with that?"

Ethan nodded. "Yes, I just wasn't sure if you were."

"We can come back up the inside stairs. I just know from experience that scaring the fuck out of a tattoo artist causes issues."

Ethan chuckled. "I can imagine. That ever happened to you?"

Joey nodded as he opened the front door, letting Ethan out first and following him, locking the door behind him. "Yes. My client ended up with a scratch up their thigh, far too close to where we have to be careful."

Ethan winced as they descended the metal staircase. "Ouch."

"Luckily, it was only a scratch. It could've been worse." He checked his phone, shaking his head when there were no messages or calls. When was the guy going to call him?

Joey shoved the phone into his pocket after double-checking it was not on silent and threaded his fingers through Ethan's hand, squeezing. "Ready?"

Ethan inhaled and smiled. "Always."

Every time he gifted Joey with a smile like that, Joey felt like he'd won the lottery. And in some ways, he had. He wished they had met under better circumstances because Elliott would've loved him.

The hustle and bustle of traffic was audible even before they rounded the edge of the building and headed through the alley to the street. Reporters stood waiting, grabbing their cameras or camera person when Joey and Ethan came into view.

"Joey! Ethan! Are you a couple now? Why have you been hiding? Are you guilty of Elliott's death?"

The questions kept on coming, but he studiously ignored them all, even when one of them got colourful with their words. Ethan tensed, but Joey squeezed his hand again and led him around the front of the building and into the shop entrance, closing the door on the questions. The blinds had already been closed, stopping them from being able to see inside, but it also kept out the sunlight, making the shop darker than usual for the daytime.

"Hey, I wasn't expecting to see you today," Ani said from behind the counter, wearing her trademark black clothes with tattoos visible.

"I said I'd introduce Ethan to everyone while I wait for that guy to call." He patted his pocket, checking that his phone was still there, even though he knew it was. "Who's in today?"

Ani winked at Ethan. "Everyone."

Ethan's barely audible exhale made Joey smile, and he slid his arm around his waist, pulling him closer. "You'll be fine," he murmured, pressing a kiss to his temple. "Are they busy?"

"Only Dallas has a client. You couldn't have picked a better time to visit."

"Of course, we couldn't," Ethan mumbled.

"Can you buzz them for me, please, Ani?"

"Sure."

Joey turned Ethan towards the wall of designs. "Each area and room has a little buzzer, which we use if we need an artist to come to the reception area. It's easier than shouting."

There was a muted buzz throughout the building, and then Beck shouted, "Coming!"

Joey chuckled. "Well, it's easier than Ani shouting. Some don't seem to care."

He faced the corner of the room his friends would enter from and tugged Ethan into his body as if he could shelter him. But Ethan stood straighter when two men entered. They could be described as imposing, but they were some of the nicest guys he'd ever known.

Stepping forward, he held out his hand to Beck, the man dragging him into a hug when they shook.

"Hey, man. How're things?" Beck cupped Joey's nape, keeping him from retreating, and stared at him. "Well, you look like you're all in one piece, so I suppose can't complain."

Joey snorted. "I'm okay. How are you?"

"Busy as ever."

Joey raised his eyebrows. "So I've been told."

Beck shoved him backwards. "Fuck off. I had a client cancel at the last minute."

"What's your excuse?" he asked Finn.

Finn threw up his middle finger, and Joey caught it and twisted, ending up in a tussle with the smaller man.

"Enough! You'll break something again!" Ani called, and they broke apart, laughing. "I refuse to order more furniture because you went off on one. I swear I'm a babysitter, not a bloody manager."

Joey glanced at her and caught her throwing a smile towards Ethan, who grinned back at her. He retreated to Ethan's side, sliding his arm possessively around his waist again. "Guys, this is Ethan. Ethan, this is Beck, and this is Finn." He pointed at each man in order and tried to see them as Ethan might as his boyfriend greeted his friends.

Beck had short, dark brown hair, which was always immaculately styled, a neatly trimmed beard and moustache, bright blue eyes, and his trademark dark wash jeans and tank top, showing off his tattoos. Finn had slightly longer brown hair, always hidden behind a backwards flat cap, a barely-there moustache, dark-rimmed glasses and leather bracelets, complementing the khaki trousers and T-shirt he wore. All in all, they were good-looking men who could have anyone they wanted. That they were all gay was some sort of mystical coincidence shit.

A thundering of footsteps sounded, and Joey smiled. "And here is Dallas."

A giant of a man entered the room, someone who wouldn't have been out of place on a beach surfing. Dallas's slick-backed hair accentuated his good looks, even though his face was covered by a huge beard and moustache.

"Joey!" Dallas said, punching his biceps as he stopped beside him.

"Dallas," Joey replied with a shake of his head. "I'd like you to meet Ethan."

"Nice to meet you," Dallas said, holding out his beefy hand.

Ethan shook it. "You, too. Joey has told me a little about you all."

"It's all lies," Beck said, leaning back on the counter and crossing his arms over his chest.

Ethan laughed. "I bet."

"How come only one of you has a client?" Joey asked, resting his ass on the table when Ethan turned his attention back to the designs on the wall.

"Mine cancelled. I told you," Beck said. Joey flipped him off.

"I'm heading out to Cardiff in an hour or so," Finn said. "Porter's been waiting long enough."

Joey nodded. "He has. It's nice to know we have some clients who can be patient."

"So, Ethan..." Dallas said. "What are you doing with this asshole?"

Ethan faced them again, his lopsided smile curving his lips as he shoved his hands into his pockets. "Saving him from sleeping in his car?"

Joey groaned and palmed his face. He hadn't told them where he'd been sleeping, and they'd just assumed he was in a hotel each time he stopped.

"His car?" Ani said.

Joey peeked between his fingers and grimaced at her narrowed eyes. She was worse than his mother, and that was saying something.

Ethan glanced between them and winced. "Sorry. I thought they knew."

Joey waved him off with a shake of his head. "It's fine. They would've found out eventually." He sighed. "I would've preferred eventually," he murmured.

"What the hell were you sleeping in your car for?" Beck said. "It's not like you can't afford a hotel."

Joey crossed his arms. "It would've been easier for reporters to find me. It's not like I can pay cash everywhere I go."

"But the car? Really?" Dallas said. "And not even *your* car."

"There was no point in taking my car, dumbass. It's the same as using my credit cards. Reporters would've found me in no time."

Ani shushed them before Dallas could retort, which was a good thing because they were known to argue for hours. "It doesn't matter now, does it? You're back. What's your plan now?"

Joey glanced at Ethan. "We're still figuring that out."

Dallas clapped him on the shoulder. "Well, figure it out fast. I'm out. See you later." He disappeared, and his thundering footsteps headed back up to the first floor where his studio was.

Beck and Finn stayed for a bit longer before work called for them both, and Joey breathed a sigh when it was just him, Ethan and Ani.

"Ani, we need your advice."

Ani chuckled. "Use condoms and lube. Stretch every single time. Best in a bed to avoid carpet burns. Anything else?"

Joey closed his eyes, barely withholding his laugh. She was a force to be reckoned with for sure. "No, smartass. Logistics."

Ani raised her eyebrows. "I told you. Use a bed—"

"Logistics about where to live," he interrupted, and she gaped at him.

She cleared her throat, shuffled some paper into a pile that was already in a pile and peered at him again. "Where to live?" she croaked.

Joey nodded, pushing off the table and stopping in front of her, the counter separating them. He braced his hands on it. "Ethan is willing to move here, but he loves Whitby. I don't necessarily need to live in London, even though this is our home base, because of the amount of travelling we do. I think we're too close to the situation to see a solution and wanted to know your opinion."

Ani stared down at the papers in her hands, but he could see them shaking slightly. "I think you know your answer but don't want to face it." She glanced up at him, a small quirk to her mouth.

Asking her had been the right thing to do. He peered over his shoulder at Ethan, who stood with his hands in his pockets, biting his lip. He held out his hand, and Ethan stepped closer.

"I do know the answer, but I don't think Ethan believed me." He chuckled.

Ani smiled. "In that case…" She turned to Ethan. "He doesn't need to live in London to do this job. Ninety per cent of his clients he has to travel to meet. Those that live around here, we could batch into a few days or a week at the same time so that he can only be here for a short time."

Ethan rested his head against Joey's shoulder. "I just feel like it's a lot more travelling than he had been doing."

Ani shook her head. "Not at all. It's not like some of them can't send their jet for him."

Ethan lifted his head. "Jet?"

"Of course. We're tattoo artists for the rich and famous. He doesn't just travel around this country. He travels the world."

"Holy crap," Ethan whispered.

Joey laughed. "I told you this."

"I know, but having it all laid out for me makes it more real."

"So, the question really should be…" Ani glanced between them. "Are you willing to put up with him not being at home some days? Or are you willing to go with him when he travels?" She smirked. "We can always do with having an assistant around here. Or there. Or wherever you are. He's useless at paperwork."

Joey shook his head minutely, and Ani shut up. He didn't want Ethan to feel pressured to work for him. He wanted Ethan to continue doing whatever he wanted to. But he wouldn't deny that the idea of having Ethan by his side whenever he travelled was a wonderful one.

"See? It would be fine to stay in Whitby," Joey said.

Ethan's frown showed he wasn't convinced, but Joey was glad they had asked Ani because it showed Ethan that Joey wasn't making it up.

"Talking of Whitby, though. When did you say you had to go back?" Joey asked him.

Ethan shrugged. "Two weeks."

The bell over the door rang, and Joey stepped in front of Ethan to shield him from whoever entered. It better not be a reporter.

"Hey, sorry. I wondered if you had any appointments?" the guy said.

Joey tilted his head, taking him in, but he didn't appear to be reporter material, though that didn't mean he wasn't.

Ani took over, but Joey kept his gaze on him. "Welcome to Life in Ink. When were you looking at for an appointment?"

The guy glanced at Joey again and moved closer to the counter. "As soon as you have one, really."

Ani clicked around on the computer a few times before answering. "Okay. It depends on what you want and how much time it'll take to get it done, to be honest. We're booked pretty solidly for the next few months, but we have smaller bites of time. What are you wanting done?"

The guy pulled out a piece of paper from his pocket and unfolded it. Joey couldn't see what was on it, but Ani's eyebrows rose as she nodded. She glanced at Joey and held out the paper. "How long do you think?"

Joey took the paper and saw an intricate tribal design with a repeating pattern and words intertwined between them. "Where arc you wanting it?"

"Upper arm."

Joey glanced at him, taking his measure to figure out just how big a job it would be. "Maybe six hours in total, depending on how much of his arm he wants covered." He handed it back to the guy and held out his hand. "Joey Reynolds."

The guy cleared his throat. "Sorry. I came here because you were recommended. I didn't expect to meet you, though. I expected to see someone else."

"And you are?" Joey wanted his name.

"Grey. Grey Kennedy."

Joey tightened his hold on the man's hand. "Who recommended you?" he murmured.

Grey swallowed. "Elliott," he whispered, his nostrils flaring. "He was my brother."

Joey dropped his hand as he staggered back, Ethan's hands on his spine the only thing stopping him from crashing into the wall. "Elliott's brother?"

Grey nodded slowly. "Elliott found me a couple of years ago. He didn't tell you?"

Joey shook his head. There were far too many secrets around this place for his liking. "Mother or father?"

Grey seemed to understand. "Elliott's mother. Elliott found out she'd had an affair when he overheard them arguing one evening. She gave me up for adoption as soon as I was born. He told me he started searching for me the moment he knew. Once he found me, he helped out." Grey shrugged a shoulder. "My mum didn't have a lot of money, but we managed. Elliott insisted on helping."

"Why didn't he tell me," Joey said more to himself.

Grey licked his lips. "He told me he didn't want his status to mess with my life." He looked at the floor, but not before Joey saw the shimmer of tears. "I wasn't planning on coming here, but he said if anything happened to him to come. He said..." Grey paused and met Joey's gaze. "He said to tell you he was sorry he hadn't told you. It's not that he didn't trust you with what he found out. He didn't trust his father."

Joey raised his eyebrows. "Why?"

"He's not the kind of man you tangle with."

Joey shook his head. "You must have the wrong person. John is a good man."

"I'm not talking about John. I'm talking about Robert."

Joey couldn't breathe. What the hell was going on? "Elliott's uncle?"

13

ETHAN

The man, Grey, nodded. "Elliott figured out Robert was his father when we took DNA tests. From what we could find, Melinda was with Robert before she married John, and Elliott was the result. She had an affair with him a few years later, resulting in me, but she insisted she was too old for another baby and gave me up."

"How did John not know?" Joey asked.

"I'm not sure he didn't know," Grey said. "From what Elliott observed, John and Melinda were close but not as close as she and Robert whenever he came to visit."

"If Melinda was in love with Robert, why didn't she leave John and marry him?" Joey asked.

Ethan had an idea about that, but it wasn't his place to say because he didn't know anyone.

"Robert is not one to be trifled with. He's involved in some shady shit...um, stuff." Grey's cheeks flushed.

Ethan rested a hand on Joey's back. "Was Elliott the kind of person to push Robert somehow?" he asked gently.

Joey shook his head, paused and frowned. He sighed. "Yes. I don't want to say it about him, but yes. If he felt something or someone was wronged, he would fight to help rectify it. It was something we butted heads about several times."

Ethan glanced at Grey. "Do you know if he was trying to right a wrong, Grey?"

Grey rocked on his heels and bit his lip. "He was."

Joey sank into a chair, rubbing his hands over his face. "I feel like I didn't know him," he whispered.

Ethan settled beside him, arm around his shoulders. "You knew him better than anyone, Joey. It's not your fault he kept secrets." He peered at Grey again. "What do you know?"

Tears shimmered in Elliott's brother's eyes. "He was trying to get me free of Robert."

"Why? If Melinda gave you up for adoption, Robert would have nothing to do with you."

"Except Robert instigated the adoption process. Melinda didn't know that the woman who adopted me was under Robert's thumb. The moment they finalised the adoption, Robert was basically my father figure."

"Jesus." Joey sighed and sat back, dislodging Ethan's arm. "Do you think this had something to do with him..."

Everyone knew what Joey couldn't say, and Grey shrugged. "I really don't know. I honestly just came here to get a tattoo done. I didn't think I'd see you." He held up his hands. "Not that I didn't want to, but I didn't want to spill Elliott's secrets. Though, fat lot of good that did me because the minute you asked, I told you everything." He sniffed and wiped his face. "I'm sorry. I don't mean to bring this down on you. I'll find somewhere else to do the tattoo."

"No!" Joey stood. "No. You're one of us. If Elliott was helping you, we'll help you."

Ethan's heart poured out to the man. He deserved the best of everything, but he had the feeling Joey was going to end up on the wrong side of a dangerous man.

"Did this have something to do with the bruises Elliott sported a few months back? He said he'd had a drunken brawl with someone, but I was never convinced," Ani asked.

Grey crossed his arms over his chest and looked at the floor. "Yes. Robert's men gave him a warning. He knew a lot about Robert's businesses, and Robert had become aware of it. It was to persuade him to look the other way."

"But he wasn't going to, was he?" Joey said.

Grey shook his head.

"Bloody hell!" Joey said, slamming his palms on the counter, rattling the contents before leaning his forehead on it. "You should've stepped back, Ell."

"I told him that time and time again, but he wouldn't listen. He insisted on freeing me from Robert's control." Grey stepped back towards the door. "I should go. I don't want to put you in the firing line, too."

Ethan moved closer. "Let me give you my number. If you need anything at all, call. Okay?"

Grey shook his head. "He checks my phone. He'll ask about the number."

"Say that I flirted with you at the supermarket or the coffee shop, somewhere you go a lot. He won't know."

"He'll tell me to delete it."

Ethan raised his eyebrows. "How good is your memory?"

Grey licked his lips. "Pretty good."

"Memorise it then."

Joey stopped beside them. "Mine, too."

Ethan held up a hand. "No. We don't want anyone to find out Grey has been in contact with you. Just because he came here doesn't mean he saw you. He just saw Ani. That's all. My number can be pushed aside as a random guy with nothing to do with Elliott."

Joey stared into Ethan's eyes, and Ethan tried to make him understand that he was doing this to protect Joey as much as Elliott and Grey. Joey swallowed and nodded, leaning back against the counter. Ani squeezed his shoulder.

Ethan recited his number several times until Grey had it memorised, and then Grey left, promising to message updates as he could. Ethan wanted to make him promise to contact them every day so they could make sure he was okay, but that might endanger him even more.

"Who the hell is this Robert guy?" Ethan asked.

Joey shrugged. "I just know him as Elliott's uncle. I barely saw him. When he did attend any family events, he was only there for a short time."

Ethan sighed. "Do you think Elliott was going to tell anyone what he'd found out?"

"I don't know. It wouldn't surprise me. And if Elliott's death had been anything but...what it was, I might've reconsidered the...suicide aspect." Joey's voice broke on the word, and Ethan stepped forward, sliding his arms around Joey's back and resting his head on his chest. "I still haven't heard from that guy."

Ethan frowned and then remembered the man who was supposed to call Joey. He lifted his head. "Do you think it was Grey?"

"It wasn't," Ani said. "His voice was completely different. He sounded much older."

"So, we've got a brother, a mystery man and an uncle-slash-father, all of whom we didn't know about," Joey said. "Who or what else is going to turn up?"

Ethan's phone rang, and he pulled himself away from Joey to see who it was. "Sorry, it's Christi." Joey dropped a kiss on his lips, and Ethan answered. "Hey, you."

"Hey, yourself. How are things in the world of London?" she asked.

He wasn't getting into the drama that was slowly unfolding. "Good. Great, even."

"Glad to hear it. Do you know when you're tootling yourself home?"

He glanced at Joey, who was talking to Ani and pointing to something on the papers on the counter. "No idea. Meredith has given me two weeks, as you know, but she said I could take longer if I need it."

"And will you need it?"

Ethan sighed. "I don't know yet. We're still trying to figure things out."

They were both quiet for a moment before Christi said, "You're not coming back, are you?"

"I don't know," he murmured.

Christi sighed. "Well, if that's the case, I better tell you the latest news about Di. Can you believe this? The woman—and I use that term loosely, now—mixed my customer's tint wrong. I got the blame for it!"

Christi went into a tirade about everything that happened, and Ethan listened, replying occasionally and smiling always. One day, his friend might figure out that she liked Di, and they'd become friends. One day.

After a good ten minutes, he said goodbye and went to find Joey, who had disappeared into the back room with Ani a few minutes earlier. There was far too much new information for Joey, and Ethan was worried he would take it hard. He appeared to be managing with it so far, but he could tell it was a lot. Especially the secrets. Ethan wished that guy called soon. Getting as much information as they could would only help their cause.

"Look, why don't you forget about this for a while and show Ethan your room?" Ani said, and Ethan wholeheartedly agreed.

Joey sighed and nodded. "Good idea."

Ethan followed him up the stairs to a studio that was sparse in its furniture but not in its wall decoration. Designs upon designs filled the spaces, and Ethan was entranced at first glance. They were all different: flowers, skulls, tribal swirls, everything he could imagine.

"Did you do all these?"

"Yes."

"Are these ones you've given to people or just ideas?" he asked, pointing to the designs on plain white paper.

Joey stepped beside him. "The ones that aren't people's actual tattoos are just ideas. If someone chooses a design from here, I replace the sketch with the person's picture."

Ethan glanced around. "How many tattoos do you think you've done?"

Joey laughed. "Thousands. Maybe tens of thousands by now. I've been doing this a long time."

"What do your parents think of your celebrity status?"

Joey settled onto a black stool, spinning slightly. "They stay out of the spotlight as much as possible. They're not interested in fame and fortune. They're happy with their cottage in the countryside, away from the hustle and bustle of city life."

"What do they do?"

"They both retired early. I bought them the house and told them to get out of London. They want for nothing, which is the best thing about this so-called fame. I was able to get them to stop working and relax."

"I bet they loved you for that."

Joey chuckled. "They did. They're more than happy now. Mum knits blankets and clothes for the babies at the hospitals that need them, and Dad, well, let's just say he's enjoying his garden."

"Sounds like heaven."

Joey tilted his head and stopped spinning. "Is that what you want? A quiet life?"

Ethan studied the designs as he thought about his answer, and he was grateful Joey didn't rush him. What did he want? "I want to be happy. I don't think it matters where I am or what I'm doing. I'll know it when I see it." He already knew it. He wanted to be wherever Joey was. No matter what they decide to do, he'd settle anywhere Joey wanted to.

Joey stood, the stool sliding away behind him, and came to a stop in front of him. "Every time I don't think I could fall harder for you, you say or do something to make me drop off that cliff again." He cupped Ethan's jaw with his gorgeous tattooed hands, staring into his eyes, and Ethan's stomach swirled. "I know it's a hard decision to make, but I promise you, I'm happy with wherever we are."

Ethan swallowed, his gaze blurring Joey's face. "I do love Whitby, but I've found that I don't mind the idea of not living there. Maybe we could visit often, but I'd be happy anywhere. As long as I'm with you."

"And I've found I don't mind living in Whitby as long as I'm with you," Joey replied.

Ethan snorted, and his tears overflowed. He hated crying when he was overwhelmed. It felt like he was being a crybaby. "We're a right pair." He slid his arms around Joey's waist and nuzzled his cheek into his hands. "So, we've determined it doesn't matter where we live. Where does that leave us?"

"Still trying to decide where to live," Joey said, chuckling.

Ethan sniffed. "Okay, I say we need to write a list of the pros and cons of both places or other places if there's somewhere else we might want to live."

Joey studied him. "Are you sure you're ready to uproot your life and shack up with me?"

"I've never been more sure of anything," Ethan said. And it was the truth.

Despite the sadness hanging over them from the reason he'd met Joey in the first place, he had never been happier. Yes, he'd miss his family and friends, but it wasn't like they were on the other side of the world. He'd be able to visit them. And maybe he'd see more of the country if he travelled with Joey. He already knew how to keep track of things as a busy hotel receptionist. Surely, a tattoo artist's assistant wouldn't be harder.

As those thoughts flew through his head, he realised he'd already made up his mind. Now, to show Joey what they could be.

"I think we should keep our base here, visit Whitby as often as we can, and as Ani suggested, I could be your assistant or the business's assistant as I travel with you."

Joey's eyes widened, and Ethan had the impression he wasn't breathing. After several long moments, Joey said, "You'd do that for me?"

Ethan lifted to his toes to close the slight distance between them and kissed him. Already getting used to Joey's scent and taste, he closed his eyes and sank into the embrace. When they pulled back, panting, he said, "I would do that for *us*."

Joey took his mouth again, and Ethan gripped Joey's back, holding himself upright as Joey devoured him. He was glad he'd decided to keep his stubble longer. Beard burn was no longer an issue, especially with how deeply Joey kissed him. This was the right decision for them, and although he would change their plans if Joey gave a good argument, he honestly thought they would make it work. He'd have to speak to Ani about what being an assistant would involve. But his thoughts disappeared when Joey's tongue tangled with his, and he held on for his life.

"Oops, sorry!"

The man's voice broke through the haze in Ethan's mind, but Joey didn't stop the kiss. Instead, he gentled it, bit by bit, until they rested their foreheads together.

"What do you want, Beck?"

"I wanted to talk about the schedule for the Bonser event. Can you drag yourself away for a bit?"

Joey sighed, and Ethan felt the tension in his entire body. "Go talk. I'll speak to Ani," he said, dropping a last kiss on Joey's lips before disentangling himself.

"This shouldn't take long."

Ethan smiled at Beck as he passed, and he descended the stairs to where Ani was talking to a customer. He wandered around the reception area—was it called something different in a tattoo shop? There were designs on the walls here, too. Recognising some as Joey's work, he tried to see if the other designs had some sort of "calling card" in them to identify who drew them. He wasn't sure, but he had a feeling he saw a few that had the same style.

"Their styles are very reminiscent of their personalities," Ani said, stopping beside him. "Have you figured out whose is whose?"

Ethan pointed at the ones he thought were by the same person. "There are lots of lines, an almost chaotic but beautiful experience in these."

Ani nodded and smirked. "They're all by the same person. But who?"

Ethan thought about it. "Dallas."

"Correct. Next?"

He studied the designs again, finally pointing out three. "Very to the point and tidy. Finn."

"Well done. You've got a good eye. Can you find Beck's?"

He grinned. "These." He pointed to four designs, which were highly extravagant and extensive.

"Congratulations. You've got all three tattoo artists pegged correctly. Joey will be proud." Ani laughed, tucking her green hair behind her ear. The style suited her petite frame.

"That's a good thing, I think." He raised his eyebrows. "What were you saying earlier about an assistant?"

Ani cocked her head. "You're serious?"

Ethan shrugged. "Nothing has been set in stone, but I think the best choice for us is for me to travel with him. I could find virtual assistant work, which I could do from anywhere, but if you need help anyway, and it fits in with what I can and want to do, then I don't see why we can't both benefit from it."

"What did Joey say?"

"He didn't say no."

Ani threw her head back and laughed. "He wouldn't. He would feel like he was pushing you to choose what he wanted, even if you were the one to offer the option first."

"That's why I told him I was going to talk to you. You seem to help him see sense. But I wanted to talk about the potential job first."

Ani waved him behind the desk. "We definitely need someone to help. I'm becoming overwhelmed by the workload, but these guys don't like bringing strangers in and finding someone who we know who wants to do it isn't easy. We can go through what the job would involve, but it can be tweaked and changed to fit you and me and the business. That's what I like most about working for Joey. He cares about staff retention and making a family out of the business. He's happy for us to work with our strengths, and then we share the weaknesses between us, or we work together to do them."

"Sounds like a great way to run a business."

"I agree." She huffed. "It's probably why I'm still here. Oh, I will mention that you will have babysitting duties, too."

Ethan frowned. "Babysitting who?"

Ani pointed above them and rolled her eyes. "These guys. I told you before. It's more like being a babysitter than a manager."

Ethan laughed, covering his mouth with his hand and holding his side. "Ah, I understand now."

"You don't, but you will."

They went through what Ani had to do during a normal day and then the things involved in the events they did and the events they organised. The travel schedule worked well, but Ethan could see a couple of things that he could tweak to make it even better.

He was making some notes when Ani said, "You do realise if you ever get married, you'll have to have a huge wedding, don't you?"

Ethan stared at her, mouth gaping. "What?"

14

JOEY

"He seems like a nice guy," Beck said when Ethan disappeared.

"He is." Joey shook his head. "I have no idea how I found him when I did, but I'm not letting go now unless I have to."

"What does he say about that?"

Joey grinned. "He's willing to travel with me. To work as an assistant if it fits what he enjoys doing."

"He's giving up Whitby?" Beck raised his eyebrows.

"He's willing to."

"And what about you? What do you want?"

Joey smiled. "To make Ethan happy."

Beck laughed and shoved him away. "You sappy shit."

"When you meet your man, you'll know what I mean."

Beck scoffed and held up his hands. "No way, man. I'm staying free and single forever. No chains keeping me from being free."

Joey didn't reply. Instead, he changed the subject to the event Beck wanted to talk about, and they went through the plans to make sure everything was in place. As Beck turned to leave, Joey stopped him.

"I felt the same way, remember? Look at me now."

The corner of Beck's mouth curled. "It's not for me." He nodded and left, closing the door behind him.

Joey had a feeling the man would eat his words one day, and Joey would be there to rub it in. As he tidied away the documents they'd been looking through, Ethan came back.

"Did you get everything you needed?"

Ethan nodded. "I think I'd enjoy it. At the very least, I'm happy to give it a try. I won't ever leave you in the lurch, so if I didn't enjoy it, I wouldn't leave until you'd found someone you could trust to take over." He slid his arms around Joey, staring into his eyes, and Joey couldn't look away. "I think this could work, Joey."

Joey blinked at the sudden burning in his eyes, and he buried his head in Ethan's neck. "I hope so."

After spending the remainder of the previous afternoon and evening together—without any of his friends bothering them—they lazed in bed the next morning. Joey had a fitful night's sleep and had woken several times. Each time, Ethan wrapped himself around him and soothed him back to sleep, but Joey felt bad for disturbing him.

He skimmed his fingers along Ethan's arm, where it draped across Joey's stomach. Ethan's head rested on his chest, his warm breaths puffing over his nipples. Although they had spoken about Ethan's choice at length, Joey still couldn't believe he was willing to walk away from his life in Whitby.

"Are you sure, Ethan?" he asked for probably the hundredth time.

Ethan chuckled, and Joey couldn't help but smile in response. "I'm sure. It's not like we're moving to another country, Joey. I can still visit everyone."

"I know. It's just a big step."

"It is. But it's one I'm willing to take."

"Are—" Joey's phone rang, and he reached past Ethan to unplug it from the bedside table. "Unknown number." His heart raced as he answered. "Hello?"

"Joey Reynolds?"

"Yes. Who's this?"

"Denny. I knew Elliott."

Joey scooted up the bed, the cold of the headboard taking away some of the warmth Ethan had provided. Ethan did the same. "How did you know him?"

"We were...intimate. I originally met him about a year ago at a party. We hooked up. After that, whenever our paths crossed, we would sneak away and find a room. I'm assuming you don't need more information than that."

"No, I'm good. Why didn't he ever tell me about you?"

"I asked him not to make it public."

"Why? Was he not worth your time?"

Denny sighed. "He was, but I'm not out. Or rather, I wasn't."

His voice rippled on the last words, and Joey softened towards him a little. "What happened?"

"When?"

"That night, and I'm assuming you had a coming out you weren't planning on."

Denny huffed. "You could say that. I'd rather we talk in person than over the phone. Can you meet me?"

Joey stared at Ethan. "Where and when?"

"Today, two o'clock. Battersea Park bandstand."

"Okay. I'll be bringing a friend."

"Who? I don't want the police involved yet. I need to talk to you first."

Joey frowned. "It's not the police. It's my boyfriend."

Denny was quiet for a moment. "You have a boyfriend. Elliott didn't mention it."

Joey gritted his teeth. "Yeah, well, Elliott didn't tell me a lot of things, so it seems."

"Okay. I'll see you there."

The phone went dead, and Joey let his hand fall to his lap.

"Everything okay?" Ethan asked, covering Joey's hand with his.

Joey nodded. "We're meeting up with the guy at two o'clock. He didn't want to talk over the phone."

"That's understandable if there's something important." Ethan glanced over his shoulder. "It's eleven o'clock now. How about we get dressed and go for some brunch?"

Joey raised his eyebrows. "*Brunch*?"

"It's too late for breakfast and too early for lunch; therefore, brunch."

"I can think of something to tide us over until lunch," Joey said and rolled them until he caged Ethan beneath him. "I'm thinking...ties. One for each wrist and ankle. One for your eyes. One for your mouth." He lowered his head and voice. "Maybe something to cover your ears. You won't know what I'm going to do to you until I've done it." He skimmed his lips over Ethan's jaw. "What do you think?"

"I don't think I'm going to last long if you do that to me," Ethan whispered.

Joey raised his head, staring into Ethan's eyes. "You'll last as long as I make you."

Ethan's eyes flared, and he licked his lips. "Are you sure this is the right time?"

"It helps me push aside everything else and concentrate on you."

"Okay."

Joey dropped a kiss on his lips and then climbed off him. "Strip the bed down to the sheet and lay on your back. I need to get supplies."

As he rummaged through the drawers, he could hear Ethan moving behind him, but he didn't look to see if he was doing what he was told. Joey had no doubt he would. He picked six ties from one drawer and noise-cancelling headphones from another. When he faced Ethan again, his lover was lying on the bed as he'd been asked to, and Joey's gaze ran the length of him. His muscular physique might be seen by many as butch—or a giant, as Christi had called them—but he was in perfect proportion everywhere. His chest tapered into the V of his abdomen, heading into his groin, where his cock stood proudly. Joey couldn't help the smile that spread across his face at the sight.

He wrapped the ties around his hand as he stepped closer, dragging out the moment. As much as he wanted this to last hours, he was on borrowed time. He put everything on the bed beside Ethan's hip and chose the first tie. He slid the fabric around Ethan's ankle, tying it tight enough for him to feel it but loose enough not to stop the blood flow. Then he moved on to the second ankle. He repeated the action for his wrists, tying them low enough that it wouldn't strain Ethan's arms as they continued.

"I've left a long tail that you can pull to free yourself should you need it," he said.

"Thank you, Sir."

Joey ran his hands down Ethan's arms, the goosebumps flowing in the same direction, and then he straddled Ethan's thighs. Grabbing another tie, he placed it over Ethan's eyes and beneath his head, bringing it back to the front to tie off.

"Colour?"

"Green, Sir."

"When I put this final tie on, you're not going to be able to talk easily. I will assume everything is fine unless you use your fingers. One finger means green. Two fingers mean yellow. Five fingers mean red. Understood?"

"Yes, Sir."

"Repeat back what I said." Ethan did. "Good. If for some reason that doesn't get my attention, I want you to make as loud a noise as you can for as long as you can, however you can. Be it with your limited voice, hands banging on the headboard, or anything else you can think of."

"Yes, Sir."

He leaned down and ran a hand along Ethan's jaw. "I never want to hurt you."

"I know, Sir. Hurt is only allowed during play, not when someone wants out."

"Good."

He smoothed the tie over Ethan's mouth, which opened without being asked. Joey knotted the tie, making a mental note to get some sort of hood or ball gag in the future. He nipped at Ethan's lips. "Right, final item. These will block out all sounds. You'll be completely deprived of everything but feel. Are you ready?" Ethan put up one finger. "Good." Joey slid the headphones over his ears, and Ethan stilled. Joey ran his fingers down Ethan's jaw to his chin and nipped at his lips once more. Then he pulled back and climbed off the bed.

He'd purposefully not grabbed everything he wanted to use when Ethan could see because it would spoil the surprise. He went back to his drawer and pulled out a Wartenberg wheel, a feather and a cock sleeve. When he turned back to the bed, Ethan's chest heaved, but his cock strained. Joey placed everything on the bed except the feather. He held it just above Ethan's ankle and then skimmed it slowly across his skin. Ethan flinched, which Joey expected, but then settled as Joey continued to weave the feather up his leg. When he reached Ethan's groin, his cock bobbed, precome leaking down the swollen red shaft. Joey kept going past it, without touching, and down his other leg.

Then he removed it and grabbed the wheel. Again, Ethan flinched when it first touched his abdomen, but he stayed as it made its way across his stomach and chest. Joey made sure to run it over his nipples, and they tightened in response. Joey catalogued every response to the stimuli.

Picking up the feather again, he ran the feather down one side and the wheel down the other several times before swapping over. Ethan panted through the tie in his mouth, his nostrils flaring, and Joey put down the wheel and feather and wrapped a hand around his cock, smearing the fluid around to coat it for what he had planned next.

The cock sleeve had bobbles on the inside, so it would stimulate him even more. Joey rested it against Ethan's tip, and Ethan froze—even his chest as if he wasn't breathing. He slid just the head of Ethan's cock into it, and Ethan bucked, but Joey pulled it free again. Ethan groaned behind the tie, and Joey smiled. He repeated it, rotating the sleeve so it hit all the nerve endings beneath the head. Ethan writhed, and sweat beaded on his skin. Lowering the sleeve onto his cock fully, he paused, keeping it still and making Ethan mumble behind the tie. Joey was determined to make him lose control.

Holding the sleeve in place, he grabbed the wheel again and ran it across Ethan's nipples. Ethan's neck strained as he pressed his head into the mattress. Joey chose one nipple to focus on and slid the wheel back and forth over the tip. He added the sleeve into the mix, lifting and lowering it. If only he had three hands, he would've used the feather on the other nipple, giving him three sensations to deal with.

The sleeve made a slicking noise, and Joey knew Ethan was already close. But Joey wanted inside him before he could come. He wanted to feel him tighten around him.

He left the sleeve around Ethan's cock, though he didn't expect it to stay on. It would slowly work its way off, but the sensations would keep going until it slid free. He reached for the lube and prepared Ethan as quickly as he could while still using the wheel on him. When he was ready for him, Joey slid a condom on and slicked it and wrapped his hand around the sleeve, which had fallen off during his ministrations.

He held his cock at Ethan's pucker and the sleeve at his cock. He slid inside him at the same time he slid the sleeve down his cock. Ethan shouted behind the tie, but his fingers were inside his fist. When Joey sank deep inside, he paused. He crawled closer, lifting Ethan's ass to rest on Joey's thighs, keeping them tightly bound together. He wasn't planning on going anywhere. The feather skimmed across Ethan's nipples, and the sleeve slid down Ethan's cock repeatedly. But still, Joey didn't move. He could feel Ethan rippling around him, but he was going to send Ethan over the edge without fucking him more than he already was.

Ethan writhed and squirmed on the bed as Joey continued with the feather and sleeve. Ethan's ass tightened on him with each slide until Joey's cock was strangled. Ethan tensed all over, his body becoming a block of ice before he let out a muffled yell, and the contractions around Joey's cock had him needing to move. He gritted his teeth through the need until Ethan's body relaxed a little, and then he put everything down and gripped Ethan's hips. Moving back a little, he withdrew once and slammed into him. After that, he couldn't stop and fucked him hard and fast to his own orgasm. Just before he went over, Ethan contracted around him again, and Joey's eyes widened at the second release of fluid over Ethan's stomach.

"Fuck," Joey groaned as he released into the condom. He gave himself a second's breather and then pulled free. Throwing the condom over the side of the bed, he leaned down and lapped up every splash of come on Ethan's body. If he paid special attention to his nipples and cock, who could blame him?

When he was done, he pulled Ethan's wrists and ankles free first, and then his mouth, which he kissed and kissed to help with his dry mouth—at least that's what he told himself. He removed the headphones, kissed him again, and untied the tie around his eyes.

Ethan blinked lazily at him. His body splayed over the bed when Joey had left his limbs as if he couldn't get the energy to move.

"Hey," Joey said.

"Hi," Ethan croaked.

Joey leaned across the bed to reach the glass of water he'd put there and helped Ethan to sit up. His lover rested fully against him while Joey held the glass for him to drink his fill.

"Thanks."

Joey nuzzled his cheek against Ethan's head. "You're welcome."

Despite the uncertainty of what was to come that afternoon, Joey's body was humming. Yes, the orgasm helped, but his mind, too, was calm and ready for whatever was going to be thrown his way. He had no idea what Denny was going to tell him, but he was pretty sure he wouldn't like it. With Ethan by his side, he could manage anything.

"You okay?" Ethan mumbled.

Joey tightened his hold on him, rubbing his hands over his body to help centre him. "Yep. Let's get you into the shower."

Holding a rag doll under the spray would've been easier than keeping Ethan from folding himself onto the floor. He was completely loose and flopping all over the place. Eventually, though, they were washed and dried, and when they climbed out, Ethan was steadier.

"We need to do that again," Ethan said as they dressed.

Joey glanced at him, but Ethan was staring at the bed and the discarded ties and equipment. "We will. Maybe next time, though, we do it when we don't have to be anywhere. You were far too relaxed afterwards."

Ethan wrinkled his nose, and Joey chuckled. "Sorry. That was intense. And I loved every minute."

"I could tell."

Ethan's stomach rumbled. "We need lunch."

"Oh, it's lunch now, is it?"

Ethan pointed to the clock. "It's twelve-thirty. It's no longer brunch time."

Joey laughed. "Okay. Lunch it is."

Before they left the apartment, Joey dragged Ethan into his arms. "Thank you for coming with me. For all of this, really. When you first met me, you couldn't have known what you were getting into, but you're still willing to go wherever this takes us, and I can't thank you enough."

"I'm glad I'm here. That you're not doing this alone."

Joey kissed him. What else could he do?

After they'd grabbed some lunch from the cafe Joey visited often, they headed to Battersea Park. They wandered through the grounds, hand in hand, until they reached the bandstand. Joey slowed, staring at the man sitting on the steps. A man he hadn't expected.

"You could've warned me," Joey said when they stopped in front of him. "Using Denny was a bit of a misnomer."

The man spread his hands. "What did you want me to say?"

"That you were Dennis Carter, the billionaire, playboy guitarist of the biggest band in the country."

"And would you have come?"

"Probably not."

"Exactly my point. Who would believe this playboy was gay, huh?" Dennis said, waving a hand towards himself.

That was the exact thought going around and around in Joey's head.

Dennis freaking Carter was gay?

15

ETHAN

Dennis Carter was gay?

How in the hell was the lead guitarist for The Ports—as in a "girl in every port"—gay? Ethan had seen him on the front cover of magazines, news sites and social media with a different girl every week. How had he kept that quiet?

"Are you likely to be swarmed by reporters soon?" Joey asked Dennis.

Dennis shrugged. "Who knows. They seem to find me no matter where I go, but hopefully, they'll leave us alone for now. No guarantees there won't be photos somewhere, though." He paused. "I'm surprised you didn't know I was gay. It's headline news at the moment."

"I'm sorry about that."

"Wasn't your fault. I just wish I could've done it when Elliott was…still here."

Ethan could see the pain flow across Dennis's expression. There was more to his story than he was sharing. Joey settled onto the steps, a couple down from where Dennis was, and Ethan sat at Joey's back, giving him strength through touch instead of words. It wasn't his place to say anything, anyway.

"Dennis, what—" Joey started.

"Denny. Please."

"Denny, what happened the night of the party? One minute, Elliott disappeared into the crowd. The next, we were going home. What happened between the two?"

Denny sighed and threaded his fingers, rubbing his thumbs together. "We hooked up. I'd sent him a message to meet me in an upstairs bedroom. We'd done it before. Several times, in fact. We were there for probably...an hour. Maybe less. Elliott kissed me goodbye before he left the room, and I waited ten minutes before following. Again, we'd done it before."

"You make it sound like something different happened this time?" Ethan leaned harder against Joey's back when his voice broke.

Denny nodded. "When I exited the room, there was a man waiting for me. An older man I'd never met before."

"Who was he, and what did he want?"

"He said his name was Robert, and he," Denny huffed a laugh before continuing, "*offered* me money to stay away from Elliott. Said it was up to him to keep an eye out for him, and what we were doing was irresponsible and disgusting."

Joey leaned forward. "What did you say?"

"Why would I need money? I told him to get lost, in not such pleasant words. I had no idea who he was." Denny shook his head. "Not until Elliott's funeral. Robert is his uncle, and from what I dug up about him since, he's not a man to be trifled with."

Was Joey going to be truthful about Robert's relation to Elliott? Ethan wasn't sure if it would be beneficial to the investigation or not.

"So I've been told," Joey said. "Did anything else happen that night?"

"No," Denny said. "I only saw passing glances of Elliott with other people at the party. The last time I remember catching a glimpse of him was around eleven o'clock. He looked trashed, which was unlike him."

Joey nodded. "That was roughly what time we went home." He sighed. "I should've known something was wrong."

Ethan squeezed his shoulder. "Elliott appeared to be adept at hiding things, Joey. If he didn't want you to know, you wouldn't."

Joey stood, pacing from one side of the bandstand to the other, sliding his finger through his hair. Ethan hated seeing him so ravaged by grief. He wished there was something he could do to help, but he was working blind from this. He didn't know Elliott when he was alive, and he only had his impartial opinion to add.

"I wonder if Robert cornered him?" Joey asked suddenly.

"What difference would that make? They're family," Denny said.

Joey glanced at Ethan, who nodded once. "I've recently found out that Robert is not actually Elliott's uncle. He's his father."

Denny's eyes widened, and he sat up straighter. "Holy shit."

"Why did you have to come out?" Ethan couldn't keep the question from escaping his mouth.

Denny glanced at him and then away into the distance. "When I declined Robert's offer, he threatened to out me. I told him to shove it, saying it was Elliott's choice. The day after Elliott..." He cleared his throat. "The newspaper ran the news about me. I assumed it was Robert, making good on his threat."

Ethan frowned. "But why would he have done that when Elliott was dead? You wouldn't be seeing Elliott anymore. He didn't need to throw you to the wolves."

Denny turned sad eyes to him. "Some people don't need a reason. They enjoy throwing their weight around and making others see what they're capable of. Maybe he wanted me to know just how much reach he had."

"How has it been since?" Joey asked, settling back onto the step.

Denny blew out a long breath. "Rocky. The band is fine about it. The management, not so much. After all, it's not 'appealing' to change our tagline to 'a girl *or boy* in every port,' so I'm told."

Ethan rolled his eyes. It wasn't anything he hadn't heard before, but it still stung when people didn't just accept them for who they were. He narrowed his eyes, looking in the distance, where he could see some people heading their way.

"We're about to have company, I think," he told them.

Denny stood, brushing off his jeans. "I better go."

Joey rose to meet him. "Have you told the police anything?" Denny shook his head. "Am I able to tell them about you if it might help them?"

Denny frowned. "Help them with what? I thought it was a suicide."

"It was, but I've found some inconsistencies that I'm considering taking to the police. I'm less and less convinced he did it on purpose. With all the information coming to light, he had things to live for."

The war inside Denny was evident, but he squared his shoulders. "Yes. I'll do whatever it takes to help."

Joey held out his hand. "Thank you."

They shook, and before Denny walked away, he hesitated. "I never got the chance to tell Elliot...I loved him," he finished in a whisper.

"I can tell," Joey said, pulling Denny into a hug before letting him go.

They watched him walk away, and several of the people who had been heading towards them changed direction. Before Denny met them, several large, imposing guards joined him, holding them at bay. Ethan hadn't seen them anywhere, so wherever they had hidden had been good.

"Things are not adding up," Joey repeated.

"I don't know Elliott, but he seemed to have too many things going on to want to leave this place," Ethan conceded.

"He wouldn't have left Grey, not with Robert still around. If he is the threat he seems to be."

Ethan sighed. "We won't get any more answers here. Shall we go home?"

Joey smiled and slid his arms around Ethan's waist, lowering his face to his neck. "I love the sound of that."

"What?"

Joey lifted his head, spearing Ethan with his gaze. "Home."

Ethan's heart skipped a beat at the happiness in Joey's eyes. Where had this man come from? He'd appeared in Ethan's life when he had needed him, even though he hadn't realised it then. Since that moment, Ethan's life had changed for the better. Not that it had been bad before, but he'd been lonely. He'd wanted more than what he had, and then Joey had shown up and sent everything spiralling out of control.

The kicker? Ethan wouldn't change any of it. He would be away from his family and friends for extended periods, but he couldn't give Joey up. Wouldn't give him up.

As he stared into Joey's eyes, Ethan knew he would never be the same.

"Let's go home."

Joey beamed, and they wandered back towards their car, hand in hand.

"Joey! Joey Reynolds! What were you doing meeting with Dennis Carter? How do you know him? Ethan, do you have any problems with Joey's past? Can you forgive him?"

The reporters came out of nowhere, and Ethan jumped at the first shouted question. Joey tightened his hold on Ethan's hand and increased their speed. There was no getting away from them, though. They surrounded Joey's car. They pushed through them, and Joey shoved several out of the way, no less hard than they deserved. Joey unlocked the car and opened the door for Ethan while the reporters threw more and more questions at them. Joey climbed into the driver's seat. He revved the engine, giving the reporters enough warning that they were going to move, but they barely stepped back an inch. Joey shrugged.

"It's their toes."

He inched forward and then squealed onto the road, leaving them behind. Ethan doubted it would take them long to follow, but for now, at least, they were free of prying eyes. He rested his hand on Joey's tense thigh, and it was enough to relax him. Marginally.

"Sometimes, I wish I'd chosen a different career. Or at least, a quieter business. I could have still done tattooing, but for regular people."

Ethan squeezed his leg. "It doesn't matter. We'll deal with it as we've dealt with everything that's been thrown at us so far."

Joey peered at him for a brief moment and faced the road again. "How are you taking everything so calmly?"

Ethan snorted. "There's no reason to do anything else. It's not like I can do anything about it. It's your life."

"You could leave."

Ethan removed his hand and stared out of the window. "Do you want me to?" He was afraid of the answer.

"Not in the slightest."

There was no hesitation in Joey's voice, and that, more than anything else, removed the tension in Ethan's body.

"I was just saying you could leave if you wanted to."

"No, I can't."

"Why?"

"Because I love you too much to leave you alone with this. You're stuck with me." Though he had some more questions. Mainly, what did the reporter mean about forgiving Joey for his past? What had he done that needed forgiveness?

"You love me?" Joey asked.

Ethan smiled. "I do."

"I love you, too."

There were reporters hanging around the entrance to the car park when they arrived back at Joey's house, and after inching the car forward enough to tell them he meant business, Joey got them parked. They ignored the questions shouted at them and climbed the steps. When they were secure behind closed doors, Joey pulled him in for a hug.

"Thank you for being here."

Ethan tightened his hold. "You don't have to thank me for that."

Joey lifted his head. "Still, thank you." He dropped a kiss on his lips and tugged Ethan towards the sofa. "So much has happened. I don't know what to do with it all." He rested his head back.

Ethan snuggled beside him, listening to his heartbeat beneath his ear. He didn't want to bring up his questions, though he would eventually. "It's a lot to take in. First Grey being Elliott's brother, and then Robert being their dad, and then Denny being Elliott's lover. It's a lot."

"What else didn't I know about Elliott? Why was he hiding this all from me?"

"He could've been trying to protect you."

"From what?"

"Robert would be my first guess. It seems like he's trouble from what Grey and Denny have said."

Ethan let Joey have the silence while he digested everything. He couldn't even begin to understand what Joey was going through. If Christi or Kole had secrets like that, he would probably react the same way. He would want to know the truth, just like Joey did, and that meant he would need to broach the subject of his past at some point. He wasn't sure he wanted to be blindsided by revelations later when they could be cleared up in the beginning. Joey had enough on his plate at the moment. It could wait a few days.

His gaze caught on the wall. "Is something missing there?" He pointed at the wall where it appeared faded.

Joey chuckled, though it was tinged with sadness. "Elliott had a painting there when he lived here. He took it with him when he moved out. I've never replaced it with anything, even though I should."

"It doesn't need covering," Ethan said. "It looks perfect to me."

Ethan sat on the comfortable chairs in the reception of Life in Ink and checked his emails while Joey tattooed his client. He'd received one from Meredith asking when he was likely to return, and he'd replied that he didn't know. She had given him two weeks and had said he could have more, but he knew they were short-staffed. He hated leaving things so up in the air, but until he and Joey had more concrete plans, he couldn't give her a more definitive answer.

He had one from David, too. Rolling his eyes because David was probably asking the same thing as Meredith, he opened it, eyes darting across the screen as he read. He went rigid when he finished.

"Everything okay?" Ani asked from her perch behind the counter.

Ethan closed the phone and rested it on the arm of the chair. Blowing out a breath, he said, "Yeah. My assistant manager is being an ass. As always."

"What's he done?"

Ethan stared at the phone, contemplating what he should do about it. "He's threatening to go to the media about Joey's...activities while he was in Whitby."

"Activities?"

"The work he did, where he stayed, everything he knows and has gleaned from other people. He's always been an ass, but this takes it to the next level."

"Isn't it illegal for him to talk about employees?"

"Probably, but Joey was only a temp. He was just a handyman."

Ani snorted. "It's funny to think of Joey doing that, but I don't know why. He's always been doing stuff like that here."

"I need to ask him what he wants me to do about it."

"He'll probably tell you to ignore it."

"Maybe." Ethan wasn't so sure. He couldn't say what David was capable of. He'd always thought the man was slimy, especially with how often he touched Ethan's arm without him saying he could. He stood far too close to employees and guests alike, but Ethan had never said a word about it. Should he speak to Meredith?

He grabbed his phone, opening the email again.

Ethan,

Hope you're doing well on your holiday.

I would like to remind you I have photographic evidence of Mr Reynolds' actions during his time here, and I would like you to consider remuneration for keeping those details from the media.

Take your time to respond. I know you must be busy figuring out how to live in the limelight. This is just a way for that to happen sooner rather than later.

Have a wonderful time.

David.

Ethan stopped himself from deleting the email and, instead, closed out of his account. He'd talk to Joey about it once he was done for the day. After all, Ethan was no longer alone in this. Certain decisions needed to be discussed before he could make them.

"Hey." He glanced at Ani. "Don't worry about it. Whatever happens, happens. You'll both get through it. It's nothing he hasn't been through before."

"I know. I just hate that I'm the one bringing it to his door."

"Honestly, don't worry." She shuffled some paper. "Come on over here, and I'll talk you through some more things you might get to do if you decide to take the job."

Ethan allowed Ani to distract him for the rest of Joey's two-hour tattoo session. The more he learnt about the job, the more he believed it would be a good fit for him. It would encourage the organisational side of him, and he could change things as he needed to, which gave him more scope for making the role his while still ensuring everything gets done that needed to.

"Do you know what, Ani?" Ethan said, leaning a hip against the counter. Ani raised her eyebrows at him. "Go for it. I'm in."

Ani's eyes widened, and Ethan could barely keep himself from chuckling at her. "Seriously?"

"Yep. Why not? I'm staying with him, and regardless of where we end up, I might as well do the job. If it doesn't work out, it doesn't work out. But I'll give it my best go."

Ani threw her arms around him and held him in a vice grip. "You're bloody amazing, Ethan. You won't regret this, I promise."

"Won't regret what?"

Joey's voice sent shivers down Ethan's spine, and he glanced over his shoulder as his boyfriend walked over to him. As Joey's arms slid around his waist and his head rested on his shoulder, Ethan closed his eyes and sighed.

"Ethan's agreed to the job," Ani said, pumping a fist in the air.

Joey turned Ethan to face him. "Really?" His expression showed he was teetering on the edge of hope.

"Really." Ethan cupped Joey's face. "I want to be with you, and this is a job I know I can do and will enjoy. Why not?"

Joey kissed him, stealing every bit of air from his lungs before pulling back. "I love you."

Ethan grinned. "I love you. So, where do I sign up?"

"I'll sort the paperwork for you," Ani said.

"I need to let Meredith know," Ethan said. "I don't think she'll be too surprised about it."

Joey tightened his hold on Ethan. "I'm so glad you decided to join us."

Ethan was, too. He shared a glance with Ani, who nodded towards Joey, and Ethan looked away. He would bring up David's email soon.

Ethan's phone rang, and he disentangled himself to pull it from his pocket. He frowned at his dad's name. "Hey, Dad. How are you?"

"I've been better. Your mum's taken poorly. She's okay, but she's staying overnight at the hospital."

Ethan's heart skipped several beats. "What's wrong with her? What happened?"

"She had a fall. She caught that uneven slab in the back garden and broke her arm. The doctors aren't worried. They're only keeping her here because they found her to be dehydrated."

Ethan settled the more his dad said, but he needed to see her for himself. "Okay. I'll get there as soon as I can."

"No. She wouldn't want you to bother yourself. You know that. I just wanted to let you know in case someone else told you and didn't have all the information. I didn't want you worried."

Ethan snorted. "Yeah, like that'll happen."

"It's not us you nccd to worry about."

He frowned. "What do you mean?"

"Have you heard from Kole lately?" his dad asked.

"Not since I came down here. Why?"

"You might want to call him or Christi."

Ethan's heart picked up again. "What happened?" he asked for the second time.

"Someone attacked Kole during one of his tours."

16

JOEY

E than's wide eyes met Joey's, and he immediately stepped closer, resting his hand on Ethan's shoulder. He couldn't hear what Alan was saying, but the lines on Ethan's face deepened the more he listened.

"Okay. I'll call Kole and, if he doesn't answer, Christi. I can be there in a few hours."

Joey's heart skipped a beat. What had happened? When Ethan said goodbye and dropped his arm, his chin trembled, but his lips pursed. A sure sign that he was angry.

"Kole was attacked during a ghost tour. Dad doesn't have much information, so I need to call Kole." He punched at the screen of his phone and put it on speakerphone. It rang and rang. When the voicemail came on, Ethan left a brief message and hung up, and then called Christi. "Christi! Is Kole okay?"

"Hello to you, too." She yawned. "God, sorry. I'm knackered. Yes, he's fine. A little bruised, a lot pissed off, but he's good."

"Who was it, and did they catch them?"

"It was a guy who Kole had spent a night with. He didn't want to take no for an answer about a second date. He jumped him during the tour. Initially, the customers thought it was part of it, but when the guy started screaming at Kole, some of them pulled the guy off and held him until the police came."

"Jesus Christ." Ethan swiped a hand over his face. "I'm glad they caught the fucker. I'll get on the road tonight and be there in a few hours."

"No, you won't."

Ethan frowned. "Why?"

"Because Kole is fine. He's bruised, but he's fine. He's going out again tonight."

"What?" Ethan stared at Joey as if he could smash some sense into Kole, which was exactly what Joey was thinking.

"He doesn't want this one thing to affect him, Ethan. He believes if he doesn't get out there again tonight, he never will."

"That's not true. He's—"

"Isn't it? It scared the fuck out of him, Ethan. If he doesn't go back out there sooner rather than later, he's going to make it a big thing, and then all we'd get is moaning and groaning from him." She chuckled, though it sounded forced. "He needs this. I'll be with him, and so will a plain-clothed police officer. Although they've caught the guy, they want to have someone with Kole for the next three days to make sure. Nobody knows this but us, though."

Ethan sighed. "That's something, at least."

Joey slid his arm around Ethan's shoulders, pulling him into his chest. "If you need anything at all, Christi—you or Kole—you let us know, okay?"

"Oh, hey, Joey. Yes, thank you. We appreciate it, but we'll be just fine."

"Ethan, why don't you take this upstairs? I'll finish up down here and be there soon," Joey said, pressing his lips to Ethan's temple.

Ethan nodded and lifted his head for a kiss before heading out of the reception area. Joey knew that Ethan being so far from his friends would come at a price—like that day when Ethan couldn't get to them as quickly as he used to—and it was an added complication that Ethan would need to decide he was ready for.

"Stop frowning. You'll end up with more lines," Ani said.

Joey glared at her. "Do you need anything from me?"

Ani leaned on the counter and stared at him. "You know I don't. You wanted to give Ethan some time alone with his friend, so sit your butt down and wait patiently."

"Why did I ever employ you?" he grumbled as he sat.

"Because nothing would've ever got done if you hadn't."

She wasn't wrong. Joey rested his head back against the window and closed his eyes. He didn't have an appointment until the following day, so he had time to kill. The bell tinkled as someone entered the shop, and Joey glanced over. Two men entered wearing black suits and long coats, and he immediately recognised them as police officers. Or detectives, whatever they wanted to be called.

"Good afternoon. How can I help?" Ani said with a smile.

"We'd like to speak with…" The first man paused when he met Joey's gaze. He turned towards him. "Joey Reynolds." He moved closer, lifting his identification with one hand and holding out his other hand. "Detective Harmon. This is Detective Keith. Can we ask you some questions, please?"

Joey stood and shook hands. "What's it about?"

"Elliott Kennedy."

"I thought the case was closed."

Detective Harmon nodded. "It was, but we have had new information come to light. We're following up on it."

"What kind of information?"

Harmon glanced at Ani. "Can we go somewhere private?"

Joey frowned. "My studio is this way." He headed for the stairs. "Ani, can you let Ethan know where I am when he's done, please? He can come in at any time."

"Sure thing."

He led the officers to his tattoo studio, and Keith closed the door behind him.

"So, what's this about?" Joey asked, resting his hip against the sideboard and crossing his arms over his chest.

"Some pictures have come to our attention. From the night of the party," Harmon said. "We'd like you to look at them and see if you can identify the people in them."

Joey nodded. "Sure."

He handed over a folder, and Joey opened it. A large picture with Elliott front and centre sent a wave of grief through him. He stared at his best friend for a long moment, wishing things were different, and then focused on the others.

"Anyone in particular?" he asked, ignoring the crushing sensation in his chest.

Harmon stopped beside him. "Him and him," he said, pointing.

"That's Dennis Carter. You know the guitarist from The Ports?" The detective nodded. "The other is..." He stared at the face, mind whirling. "The other is Grey Kennedy."

"A relation to Elliott?"

Joey swallowed hard. The true relation was not known by many. So, did Joey tell them the lie about Grey being Elliott's cousin—as no one knew Grey was Melinda's son, though they did know he was Robert's son—or the truth about them being brothers? Before he had to answer, there was a knock, and Ethan came in.

"Hey, Ani said I could come in." Ethan looked unsure but strong, and Joey waved him over.

"These are Detectives Harmon and Keith. They have questions about the night of the party." Joey showed Ethan the photo when he stopped beside him. "They want to know who these are."

Ethan tensed, but Joey doubted anyone else had noticed. "Dennis Carter and Grey Kennedy. I'm assuming you know who Dennis is, but Grey is Elliott's cousin."

There was the answer Joey needed. They were going with the lie for now. Had Ethan come to the same conclusion Joey had?

"Father's side or mother's?" Harmon asked.

"Father's. Robert Kennedy is Elliott's uncle," Joey said.

Harmon glanced at Keith, who nodded. "We have reason to believe there was an altercation that night, but we don't have information as to who the involved people were besides Elliott. We're trying to find out because there was additional bruising found on Elliott's body that was unaccounted for. Initially, we put it down to—" Harmon stopped himself and blinked before continuing. "We put it down to cause and effect, but now we're not so sure."

Keith's phone rang, and he excused himself to a corner to answer it.

"And you think one of these men had something to do with it?"

Harmon shook his head. "We just want to talk to them."

Keith came up to them. "And we'd like to know what you and Dennis Carter spoke about today."

That's what the phone call had been about. They'd found out about their meeting.

Joey stared down at the photograph. As much as he wanted to keep Elliott's secrets, he needed to find out the truth. He glanced at Ethan and sighed. Refocusing on the officers, he said, "Dennis and Elliott had been seeing each other for a while. I don't know exactly how long. Dennis was in the closet, and they met up at the parties. I don't know if they met up outside of them as well." He sighed again and pointed at Grey. "Grey is not Elliott's cousin. He's Elliott's brother. Grey visited us yesterday and told us that Robert had an affair with Elliott's mother. They had Elliott, although John claimed him, but when Melinda fell pregnant with Grey, Melinda insisted she put him up for adoption. I'm only going by what Grey told us Elliott had found out." He stared at Harmon. "I'm not convinced Elliott's death was a suicide."

"Why?" Harmon asked.

"He had too much to live for. His relationship with Dennis, his brother, and Grey said Elliott was trying to keep him out of Robert's clutches."

Harmon's jaw clenched. "Yes, we know about Robert's possible activities." Harmon scratched his head. "Anything else you think we should know?"

Joey shook his head. "Not that I can think of."

Harmon handed him a card. "Call me if you think of anything or if anything else happens."

"Will do." Joey handed the folder back to him.

After they'd seen the officers out and filled Ani in on the events, they went back to the apartment. Ethan didn't talk, but he took Joey's hand and led him to the bathroom. Ethan set the bath running. Pushing Joey back against the sink, Ethan tugged Joey's shirt over his head and nuzzled into his chest. He dropped to his knees and kissed above Joey's waistband.

Peering up at him, Ethan said, "I bet I can get you off before the bath overflows."

Joey's breath stuttered from his lungs as Ethan went to work on his zip. By the time he was naked, Joey's cock was throbbing. He doubted it would take long at all. Ethan wrapped his hand around the base, opening his mouth to take him in, but Joey gripped his hair and tugged him away.

"Just your mouth," Joey ordered.

Ethan's eyes darkened. "Yes, Sir."

He removed his hand, and Joey guided him forward. Ethan's tongue licked at the head of Joey's cock, and Joey stared down at him, needing more but knowing he was making himself wait. Making them both wait.

"Hands behind your back."

Ethan did, while his tongue and lips marked every inch of Joey's shaft they could reach. It wasn't easy when Ethan couldn't use his hands to keep it still, and Joey certainly wasn't going to help him. After all, Ethan had made the bet, but he hadn't stated the terms.

Joey rested both hands behind him on the sink and let Ethan do what he could with what he had. Ethan rose on his knees and opened his mouth over the head, taking him in. Then he sucked at it, using his tongue to rub against the underside.

"Fuck," Joey growled, tightening his abs so he didn't thrust, no matter how much he wanted to. He glanced at the water level. Only halfway. Fire streaked through him, and he hissed in response to a strong suck.

Ethan bobbed up and down, taking him into his throat and back out again at a rapid pace. When he stopped with his throat full and swallowed around Joey's dick, Joey palmed the back of Ethan's head and thrust further. Ethan choked, and Joey pulled him off. Tears streamed down his face. Joey smeared them across his cheeks.

"Again."

Ethan took Joey down again, swallowed, and Joey held him in place. The flexing of Ethan's throat triggered him, and he pulled back a bit and came into Ethan's mouth. As Ethan was trying to breathe, he couldn't keep everything in his mouth, but he caught it with his hand. Joey dropped his head back against the mirror as his orgasm released him. Peering down at Ethan, Joey watched him lap up his release until his hands were clean.

"Your turn," Joey said, pulling him up.

Ethan's nose crinkled. "No need." He glanced over his shoulder and pushed at Joey, switching off the taps not a moment too soon. "Bloody hell, that was close." He pulled out the plug, letting some of the water out. There was no way they'd be able to climb in without the water flooding the bathroom. "Maybe that wasn't such a good idea."

Joey pulled him closer, palming his groin and feeling the wetness from his release. "You came."

Ethan lifted his head. "I did. That was fucking hot."

Joey kissed him. "I'll remember that."

"Please do." Ethan slid his arms around Joey's neck and fused their mouths. The sensation of Ethan's fully clothed body against his own naked skin was arousing, to say the least.

"Let's forget about the bath. I can think of a better way to spend our hours," Joey said.

Two hours later, they lay in bed with Ethan's head resting on Joey's chest. Joey's fingers trailed up and down Ethan's arm as he stared at the dark ceiling.

"I wish I knew what the hell was going on," he said. "It reminds me of a film I saw called *The Thirteenth Floor*. It was about a man who worked for this company to create an alternate universe, a world within a world type of thing. Eventually, he found out he was in one of those worlds himself, and it blew his mind. That's where I am."

Ethan's hand smoothed across his skin. "It's understandable. Elliott wanted to protect you from this, but you've been brought into it, anyway. My concern is that Robert is going to do something. We don't yet know what he's truly capable of, only what we've been told."

"As if we didn't have enough to worry about already." Joey sighed. "Why didn't Grey tell us he was at the party?"

"I don't know. Did you see his expression in the photograph?"

Joey had, and he didn't like it. "Almost like he was pissed off or disgusted?"

"Yeah," Ethan murmured. "It looked like he was looking at Elliott and Denny, but we can't be sure. For all we know, that picture could be a fake."

"I took everything Grey told us at face value. I didn't check anything. Maybe I should have. Maybe Grey is the one pulling the wool over our eyes. Or maybe Denny is. I've no idea."

"Hopefully, the police can find out more information. I'm sure they'll let us know if they're telling the truth or not. Grey hasn't messaged any updates like he said he would."

They dropped into silence, and Joey's mind went over everything that had happened since Ethan turned up at Elliott's funeral the previous day. Had it really been only two days since he'd been back with him? With everything that had happened, it seemed like they'd been to-ing and fro-ing for weeks.

"I'd like us to go to my parents' for dinner tomorrow. Is that okay with you?" he asked into the quiet.

Ethan blew a hot breath across Joey's chest. "Sure. I made you meet mine, so it's only fair, after all."

Joey chuckled and pressed a kiss to Ethan's hair. "True. But if you're not ready, we can do it another day."

"I'm ready. It's fine. I look forward to hearing all about your childhood."

Joey groaned. "On second thought..."

They laughed and settled down again.

"Get some sleep, sweetheart," Ethan said. "I'm right here and going nowhere."

Joey wrapped his arms around Ethan and sighed. "I love you."

"I love you. Now sleep."

Joey closed his eyes, listening to Ethan's breathing, and allowed himself to relax. He wouldn't be able to sleep, that much he knew, but he could pretend so that Ethan could get some rest.

He went over every piece of information he had about the party, the events afterwards, the new people involved, and he kept coming back to one thing: who was telling the truth and who was lying?

Denny seemed like a good enough guy from what Joey knew of him, but he had a reputation to protect. Grey was a clean slate, someone he didn't know and hadn't researched. He could be working for Robert or running from him. Robert was an issue Joey had never considered.

As another thought crossed his mind, he frowned. Had his visit to Whitby set more in motion for Ethan's friends and parents to deal with? He'd speak to his lawyer to find out what he could do, or maybe he could just employ a private investigator. It wouldn't take much to find out if there were problems there, surely. Ethan hadn't mentioned any blowback from Joey's presence, other than David's taunts, but that was easy enough to deal with. Unfortunately, it seemed that the main problems were from right on his doorstep.

Was he putting Ethan in more danger by having him there with him? Probably.

Could he give Ethan up to protect him? Probably not.

Would he if he had to? Absolutely.

He just hoped he wouldn't have to.

17

ETHAN

After the upheaval of the funeral, people coming out of the woodwork, the media and David's email, Ethan and Joey had an early night and a lie-in the following morning. Being Sunday, the only plan they had was to go to Joey's parents' house for dinner, which Ethan was trying not to think about. Instead, as they lay in bed, Ethan's head on Joey's chest, he explained about David's email.

"Ani said you would say I should ignore it, but I don't know David well enough to know if he's capable of anything more."

Joey's chest lifted and fell as he sighed. "Under normal circumstances, yes, I would've said ignore it, but David gave me a slimeball feeling right from the beginning, and the way he was with you was just plain wrong." He paused. "The least you should do is tell Meredith. I'm sure she could think of something to give her an excuse to fire him."

"Won't that exacerbate things, though?"

"Possibly. I'm happy to pay him to keep his mouth shut, but one, there's no guarantee he will stay quiet, and two, there's always the chance he'll keep coming back for more and more."

"True." He wasn't sure what the best route was, but he'd definitely speak to Meredith. Maybe she could speak to other employees and see if they'd had similar experiences to him. It might stop him from focusing so much on him and Joey if he had something else to worry about. Maybe.

Far too many maybes around there lately.

Joey slipped out from beneath him and braced himself on his elbow. "Tell you what. Go for a shower, and I'll cook us a late breakfast. Sorry, brunch. We're not due at my parents' until three o'clock, so we have time to relax."

"Deal."

Joey leaned over and kissed him, soft and far too chaste for Ethan's liking, but a shower sounded nice. Some warmth to help keep away the chill of what David was trying to do. He truly was an asshole. He watched Joey walk naked to the drawers before he slipped on some boxers. Catching Ethan staring, he winked and left the room, and Ethan headed for the shower. As the hot water pounded down on him, he closed his eyes and let it wash away his worries, at least for now. He was where he wanted to be and would soon be doing what he believed he might enjoy—which was another reason he needed to speak with Meredith. He shivered as he climbed out of the shower and dried off as quickly as he could, and then he sat on the bed and held his phone. He wasn't sure what Meredith's reaction would be to him handing in his notice, but he'd soon find out.

"Hey, Ethan. How are things down there?" Meredith said, and just hearing her voice made Ethan realise it would be fine.

"Hi. They're great, Meredith. Really good."

Meredith sighed. "You're not coming back, are you?" She echoed Christi's words.

She always had been quick on the uptake. "I'll be back to work my notice, but then, no. I'm moving to London."

"I'm happy for you, Ethan. I truly am. And...I knew it was coming. I've checked and you have enough holiday days accrued to use for your notice period. I'm not saying that I don't want you back, but you have the option if you want a fresh start from now."

Ethan swallowed hard, and everything went blurry. "I don't know what to say."

"Say, 'Meredith, I'd like you to use my holiday as my notice period, please.' It's not that hard when it's truly what you want."

Ethan chuckled and inhaled deeply. "Meredith, I'd like you to use my holiday as my notice period, please."

"Good boy. I will sort it. I want you to keep in touch, yeah? Let me know how life is in the limelight."

Which reminded him of his other reason for calling. "Talking of. I have something to talk to you about."

"What's that?"

"David."

Meredith sighed. "What's he done now?"

Ethan paused. Had he done something before? "Blackmail doesn't look good on him."

"Fucking asshole," she murmured quietly enough that Ethan was sure he wasn't supposed to hear. "I don't know what to suggest."

"I need to tell you about other things he's done, too." He went on to explain David's behaviour during working hours, the innuendos they put up with, and anything else he thought was pertinent to the conversation.

"Why is it only now I'm hearing about this?" Meredith said. "I knew what I saw, but I never knew it bled into work."

"We didn't think it mattered. It appeared harmless, to begin with, but now, with the blackmail, I'm wondering if he's getting worse."

"I'm going to investigate it, Ethan. I know you won't be working here any longer, but I'll keep you updated so you know if there's likcly to bc any backlash from it. If I have to let him go, he might up the heat on the blackmail."

"Okay. Thanks, Meredith, and sorry for throwing everything at you."

"It's fine. I'm just so glad you're happy."

Ethan smiled. "Yeah. Life throws things at you when you least expect it."

"So true."

They spoke for a few more minutes, and then they ended the call with Meredith promising to send the final paperwork to him in the week. He couldn't believe that was it. His years at The Cliff End Hotel were done. He stared down at the phone for a long moment, remembering the people and events he'd seen and taken part in. It was a wonderful place to work if he excluded David's being there. Though, hopefully, he wouldn't be there for much longer.

"Hey," Joey said, stepping into the bedroom. "I heard you on the phone, so I gave you some space. Everything okay?"

Ethan leaned against Joey's arm and smiled. "I'm using my holiday as my notice period, so I don't have to go back. I've also told her about David. She's going to look into it."

Joey slid his arm around him, and Ethan sighed. "Wow. I was expecting to have to part with you for a few weeks while you finished up there."

"Me, too. The only thing I really need to go back for is to pack up the house and get it on the market. I'm sure Dad and Mum will help if I need anything during the sale."

He'd spoken to his mother late the previous evening, and although groggy, she sounded in good spirits. It lessened the worry about her, but he still hadn't spoken to Kole. He'd received a few messages from Christi, though, updating him as much as she could. He had done his tour the previous evening, and Christi had sent him a thumbs up, so he believed it went okay.

So many things were happening at once.

"I would offer to slow time down, but I don't think that would help," Joey said with a chuckle.

Ethan laughed. "I didn't even realise I'd said that out loud." His stomach growled, and he pressed his palm against it. "Oh god. Has breakfast gone cold?"

"No, I put it in the oven. It'll still be hot enough."

"Okay, let me get dressed." Ethan moved to stand, but Joey grabbed his arm and tugged him to the bed.

"I can think of something much better to do with this towel." Joey growled and kissed him, and Ethan let himself be distracted—because who wouldn't if they had a "Joey" in their arms?

An hour later, their breakfast was far crisper than Ethan liked, but he ate it anyway. Joey had offered to make some more, but Ethan declined. No point wasting food, especially as his stomach was churning enough about meeting his parents. He hadn't thought about how nerve-wracking it was when he'd taken Joey to meet his. He felt like he needed to apologise again, but Joey wouldn't have it.

"You don't have to worry about it, you know," Joey said, proving he was a mind reader.

Ethan chuckled. "That transparent, am I?"

"Not really. I'm just getting to know you." Joey leaned his head down onto Ethan's shoulder. "They're lovely people. Much like your own. I'm sure they would get on well together." Joey hummed. "Maybe too well. We might need to keep them apart."

Ethan snorted. "Two of my mum? Definitely."

"I suppose there is one thing. If we ever get married, we won't have to do anything."

Ethan's heart raced at the thought of marrying Joey. They'd barely known each other, but the idea wasn't as far-fetched as he would've thought at another point in his life. He glanced down at Joey, imagining their lives completely intertwined forevermore, and it wasn't a bad thought.

Joey lifted his head. "Are you thinking how it sounds too sudden or too right?"

The man's bright gaze met his, and there was no hesitation. Ethan realised that if Joey asked him to marry him right then, he would've said yes. How crazy was that?

"Both," Ethan answered.

A smile crept across Joey's face. "Duly noted." He sighed. "I really need to start getting up earlier again. I've not jogged or done weights for days. But I'm finding I don't want to leave my bed for some reason." He winked.

"Same with me and yoga," Ethan said.

"You definitely need to do yoga again. Definitely."

They spent the next couple of hours talking about what needed to be done for Ethan to join Joey in London and what Joey's schedule looked like over the next couple of weeks. Ethan would need to return to Whitby sooner rather than later to get some more things. He'd only brought one bag, after all. They decided he would drive back on Tuesday and grab whatever was essential and could fit in his car, and he would return on Thursday so he could spend a night each with his friends and family. Joey was due to visit Bath on Tuesday and Cardiff on Wednesday, so it was the perfect time. The next time Joey travelled, Ethan would be going with him. It was a crazy but exciting thought.

The drive to Joey's parents took around an hour. They were on the outskirts of London in a lovely detached house that should've scared Ethan with its size. He was used to Joey being so down-to-earth despite his money, and he hoped his parents were the same.

"They'll love you. I promise."

Joey snuck a kiss as they headed, hand in hand, to the front door, which was opened by a butler—there was no mistaking who it was. He even wore the uniform.

"Good afternoon, Master Joey. Your parents are in the lounge."

"Thank you, Percy. I'd like you to meet my boyfriend, Ethan."

The butler, Percy, bowed his head and held out his hand. "Nice to meet you, Master Ethan."

"Likewise." And he found it was true. As they headed for the lounge, Ethan said, "You never told me they had money. I thought this was from you."

Joey glanced at him. "The house is. Everything in it was bought by them."

"Percy seems to have known you for a long time."

Joey grinned. "We didn't always have money, but I was about ten when Dad made a wise business choice and reaped the rewards." Ethan raised his eyebrows at him. "Investments. Dad has a way with them. They're not famous by any means."

"Not like you." Ethan nudged his side.

Joey chuckled. "Definitely more subdued than me."

They entered a large, bright room with plenty of seating space, a large coffee table and a bar in one corner. Ethan inhaled and braced himself for meeting the two people deep in conversation.

"Mum, Dad?"

Joey's mum glanced up, and Ethan could see the resemblance immediately. They had the same facial features, though Joey's were more masculine than his mother's. She smiled in the same way, too. Rising from her chair, she opened her arms as Joey went towards her.

"Joey! I'm so glad you came."

At the words, some of the nervousness disappeared. He'd been worried they would be stuck up and grandiose because of their money, but he could see where Joey got his down-to-earth personality.

"Hi, Mum. This is Ethan."

Ethan stepped closer and held out his hand, but she grabbed it and tugged him in for a hug.

"Ethan, my dear. I haven't heard as much about you as I want to know, so be prepared to be interrogated over dinner."

"Yes, ma'am."

"Pfft. Hazel, please."

Ethan smiled. "Hazel."

"Sweetheart, come meet Ethan. He's adorable, just like Joey told us."

Adorable? He glanced at Joey, whose cheeks had darkened, and he wouldn't meet Ethan's gaze. He'd tease him about that later.

Joey's father rose from his seat and stepped forward, hand outstretched. "Nice to meet you, Ethan. Please call me Jonah."

"Thank you for having me, Jonah."

"You're most welcome. Come, sit." Jonah waved to the sofa opposite them. "Tell us about you."

Ethan cleared his throat as he sat. "Um, well, there's not much to say, really."

"Of course there is. Joey said you live in Whitby?" Hazel said.

Ethan shared a glance with Joey, who smiled and gave a small nod. He refocused on Hazel. "I do, yes. Although, I've decided to, um…" He stared at Joey, wanting his help to explain their crazy, fast decision.

Joey chuckled and wrapped an arm around him. "Ethan is moving in with me. We've had a long talk about it, and we've agreed that it's a good decision. He's going to work as my assistant when I'm on the road."

Hazel frowned. "It is a bit quick. Are you sure about making such a big decision?" She held out her hands. "Please don't think I'm against it. I'm not. I'm just concerned."

Ethan nodded. "I was, too. I kept thinking we were moving too fast, but I think living with someone is the best way to find out if you're compatible or not. Or at least, the quickest way." He exhaled and stared at Hazel, seeing the worry and love shining in her eyes for her son. "I love him, Hazel. I know it's quick." He stared at Joey, smiling. "But I also know my heart."

He heard sniffing, and Hazel wiped her eyes. "Oh, I'm just a big softy. Don't mind me." She waved him away. "I don't think we have anything to worry about, Jonah."

"Me either."

"Madam, Sire, dinner is ready," Percy said from the doorway, proving he had impeccable timing.

"Wonderful," Hazel said, standing. "Let's eat."

When they were settled at the dining table, their conversation continued, and Ethan felt as comfortable with Joey's parents as he was with his own. They covered so many topics, including Hazel's knitting and Jonah's garden, and they gave them advice about how to live with someone, which was cute. He wouldn't turn down any advice, though, the same as he wouldn't when he spoke with his mum. That thought reminded him of her fall and everything that was going on with Kole. Despite having to leave Joey for a few days, he was looking forward to being able to check in with everyone and ease his worries.

"It was so lovely to meet you, Ethan," Hazel said as they got ready to leave. "I know you'll miss having your parents close by, so I want you to know that you are always welcome here. With or without Joey."

Ethan's throat closed, but he smiled. "Thank you," he rasped.

Hazel pulled him in for a hug and then patted his face before turning to Joey. "And you, mister, don't be a stranger. We're not far enough away to warrant months between visits." She wagged her finger at him, and Joey chuckled.

"Sorry."

Ethan nudged him. "I'll start adding you to his calendar, so he has no excuse."

Joey gasped. "So cruel."

They waved and climbed into the car. Ethan exhaled. "Your parents are lovely."

"They are. Their money didn't change them in any way. Our original house was a place they had hoped to fill with more children, but Mum developed endometriosis, and she struggled to conceive. After several years, they stopped trying, as the emotional toll was too great. She's now got her eyes set on grandchildren." He glanced at Ethan. "I should've warned you about that."

Ethan laughed. "Throwing kids at me already, huh?"

"You don't want kids?"

Joey's neutral tone made it difficult to determine his opinion on the matter, but Ethan would be honest. "I do. At least two so they can grow up together, but I'd be happy for more."

Joey exhaled. "I'm glad. I was worried for a moment."

"Would it have been a deal breaker?" Ethan peered at him, the sun sending shimmers of gold through his hair.

"Nope, but I'm glad you do."

Ethan inhaled, gathering his courage. "I can't seem to find a good time to ask this, so I'm just going to ask. What did the reporters mean when they asked if I'd forgiven you for your past?"

Joey sighed, and his knuckles went white on the wheel. "When I was a teenager, I was a passenger in a car that was involved in a hit-and-run. The driver, a friend at the time, didn't stop, even when I tried to make him. As soon as he dropped me off, I called the police. The person we hit survived but not without injuries. They bring it up every chance they get."

Ethan shook his head. "It wasn't your fault."

"Doesn't matter to them. Or anyone, really."

"It matters to me. It wasn't your fault," he said again. He changed the subject back to where they had been. "We wouldn't be able to take a child on the road as much as your schedule does now." He pulled out his phone. "Ani gave me access to your calendar." He checked his emails while he spoke. "Do you always make your journeys more difficult by scheduling each side of the country the day after each other? It would be easier to streamline..." He trailed off as he read an email from an address he didn't recognise.

Ethan,
You really shouldn't have brought Meredith into this. Or anyone else, for that matter. Now, I don't have a job, and that is your fault. Good luck trying to dampen this down.
David.

Attached were several pictures of Joey and some of them both doing various things, including the pictures of them in the kitchen at his house when that reporter got into the back garden.

"How the fuck did he get those photos?" he murmured.

18

JOEY

J oey was steaming by the time they arrived back home. How dare that man threaten to put those photos online? That was if he hadn't already. When they locked the door behind them, he pulled his phone out and called a woman he sometimes used to help with his media presence. Ani did a fantastic job, but she wasn't a professional. Polly, on the other hand, had many years under her belt working with reporters and dampening down stories.

"Hey, Polly. Sorry to disturb you on a Sunday, but we have a situation." He spent the next half an hour explaining what was happening and how David fit into everything.

"Okay. Leave it all with me, and I'll see what I can find out before I come back to you. We might not be able to stop the photos from being leaked, but we can cause an uproar to whoever does it."

Joey wished there was a better answer. "Thanks, Polly. Anything you can do is great."

It took her nearly two hours to come back to them, but when she did, it was with some good news and some bad.

"I've spoken to several news outlets. They said they won't run the photos if they're sent to them, though take it with a grain of salt. And there were several who declined to stop their stories from printing, so I don't have great news. But I've emailed you a statement you can put out if they leak the photos. It will call out the man who took the photo and the ones trying to make money from them." She sighed. "I'm afraid there's not much more we can do until we know if the photos are online or not. It could be smoke and mirrors to distract you from something else, so keep your eyes and ears peeled."

"Will do. Thanks, Polly." Joey turned to Ethan. "I'm sorry about this. If I wasn't in the limelight, none of this would matter."

Ethan slid his arms around Joey's waist. "It still doesn't matter. What happens, happens. We'll deal with it. Do I want everyone to see us in a compromising position? No, but it doesn't matter if they do." He grinned. "Everyone will want what is mine." He winked.

Joey chuckled, letting some of the tension release from his body. "And what is *mine*."

"Someone who's 'adorable?'" Ethan teased.

Joey swallowed hard as his cheeks heated. He shook his head and closed his eyes. "You won't ever let me live that down, will you?"

"Nope."

Joey kissed him. It was the only thing he could do. Because he *was* adorable. Damn adorable and sexy and amazing and submissive and...everything Joey ever wanted in a person.

Two days later, they stood between their cars in the car park behind the shop, clinging to each other. Why was it so hard to let him go when they'd only been together less than two weeks? And some of that was spent apart, anyway. Joey didn't want to let Ethan go, but he had to work, and Ethan had to see his family.

"It's two days, but it feels like more," Ethan said into his neck.

"I know. How crazy is it that we've only known each other a short time, but we're already not wanting to be apart?"

"Super crazy." Ethan pulled back and inhaled. "Okay. I'm going." He kissed Joey, and when he went to pull away, Joey clung to him again, kissing him deeper before letting him go.

"Have a safe journey," he said, brushing his thumb across Ethan's cheek.

"You, too. Call me when you get there."

"Make sure you stop along the way, Ethan. It's a far longer drive for you than it is for me."

Ethan chuckled. "I will. I couldn't do what I did on the way down here. That was nuts."

"Exactly my point." Joey kissed him again and then pushed him towards his car. "Go."

"Yes, Sir."

The way he said it made Joey's blood heat, and he cursed the man as he reversed out of the parking space. Ethan waved, and Joey returned it, watching until the car turned out of the alley. Joey exhaled hard and then inhaled and climbed into his car. Ethan had over five hours of driving to do, whereas Joey only had around two and a half, depending on the traffic.

They hadn't heard anything more from David and his threat to release the photos, and Polly had kept in touch to say none of the news outlets she'd been in contact with had heard anything either. Yet. It gave them a sense of standing on the edge of a cliff and waiting for the wind to blow them off.

He'd just entered Bath when his phone rang, and he smiled, anticipating Ethan's name on the screen. That smile disappeared when he saw a number he didn't recognise. He pressed the button on his steering wheel to answer as he concentrated on the road towards his client's house.

"Hello?"

"Joey? It's Grey."

Joey's body didn't relax. "Hey, Grey. How're things?"

"Yeah, not bad." His voice was less than convincing. "I'm sorry to call, especially as we agreed for me to contact Ethan, but... I'm not sure what to do, Joey."

"Give me a minute, Grey." Joey spied a layby and pulled into it, giving him a few much-needed seconds to gather his concerned façade so he could figure out if Grey was telling the truth or not. "Right, talk to me. What's wrong?"

"I don't know. Robert's acting strange. He's been around here more than usual. As if he's checking up on me."

"Has he said anything?"

"Nothing unusual." Grey sighed. "I'm probably overreacting. I'm just so..." He didn't finish, but Joey heard the exhale.

"Just carry on as normal, Grey." He purposefully didn't mention that the police were still investigating. "Don't do anything that might spark his interest."

"I think something already has. What if he's gearing up to bring me into whatever he's involved in? Elliott didn't want that, but how can I stop it?"

"Stand your ground. If you stick up for yourself, it'll be harder for him to wear you down."

Joey wanted to ask why Grey hadn't told them he'd been at the party, but he didn't want to tip the guy off if he was playing them. He needed to keep pretending that he believed everything Grey said, even though his belief was tenuous at best at that moment.

"Okay. Thanks. Sorry to have bothered you."

"Not at all. Call anytime. Oh, have you made the tattoo appointment yet?"

"No. I'm working up the courage."

Joey forced a chuckle. "It hurts more in your head than in reality."

"Probably." Grey huffed. "Where are you headed?"

Joey frowned. "Sorry?"

"I can hear the engine." He paused. "Sorry, it's none of my business."

Joey cleared his throat. "I'm in Bath. I have an appointment."

"Oh, nice town, I'm told." He sighed. "I'm going to go. Thanks, Joey."

"You're welcome."

The call ended, and Joey stared out of the windscreen, thinking over their conversation. Something niggled at him, but he couldn't figure out what it was. Shaking his head, he started back off, heading for his client, a rough-and-ready motorcycle club member who didn't venture far from his hometown. Joey had been tattooing him for years. There wasn't much skin left to decorate.

When he arrived, he sent a message to Ethan, letting him know he'd arrived and to remind him to stop and eat along the way.

"Joey!" Ryker said, clasping his hand and bringing him in for a back-slapping hug.

"Hey, Ryker. How're things?"

Ryker grinned, his gold teeth gleaming in the sunlight. "Ah, same old, same old. Old being the operative word here. My bones creak a little more, but my bike stays true and pure."

Joey chuckled. "That's all that matters then."

Ryker led the way to his study, his burly body leading him to a room Joey had been in many times, and Joey started setting up as Ryker brought him up to speed on his news.

"I'm sorry to hear about Elliott."

Joey paused and flared his nostrils, trying to reign in his emotions. Elliott had joined him on this particular visit a few times. "Thanks."

"He was such a bright light in this world. He'll be sorely missed. Even here."

Joey couldn't respond, so he concentrated on finishing the set-up. When he was under control, he turned to Ryker. "So, what're you having done this time?"

"I want motorcycle handlebars on my lower back."

"Okay. Let me see what space I have to work with."

They talked specifics of the design, and Joey drew something for him, adjusting it with details Ryker asked for until he was happy. Once he started, they fell into easy conversation with periods of silence.

After one such silence, Ryker said, "How are you really, Joey?"

Joey lifted the needle and sighed, giving his back a stretch as he considered his words. "I've been better, but I've been worse, too. I have someone important helping me to heal."

Ryker craned his neck and raised his eyebrows, and Joey chuckled. "Lay down, and I'll tell you the story." He waited until Ryker was back in position, and he started back on the design. "I went a bit off the rails after I found Elliott. Started driving and just carried on. Stopping here and there to sleep and get food when I had no choice. I was in a bad place." He sighed again. "I stopped in Whitby and headed for a bar, trying to drown my sorrows and sleep it off. But a guy approached me. He offered me a sliver of light. It was supposed to be one night, that's all, but he saw me sleeping in my car and decided it was his business to get me out of my funk." He chuckled. "His name's Ethan. We spent a few days together in Whitby until the reporters found me, and then I split, thinking it would be better if I wasn't there."

"Stupid ass," Ryker said, and Joey laughed.

"Yeah. I'm so glad Ethan took the chance and drove down for Elliott's funeral. I don't know where I would've been if he hadn't been here the past few days."

"Sounds like a great catch."

"He truly is."

"So, where is he?"

Joey wiped at the design and continued. "He's gone home for a couple of days to get things sorted. He's moving in, and he's going to be my assistant."

"Good for you, Joey. I'm so glad."

"Thanks."

It took another two hours to complete the design, and then Joey dressed it and packed up his stuff.

"Are you hanging around?" Ryker asked. "Merry is setting up the barbecue this evening."

Joey shook his head as they exited the room. "I wish I could. I have a room booked in Cardiff tonight."

"Well, at least let us feed you before you leave."

"Honestly, it's—"

"Is that you, Joey Reynolds?" a shrill but warm voice said.

Joey smiled. He couldn't help it. Merry wasn't a typical biker's old lady. She was a biker herself, first and foremost. It had taken Ryker six years to persuade her to take a chance on him, but they were perfect for each other.

"You know it, Merry." He slid his arms around her, hugging her tightly.

"I'm sorry, honey," she whispered.

Joey blinked back the tears and smiled, pulling back. "Thanks."

"Are you staying for dinner?" Joey shook his head again and explained his plans. "Pfft. You can stay for a bit. It doesn't take that long to get to Cardiff from here."

Joey didn't argue any longer, wanting to spend time with people he considered friends. "Okay. I'll drive over when we're done."

Merry patted his cheek. "Glad to hear it." She turned to leave, but Ryker grabbed her and pulled her into him, whispering something in her ear. She turned sly eyes on Joey, and he chuckled, knowing Ryker had just spilt the news about Ethan. "Ooh, story time!"

His phone rang, and he answered it with a smile. "Hey, you." Merry's eyes gleamed as she watched him, and he raised his eyebrows at her, but she just crossed her arms over her chest.

"Hey. How are you doing?" Ethan asked, the tiredness clear in his voice.

"Good. Are you there now?"

Ethan sighed. "Yeah. I've just dropped onto my sofa."

"Have a nap and then visit your parents. Don't do it while you're tired."

Ethan yawned. "I think you're right. Did you get the job done?"

He wandered over to the window and looked out at the garden, slowly filling with people attending the barbecue. "I did. Not long ago, actually."

"Ah. You're heading for Cardiff soon, then?"

"No, actually." He chuckled. "I've been browbeaten into staying for dinner."

"I heard that, young man!" Merry shouted.

Joey laughed again. "Sorry, Ryker's wife just reprimanded me."

"Ryker?"

"My client. I'll explain later." Ethan yawned again. "Okay, get some sleep, and call me later."

"Let me know when you leave there and arrive in Cardiff."

"I will."

"Love you." Ethan sounded like he was already dozing off.

"Love you more."

There was no response, so Joey ended the call and hoped Ethan would sleep long enough. He set his alarm to go off in two hours so he could call Ethan and wake him if he wasn't already. He wouldn't want to sleep through the visit to his parents.

"You're so in love with him; it's beautiful," Merry said, slipping in beside him.

"I truly am. He's the best part of me."

Merry slapped the back of his head. "No, he's not. You're the best part of you. He's the best part of him. Together, you're perfection."

"You've not seen him."

"I don't need to. I can see it in you. If he's as good as your expression tells me, he's perfect for you."

"When did you get so sappy?"

Merry slapped him again. "I'm not. I'm a realist."

Joey chuckled and followed her out to the back garden. This was a place where he didn't have to worry about reporters. The club didn't allow them into their private houses or on their land. Something they had decided upon way before Joey came into the picture. Meeting some other members that he'd not seen for a while was a boon he hadn't expected. The hours passed, and barring the phone call he made to Ethan to make sure he was awake—he had been—he forgot about everything happening back home. It was nice to relax in a different way from how he did with Ethan, though that idea brought many pleasurable images into his mind.

"Stop thinking about him," Merry teased as she passed.

Joey shook his head and smiled. "Can't help it." He checked his watch. "I really must be going now. Thanks for having me."

Ryker waved him away. "You're always welcome. You know that. Next time, bring Ethan."

"I plan to."

He shook hands with several of them, hugged Merry and aimed his car towards his next destination after sending Ethan an update. When he finally arrived at Cardiff, it was just before eleven that night, and he was exhausted, but once he'd settled into his room, he sent a message to Ethan to see if he was still awake. The phone rang seconds later.

"Hey, you."

Ethan's voice was a balm he hadn't realised he needed, and Joey lay back on the bed and closed his eyes, imagining Ethan was lying beside him, talking right into his ear.

"Hi. How are your parents?" he asked.

"They're fine. Mum is grumpy because she can't do as much as she wants to, but she's managing. I think Dad's worse off because he's having to put up with her moods." Ethan chuckled. "He doesn't mind. Not really."

"I didn't doubt for a moment he did. How is the house?"

"Same as I left it, though I should've thought to empty the fridge before I left. There was some nastiness in there I never want to smell again."

Joey laughed. "Oh, god. I can imagine."

"How was your evening? You mentioned someone called Ryker. That's an interesting name."

Joey slid an arm behind his head and explained about the whole motorcycle club thing and how he came to be the one to tattoo them. "Ryker is actually called Ryan. One of his friends started calling him Ryan the Biker, and it ended up being shortened to Ryker. And it stuck." Until that evening, he hadn't realised quite how close they had become, and he finally moved them into the "friend" category he always saved for those he knew before his unexpected climb to fame.

"Have you had any problems since you've been there?" he asked. "David's not been in contact or anything?"

"No. I've not heard anything from him. Christi called earlier to confirm tomorrow's night out, but that's it. I've not heard from anyone but Ani."

"Ani?"

"Yeah, she messaged to make sure I got here safely."

Joey smiled. "I'm glad. I had a feeling you would become best friends in no time if you ever met." Ethan's laughter filled his soul, and Joey sighed. "I miss you."

He could almost feel Ethan's smirk through the phone line. "It's only been fourteen hours." He paused. "Not that I've been counting or anything."

"Fourteen hours too many, in my opinion."

"I agree. Not long to go, though." Ethan sighed. "How has this become my life?"

"What do you mean?"

"I've found a man I love, I'm moving to London, and I've found a job I believe I will enjoy all in the space of two weeks. How is it possible to have everything fall into place in such a short time? It seems inconceivable."

"It does, but it's right for us." He remembered the phone call from Grey. "Grey called me earlier. He said Robert had been hanging around more, checking up on him. I don't know what to think about him now that we know he'd been at the party."

"Me either, in all honesty. I took everything he said originally at face value, but maybe we should find out more before deciding if to trust him completely."

"I might get a friend to look into him and see what they can find."

"It certainly wouldn't—Holy shit!"

Ethan's outburst coupled with the sound of glass smashing had Joey sitting upright. "What? Ethan? What happened? Ethan? Ethan!"

19

ETHAN

Glass shattered and splintered through the air as Ethan covered his head with his hands. The pinpricks of the shards hitting him made him hiss, but he waited until the sound ended before lifting his head again. The front window was in pieces, cool air blowing through the gap.

"What the hell?" he said, staring at the brick now decorating his living room floor. He knew better than to touch it, but he knelt closer to see if there was anything on it. White markings were on the side that he could see, but he couldn't decipher them without moving it, so he left it. No matter what it said or didn't say, he had a feeling who had sent the "gift."

"Ethan! Ethan!"

The tinny buzz of his name registered, and he dived for his phone, which he'd dropped when he'd covered his head.

"Joey? I'm okay."

"Fucking hell, Ethan. You scared ten years off my life. What happened?"

He glared at the offending brick. "Someone sent me a gift, except it missed the letterbox."

"What?"

He explained further, and Joey's curses changed the colour of the air.

"Ethan? Is everything okay in there?"

"Hang on, Joey." He stood and went to the door despite there being a new opening in his house. "Hey, Mrs Franklin. Yes, I'm okay, thanks."

The frail woman from next door scrunched her face. "Those hooligans are at it again, aren't they? They need to be taught a lesson."

"I agree, Mrs Franklin. You didn't get hurt, did you?"

Mrs Franklin shook her head. "No, dear. I was watching my documentary when I heard the noise. I wanted to make sure you were okay because I saw you drive up earlier. Have you been away on holiday?"

Ethan smiled, wishing he could hurry the conversation up but knowing she wouldn't leave until she had her answers. "Yes, in a way. I'm moving to London, so I'm back to sort the house out."

"Oh, how lovely, Ethan. It's a shame because I never know who I'm going to get living next to me, and you're wonderful. When you first moved in, I was so—"

"Mrs Franklin, I'm sorry to interrupt, but I need to call the police." He gestured to his phone.

"Of course, dear. I'll go back to my show. Let me know if you need anything."

"I will. Thank you for checking on me."

Mrs Franklin waved her hand and shuffled back to her house as fast as her walking frame would let her. He watched her until she closed her door behind her and then closed his own, shivering.

"Sorry, Joey. It was my next-door neighbour checking on me."

"You're right, though. You need to call the police. I'm getting on the road now and will be with you as soon as I can."

Ethan shook his head despite Joey not being able to see him. "No, I'm okay. You stay and do your job. I'll keep you updated with what the police say."

"You're not staying there tonight."

Ethan smiled. "I won't. I'll either stay with Kole, Christi or my parents, don't worry."

"Glad to hear it." Joey's sigh came through the phone. "I wish I was with you."

"I do, too, but we can manage two more days."

"Can we?"

Chuckling, Ethan said, "We can. It'll be hell, but we can."

"Okay. I'm going to go so you can call the police, but call me when you're settled wherever you're laying your head tonight, all right?"

"I'll message you, not call. I don't want to wake you."

"Do you really think I'm going to get any sleep until I know you're safe?"

Ethan grinned. "Fine. I'll call you."

"I love you."

"Love you back."

He ended the call, knowing Joey wouldn't do it, and called the police. When they finally had someone come around, it was two hours later, and Kole had already arrived to keep him company after his tour had finished. They took his statement, including who Ethan thought might have done it, and arranged for the place to be secured while Ethan headed to Kole's place.

They hadn't spoken much, but Ethan had immediately seen a change in his best friend. Kole was quieter, more subdued than he had been, but there was still a spark of something. As if embers were kindling and all it needed was something to fan the flames to a bonfire. He hoped he could help.

When they were finally settled in Kole's living room with a bottle of beer each, Ethan asked him how he was while he cleaned his cuts. There weren't many, but they stung. "And I don't mean your standard answer, either."

"It shook me, Ethan. There's no denying that, but I *am* okay. If anything, the tours make me feel better. What's not so great is my love life." He chuckled, though it was weak. "I'm not feeling the need to choose men when I go out anymore. I don't feel...safe, I suppose. This guy seemed nice enough, and we had a great time, but he turned out to be crazy. How can I trust my instincts now?"

Ethan patted his arm. "You'll get there again. Just think of all the other guys you were with before this. They weren't like that, and you chose well."

Kole huffed, raking his fingers through his hair. "Yeah, so well they never came back again."

Ethan could see his point, but he didn't want to make Kole feel worse than he did. "You just haven't found the right guy yet. It takes time."

"Yeah, that's what everyone says, but I'm impatient, Ethan. I want it now. I want my happily ever after to cling to me like a koala."

Ethan chuckled and patted his arm again. "It will as soon as it's time." He yawned. "I need to sleep, sorry."

"It's okay. You've had a long day. I'll be up for a few hours yet, but you have a key, so make yourself at home."

Ethan stood, pulled Kole in for a hug and headed for the stairs. He'd called Joey when they'd finally arrived at Kole's house, so hopefully, he was fast asleep, ready for his appointment the following day. Ethan, however, had a house to sort out and pack up. He wouldn't be able to take everything with him, but he could take the essentials and ask his parents to hold what he couldn't leave in the house. He had thought about keeping the house and renting it out to holidaymakers, but he didn't want the hassle of having to manage it when something went wrong. There were companies out there who could do it for him, but they would take a percentage. All in all, he thought it was better to just let it go and sell it. He could use the money he received from the sale to help towards the bills at Joey's place.

He was glad of his decision to sell when he was elbow-deep in packing boxes and bubble wrap. While he waited for the police officer to arrive, he was packing the house. So far, he'd made a pile of things to be taken to the charity shop, packed the kitchen up and put a load of washing on that he'd forgotten about before he'd hightailed it out of there for Elliott's funeral.

A knock startled him, and he almost dropped the plate he'd been wrapping. He rested it on top of the others and opened the door.

"Ethan Wright? I'm Detective Hines. I'm here about what happened yesterday."

Ethan waved him in. "Would you like a drink?"

The detective looked around. "Coffee would be great, thanks. Going somewhere?"

Ethan chuckled and headed for the kitchen. "I'm moving to London. I've just come back to pack up my stuff and get the house ready to sell."

"That's a big move."

Ethan shrugged a shoulder. "It wasn't planned, but it's the best decision." At Hines' raised eyebrows, Ethan explained his story without naming names. "I never imagined leaving Whitby, but I'm glad I am."

"Is this because of what happened with Joey Reynolds?"

Ethan settled onto the sofa, the detective copying. "In part. Joey is my boyfriend now. He's who I'm moving in with. Some people don't seem to like that."

"What? That you're moving in with him?"

"No. They think they can use photos to blackmail us into doing what they want. Joey says it's part and parcel of being in the limelight, but it's still shit. Excuse my language."

"I agree. And you think this David guy is involved?"

"Well, he's the one who's been messaging us about it. I still have the emails." He pulled them up on his phone. "I don't think Joey's received any. They seem to just be coming to me."

Hines read through the emails and then handed the phone back to him. "Can you send them to me, please?"

"Sure." He did. "I'm not saying this was David," he said, pointing to the window. "It just seems too close to coincidence to be anyone else. I'm not on anyone else's bad side, as far as I know."

Hines asked him a few more questions and then said he would be in touch. "You can go back to London if you need to. I'm not stopping you. Just let me know when you do."

"I'm here until tomorrow, but I will let you know when I leave."

Ethan exhaled once the door shut behind him, and he flopped onto the sofa. "Why does nothing ever go smoothly?" he said to no one.

He worked for another few hours, making good headway on his to-do list, and then stopped to make a trip to the charity shop to remove some of the stuff littering his floors. He grabbed a bag of chips on his way home again and ate while he spoke to Joey. After another hour of work, he jumped into the shower to get ready to meet Kole and Christi at the club.

It felt like a million years since he'd last been in the place he'd met Joey for the first time, even though it had only been a couple of weeks. He grabbed a booth when he saw it and waited for his friends to arrive. It took them as long as it took him to order for them from a passing server, and Christi squealed in his ear when she hugged him.

"Thanks for that. Make sure you're on my right side for the rest of the evening. I won't be able to hear you otherwise." He grinned when she backhanded his chest. "How are you? Is Di still giving you grief?"

Christi glanced away and settled further into her seat. "She's still there, yes."

Ethan tilted his head. "Christi?" He waited for her to look at him, and when she didn't, he said her name again.

Kole laughed. "Just tell him. He'll find out soon enough, anyway. Your lips will be spilling every secret you know after the drinks we're having tonight."

Christi sighed and faced Ethan. "The only grief she's giving me is the kind I enjoy when we're in bed together."

Ethan blinked. He hadn't been expecting that. That they would become friends, yes. But lovers? He burst out laughing. "Good for you. Now, are you going to stop complaining about her?"

Christi shook her head. "She's still a pain in the ass." Her cheeks coloured, and she sipped her drink. "She was doing it to get my attention."

Ethan slid an arm around her shoulders. "I'm glad. Are you in a relationship with her?"

Christi smiled and nodded and then blew out a breath. "I never expected it, you know?"

"I know the feeling." Ethan glanced at Kole, whose expression was carefully blank. "I can't wait to see this one fall." He tilted his head in Kole's direction.

"Pfft. I'm staying single for a while." Kole downed his drink and waved at a server, who nodded. "I'll wait for someone else to do the heavy lifting this time."

"So you should. Let them come to you," Christi said, lifting her glass to clink it with Kole's.

"Fill our lives with as much fun as we can," Ethan said, still agreeing with his motto in life.

Ethan's phone vibrated against his leg, where he'd stashed it, and he leaned back and pulled it free. An unknown number. With everything that had been happening, he was even more reluctant to answer those types of calls, but he needed to know who it was. He put his finger in his other ear to reduce the noise and answered.

"Hello?"

"Mr Wright? It's Detective Hines."

Ethan's shoulder lowered, and he excused himself and went outside to finish the call. "Sorry about that, Detective. How can I help?"

"I wanted to let you know that we've arrested David Thurl for the vandalism on your house. Fingerprints were found on the brick, and the marker that made the note on it was traced back to one found in his car."

"I never asked. What did the note say?"

Hines cleared his throat. "'*Just you wait.*' It's related to him believing you were to blame for him being let go from the hotel."

"Did he say anything about the photos?"

"Not as yet. We will find out, though."

Ethan sighed. "Thank you, Detective. I appreciate you letting me know." He finished the call and dialled Joey. "Hey. How are you?"

"Good. Just settled in with Joelle to watch some TV." Joey's voice was a balm to all that ailed him, and he smiled.

"David's been arrested. I don't know if it'll stick or whatever, but he's in trouble for the moment, at least."

"Did they find the photos?"

"Not yet. Look, Joey, it's okay. If the pictures get out, they get out. I'll live with it. We'll deal with it together."

Joey sighed. "I know. I just hate this for you."

"I know you do, but I'm sure it won't be the last time we're in the news."

"Just you wait until our wedding."

Ethan's heart skipped a beat. "Our wedding?" he croaked.

Joey's laughter warmed his soul. "When we *eventually* get married, there is no chance of it not being in the news."

Finding his voice, Ethan said, "I can imagine. I still don't care, though. Not anymore."

"Why?"

"Because I have you. Whatever else I have to deal with is worth it because I have you."

Joey was quiet for a moment, and Ethan wondered if he'd said the wrong thing. "I hate that you're so far away right now. You can't say things like that when I can't fuck you, Ethan."

Ethan chuckled, even as heat rolled through him. "You'll have to call me later and make me pay."

"Nah. You can wait until I get my hands on you tomorrow. You'll regret teasing me."

"I doubt it. I'm adorable, remember?"

Joey growled. "Go back to your friends, Ethan. I'll speak to you in the morning."

"Yes, Sir," he whispered and ended the call.

He spent the rest of the evening with his friends, and they made plans for them to visit London. Ethan could just imagine the chaos they would cause, but he was excited about it, too. Maybe he could persuade Joey's friends to come with them and show them the sights.

When he woke the following morning, despite his hangover, he was ready to get the work done so he could head to his new home. He faced a fried breakfast, chugged several glasses of water and set to work. He didn't stop, other than to speak to Joey between his clients, so when his phone rang, he answered without looking.

"You really think this is the end of it. Well, watch out. Just because I'm out of the picture at the moment doesn't mean there aren't others looking to see your and Joey's downfall. Good luck, Ethan."

David's voice chilled him to the bone, and the call cut out before he could reply. He pursed his lips and dialled Detective Hines.

"Is David still in custody?"

"Yes, why?"

"He just called me." He told him exactly what was said, and the detective cursed and apologised.

"I will see to it that he's not let out on bail. We'll see if we can't get more information out of him about who he's talking about."

"You might want to liaise with the London police, too. There are things going on down there that might be linked, though I don't know for definite. Detective Harmon and Keith."

"Thank you. I will."

Ethan glanced around him at what was left to do and decided it wasn't worth it. Anything else could be thrown away. He spent several hours loading his car, packing it so full he could only see a small rectangle in his rearview mirror and headed to his parents.

"I'm heading back now. Thank you for agreeing to help sell the house. I'm going to arrange for someone to go in and take the remaining furniture and anything else they want for the charity shop. What's left will be taken to the tip. I'll let you know when the place is empty if you still don't mind arranging for the estate agent to come in?"

His father shook his head. "Of course, we don't. You just take it easy on that journey, all right?"

"I will." He hugged his father and leaned down to kiss his mother's cheek. "I'll see you soon. If you need anything at all, call me."

His father waved him off, and Ethan climbed into the car, trying not to cry. He was never going to like being so far away from his family and friends, but he had something amazing waiting for him. Even with everything that surrounded them—the uncertainty, the blackmail, Elliott, Grey, Robert, and more—he couldn't imagine being without Joey now.

He just wished he knew what the endgame was. Who was behind everything?

20

JOEY

W aiting for Ethan to arrive home—and it would be his home from the moment he turned up—was pure torture for Joey. He'd been without him for two days already, and it was too much. He was sure, over the years to come, the need to be with him would wane slightly, but for the moment, he needed Ethan as much as he needed to breathe.

When his car pulled into the car park, Joey jumped up from his perch on the outer stairs and jogged down the rest of them and over to Ethan, opening his door before he'd even put the handbrake on. He leaned down and pressed his lips to his boyfriend's, reacquainting himself with the taste he'd been sure he'd forgotten.

He hadn't.

Finally letting Ethan up for air, Joey pulled back. Ethan exhaled with a lopsided grin. "Hello to you, too." He climbed out and stretched his arms to the sky. Joey heard several cracks in his joints and winced.

"That is a long drive," he said.

Ethan nodded. "But I'm back now." He slid his arms around Joey's back. "The stuff can wait until later. Take me to bed." He lifted his head.

Joey took his mouth again, pushing him back against the car while he ravaged him. Ethan thrust his hips, their groins grinding together, and they moaned. Joey tore his mouth away.

"Upstairs. Bed. Now."

"Yes, Sir."

Ethan slammed his car door shut, locked it and ran for the stairs. Joey took a more leisurely stroll, wanting Ethan to be waiting for him when he got there. He readjusted his groin and climbed the steps. A prickle of awareness lifted the hairs on the back of his neck, and he paused, studying his surroundings. No one was in the car park. He couldn't see anyone at the windows overlooking the area. But still, that feeling of someone watching him was there. He took one last look and then climbed the rest of the way and locked the door behind him. Pushing the feeling aside, he headed for the bedroom, and just as he'd hoped, Ethan was lying naked on the bed.

Joey leaned against the doorframe and looked his fill. The muscular, tanned body waiting for him to explore. The squirming as Ethan tried to keep still under his perusal. The cock already pointing towards his stomach. A smile crept across Joey's face. Two days was far too long.

He stepped closer, his fingers going to the hem of his T-shirt and yanking it over his head. As much as he wanted to explore the splayed body, he needed to feel Ethan around him. Submitting to him. His.

By the time he reached the bed, he was naked, but he stopped beside it, staring down at him. Ethan's breathing increased, and precome leaked onto his stomach. Joey crawled onto the bed and over Ethan, bracing himself on his hands before lowering himself on top of him. His restraint gone, he took Ethan's mouth, licking into the cavern. He ground his cock against Ethan's, and Ethan wrapped his legs around him, levering himself up in time with Joey's moves.

"I missed you like mad," he whispered when he briefly pulled back. Then he kissed down Ethan's neck and chest, circling his tongue around his nipple and sucking hard, soothing it again with his tongue.

Their hips thrust in rhythm, the heads nudging each other and taking them closer to their destination.

"Fuck, Joey. I want you."

"I've got you." Joey pushed Ethan's arm away and above his head. "Stay," he ordered.

Ethan's breath hitched. "Yes, Sir."

Joey kissed and licked every part of Ethan's body as if he was checking he was all in one piece and then lifted his ass, bending him in half while he attacked his hole. Sucking, licking, helping to prepare him for the invasion that was quickly coming.

"Oh, fuck. Oh, yes. That feels so good."

Joey lost himself in the preparation, needing to make Ethan feel as good as he could before the slight bite of pain that always accompanied his entry. He lay Ethan back down and reached for the lube. Slicking Ethan with his fingers and then his own cock, he laid back between Ethan's legs and held his cock at his hole. Ethan canted his hips, and the head nudged against the pucker, earning a gasp from them both.

He pushed forward, and Ethan froze, his mouth dropping open as Joey worked his way inside. Ethan's hands clenched above his head, and Joey's pride burst forward at him, still listening to his orders even when his body was losing control.

Joey pressed inside, bit by bit, making sure to rub across his prostate as much as he could. Ethan lifted his legs again, crossing his ankles at Joey's lower back, and Joey slid his arms around him, encouraging him to do the same. Wrapped around each other as they were, Joey couldn't thrust as hard as he wanted, but by canting his hips back and forth, he was able to stroke inside Ethan in short bursts. The fire flamed between them.

"Yes, oh, please, Sir."

Joey kept it up until Ethan was babbling, and then he lifted to his knees. He pushed Ethan's legs back, bending him in half, and slammed his hips forward.

"Ah!" Ethan screamed, gripping the headboard.

Joey kept up a hard rhythm, not changing position or speed, just staying true to his course. The one thing he did add was a smack on either ass cheek. Then he rested his hand on Ethan's lower stomach. What would it be like to feel his cock from the outside? His breath hitched. The idea of seeing and feeling his dick while it was inside Ethan was a heady thought.

"Please, Sir!"

Joey licked his lips and pushed Ethan's legs together and to one side so he was almost on his side. Then he increased his speed, their bodies slapping together. Keeping the momentum going, Joey leaned down and kissed him, muffling the noises he made and swallowing them instead.

"Come for me," Joey ordered as Ethan's pulsed around him.

Ethan's eyes rolled back, and his body reacted, constricting around Joey and sending him towards the edge. Joey thrust faster, chasing his release even as Ethan finished his own.

"Give it to me, Sir. Give me all of it."

Joey's cock throbbed, and he froze as his body flew. His vision dimmed until he could only see Ethan, and he focused on that pinprick of light while his body jerked and spasmed. He finally dragged in air and collapsed over Ethan, panting against his skin.

"I missed you, too," Ethan whispered, and Joey could hear the smile in his voice. "I do think everyone probably heard us, though."

Joey snorted and lifted his head, propping it in his hand. "Probably. I don't care."

"Me either."

Joey inhaled and exhaled, feeling like he could finally breathe again. "I'm glad you're home."

Ethan smiled. "I'm home."

They spent another hour together before Joey begrudgingly acknowledged that he had work to do. When they descended the stairs into the shop, Ani waited for them with a roll of her eyes.

"Could you have been any louder?"

Ethan's nose crinkled, and Joey slid his arm around him. "Possibly. We could try next time."

"No, thanks."

Joey kissed Ethan's temple and slipped behind the counter to check the diary. "What do I have?"

"Two so far. One is for Ade."

Joey nodded. "He wants me to fill in some more of his arm. Who's the other?"

Ani shrugged. "A new person under the name Greg. Said it's his first tattoo."

Joey gritted his teeth. "Which probably means he'll chicken out."

"Maybe." Ani smiled and nudged his side. "You'll bring him around."

Joey faced Ethan. "Are you going to watch me work, or are you going to immerse yourself in the job already?" He knew his boyfriend well enough to know he was dying to get started. Ethan gave his lopsided grin, and Joey raised his eyebrows, shaking his head. "I'll see you in a bit then." He dropped a kiss on his lips and headed back up the stairs to his studio.

He made sure he had everything he needed and cleaned the area again to make sure, by which point Ade had arrived.

"Hey, man." Ade shook his hand. "I'm sorry to hear what happened."

Joey nodded his thanks. The subject, despite how sad, was getting easier to bear when people brought it up. "Are we continuing what we started?"

"Yeah. I'd like to get it covered over as soon as I can."

Joey pointed to the chair. "Sure thing. Let's get to it. It looks a lot better already. Even those first few lines have taken the design in a whole other direction."

"I've got you to thank for that. I know I've said this before, but I don't know what I was thinking of getting a name tattooed on me. Worst thing I ever did."

Joey chuckled. "The only names worth putting on your skin are your kids' names."

"True that."

He worked steadily, using the new design to cover the name Lisbeth. It would take another session to colour it in, but even though Joey designed it, he was still impressed that it had worked how he wanted it to. It took an hour and a half, and when he was done, they couldn't see the name. Only if they really looked for it. Joey had created a mandala effect using swirls and sharp corners to intersect with the old name, making it indistinguishable.

"I can see why you're the best," Ade said, clapping his shoulder.

Joey laughed. "Don't let Beck hear you say that."

"He wouldn't be able to dispute it."

They headed down the stairs, where Ani took Ade's payment, and Ethan booked his next session. Ade said goodbye and left just as someone came in.

Grey.

Joey rose from his lean on the counter and frowned. "Everything okay, Grey?" To be honest, Grey was the last person he wanted to see that day.

Grey nodded. "I'm here for my tattoo."

Joey's heart calmed. "I have someone booked in right now. I can fit you in later, though."

Grey pointed to himself. "I'm booked in. I booked it under Greg so no one would know."

Joey failed to point out that by entering the shop using the front door as he had, if someone was following or watching, it wouldn't matter what name he was booked in under. They would know.

He feigned interest. "Oh, really? Great. Come on up, then. Ethan, do you want to watch?"

Ethan nodded, which Joey had hoped he would. For some reason, being alone with Grey was not what he wanted right then. "Lead the way," Ethan said.

They climbed the stairs in silence, and Joey opened his door, waving Grey forward. He met Ethan's gaze, who looked as troubled as Joey probably did, but Ethan wiped his expression clear and stepped in with a smile.

"I've seen tattoos being done before, but not up close. Thanks for allowing me to watch," Ethan said to Grey.

"No problem. I might need you to hold my hand," Grey joked as he settled into the chair.

Joey busied himself getting things ready while they discussed what Grey was having done.

"I'd like Elliott's name on my back, between my shoulder blades. Freehand if possible."

Joey paused, letting himself get used to the idea. He had no problem writing the name, but why would Grey want that? If he was worried about Robert and others, why would he take the risk of them seeing it? There was more to him than met the eye, and Joey needed to figure out what it was.

"What about that tribal tattoo you showed me? I thought that was what you wanted."

"I changed my mind."

"That's fine," he said finally. "I will caution you about it, though. If you're worried about Robert, having Elliott's name on your back will make things worse."

Grey shook his head, lowering his eyes. "I don't care. It's the least I can do for him. To remember him."

Joey swallowed. "Okay. Straddle the chair, facing the back, and take off your shirt."

While Grey got ready, Ethan sidled up beside Joey and lowered his voice. "What's wrong?"

Joey studied Ethan's face, wanting to tell him his concerns but unable to do so at that moment. He shook his head. "Later," he mouthed. He put everything on a tray and carried it to the table next to where Grey waited. "I'm just going to shave the area to make sure it's free from hair," he said to Grey.

"Okay."

Joey went through the motions, preparing the skin for tattooing. Knowing he couldn't do the job in silence—only because he never usually did, and it might seem strange to not say anything during it—he said, "I wasn't sure you'd gather the courage."

Grey chuckled. "I wasn't either. But then I thought about Elliott and everything he did for me. I want to remember him. I think it's a fitting memorial."

Joey frowned. Something was off. He shared a glance with Ethan, who was also frowning. "Yeah. I've seen others do similar," he said, stretching the time out. He didn't want to put Elliott's name on Grey's back, but he couldn't think of a reason to decline. Shaking his head, he wiped the area once more. "Ready?"

"No." Grey chuckled. "Yes. Go for it."

Joey inhaled, exhaled and turned on the machine. The familiar buzz filled the air, and Joey relaxed. This was just another tattoo. There was nothing to worry about. Joey laid the needle down and started the name. It didn't take long, but the moment he'd finished, he wanted to scrape it off—as if he could. Everything felt wrong about Grey now that he knew he'd been at the party.

Taking a risk, he said, "I saw some pictures of the party the night Elliott died. I'd forgotten how many people were there. Faces I recognised. Faces I didn't. It all merges together sometimes, but photos make it easier to remember."

Grey had tensed when Joey had started talking. "Did you see anyone of interest?"

Ethan shook his head at Joey, and he heeded the advice. "No. Just the usual faces."

Grey relaxed, and Joey finished covering it and talking through the aftercare.

"Thank you, Joey. I appreciate it." He turned to Ethan. "How was your first tattoo experience?"

Ethan smiled, though Joey could see it was strained. "Good. Maybe one day, I'll have one."

Grey slipped his shirt back on and tucked it in. "Fingers crossed, this won't be my last."

It would be the only one Joey ever did for him. "If you head down the stairs, Ani will sort you out."

Grey's expression tightened and then eased, and he smiled. "Great. It was nice to see you again." He headed for the door. "Did you have an enjoyable time in Cardiff?"

Joey schooled his expression, but a chill skated down his spine. He smiled. "Yes, all good. Same as always."

Grey nodded. "See you later." He closed the door behind him, and Joey leaned against the table, staring at the door.

"What's wrong?" Ethan asked, closing the distance between them.

Joey collected his thoughts. "I never told him I was going to Cardiff. I told him I was going to Bath." He met Ethan's gaze. "What the fuck is going on?"

Ethan slid his arms around Joey, and Joey nestled his face into Ethan's neck. "I don't know, sweetheart, but I have a feeling it's all coming to a head."

Joey lifted his head. "Why?"

It was Ethan's turn to stare at the door. "While you were tattooing him, Grey didn't have a grimace or anything that I would expect a first-timer to have. He was almost...smirking."

Joey's stomach churned. "I knew I shouldn't have done it. Something was telling me not to."

Ethan sighed. "I don't want to say it, but do you think Grey had something to do with Elliott's death?"

Joey stared at him. "I really don't know."

"He's hiding something."

Joey nodded. "He is. But what?"

Neither spoke, and Joey pulled his phone from his pocket. "Detective Harmon? It's Joey Reynolds. Can I ask a question?"

"You can ask, but I reserve the right to not answer."

"Fair enough. Have you found out anything about Grey Kennedy?"

The detective was silent, and Joey thought he wouldn't answer. "I have," he said hesitantly. "Why do you ask?"

"He's just been here for a tattoo, and he called me the other day." He went on to describe the phone call, the tattoo and when Grey had asked about Cardiff.

Harmon sighed. "Keep this to yourself, all right? We have reason to believe Grey Kennedy is working with his father."

Joey closed his eyes and dropped his head. "Why would he do that? Elliott had been trying to stop that from happening."

"Who told you that?" Harmon asked.

Joey's eyes sprung open, and he met Ethan's gaze. "Grey," he murmured.

"Hmm. I wouldn't believe anything he says. Everything we've uncovered so far shows him as being part of Robert's business."

"How long?"

Harmon sighed. "Three years."

"Fuck! Elliott was being taken for a fool. Grey said Elliott got in contact with him two years ago." Heat built inside him. "But why?

I don't understand why Grey was playing that game if he was already in with his father. Why not cut ties with Elliott instead?"

"I don't have an answer for you yet, Joey. We're still working on it."

Joey swallowed hard. "Do you think he was murdered?" Ethan tightened his hold on him.

"Not in so many words. It's conclusive that Elliott took his own life, but what led him to it? That's what we need to figure out."

21

ETHAN

E than's heart broke as he heard Joey's conversation with the detective. When would this all be over for Joey? Hadn't he suffered enough already? He tightened his hold on him as he ended the call, and Joey sank into him. Ethan rubbed his hand up and down his back, soothing him as best he could.

They'd been holding each other for a few long minutes when his own phone rang. He cursed. Grabbing it, he saw an unknown number, and his stomach churned. Was it David again?

"Hello?"

"Mr Wright, it's Detective Hines."

Ethan's heart calmed, and he put the phone on speaker so Joey could hear. "Good afternoon, Detective. What can I do for you?"

"We've finally finished with David Thurl's interview. I've spoken to Detective Harmon, who seems to be in charge of the case where you are. He's agreed that I can tell you what we've found out."

"And what might that be?" Joey asked.

Hines paused, and Ethan filled the gap. "Detective, this is Joey Reynolds."

"I'm sorry I'm not calling with better news, but David has acknowledged who put him up to the photographs and the brick. At least, according to him. We're still trying to confirm everything he said."

"And who was it?"

"Grey Kennedy."

The moment the words hit Ethan's ears, Joey's legs gave way. Ethan dropped the phone to catch him, and he helped him to the floor, settling him into the cradle of his arms. He reached for his phone again.

"Sorry, Detective. I'm back."

"Everything okay?"

"Not really. Is there anything else you need to tell me?" It would be a little easier now they were already on the floor.

"David said Grey contacted him through the hotel a little while back, offering substantial money for him to make your and Joey's lives difficult. The reporter was paid by David, and the other reporters were notified later. It seems he was just there to irritate you mainly."

"Well, he succeeded," Ethan bit out. "But why? What would irritating us do?"

"Exactly what it did. Sent Joey back to London. What they didn't account for was you going with him."

Ethan's heart skipped a beat, and he smiled. "I'm always willing to throw a spanner in the works."

"Harmon said this news would help you. I hope it did."

Ethan sighed. "It's certainly not what we wanted, but we were expecting something. Thank you, Detective. Oh, did David say anything about leaking the photos?"

"Yes. It was all a ruse. He didn't have the photos in the first place. Only a screenshot of one, and not a good one, either."

It had seemed good enough on the email he'd been sent. "Okay, thanks." Ethan ended the call and dropped his phone to the floor, hugging Joey. "Are you okay?"

"I just tattooed Elliott's name on his back," Joey mumbled.

Ethan closed his eyes and pressed his lips to Joey's head. "It doesn't matter."

"It matters if he was involved. I knew I should've set up that private investigator. It slipped my mind."

"You've had a lot going on, sweetheart. You can't do everything yourself. Plus, the police are looking into him. That is probably the better way to go about it."

"I don't understand," Joey said, sitting upright and resting back against the cupboard.

Ethan crossed his legs and faced him. "I don't either, but I do have a feeling that Grey is messing with us. Why else would he keep turning up and calling?" He wasn't going to mention the tattoo again.

"I think he had something to do with Elliott's death and is rubbing it in our faces."

Joey stood, and Ethan followed. "Maybe, but let the police do their job."

Joey's phone rang, and he cursed. "I don't want any more calls!"

Ethan glanced at the display. "It's Denny." He held it out.

Sighing, Joey took it and answered. "Hey, Denny. What's up?"

"Apart from being blackmailed into keeping my mouth shut about Robert, nothing."

Joey dropped his head back. "What?"

"I've had an errand boy turn up at my house, threatening my livelihood if I spill any information about Robert to anyone."

"Who was it?"

"Grey Kennedy."

"Fucking hell!"

Ethan agreed. "He's getting around."

"When did this happen?" Joey asked.

"A couple of hours ago. I've been on the phone with my lawyers and manager to ensure I'm backed up if I need to be; otherwise, I would've told you sooner."

"I kinda wish you had," Joey mumbled, heading for the door. Ethan followed him.

"Why's that?"

"Because we've realised that guy is not the person we thought he was."

"Who? Grey? He's nothing but a snake."

"Yes, I'm getting that," Joey said. "Thanks, Denny. I hope you get everything sorted out. Let us know if anything else happens, yeah?"

"Will do."

Joey ended the call, and Ethan caught his arm before he could throw the phone. "You need that," he said gently.

They descended the stairs and entered the front of the shop, where Ani and the rest of the guys were talking. Ani glanced at them with raised eyebrows. "Problems?"

"You could say that." Joey filled them in on what they'd found out about Grey.

"If he ever shows his face around here again, I'm going to rearrange it," Dallas said.

Ethan barely heard them talking. He lost himself in his thoughts, going over the information they had. Something didn't add up. Grey had been hiding his true identity from Elliott, but for what reason? What did they want with Elliott? To bring him into the business? Was Robert that obsessed with keeping it in the family? If Elliott was going to spill the dirt on Robert, it would give them a motive for his death. But the police had confirmed it was a suicide. What had happened to Elliott to make him think that ending his life was the only option? He had an idea of what might have happened, but he hoped it wasn't true. Ethan was sure an answer to the last question would destroy Joey.

"I think I need to make a statement to the media," Joey said, and for some reason, those words pierced Ethan's bubble.

"What? Why?" he said.

Joey shrugged. "I haven't spoken to them at all since I found Elliott. It might get them off our backs a bit."

"I don't know if that's a good idea," Beck said. "Keeping quiet about all of this would be the best choice right now."

"I wasn't planning on pointing the finger at anyone, although I have every right to. I just think I need to say something. I feel like I'm doing Elliott a disservice by not acknowledging him."

Ethan could see where he was coming from. "Maybe write it down first. We can't take the chance that any word is taken the wrong way."

Joey stared at him and nodded. "I can do that."

"I'll help." Ethan smiled at him.

"I'm still not sure if this is the best idea," Beck said. "Do you really want all this kicked up before the Bonser event?"

"It might make us more popular and get us more visits," Dallas replied.

"What is this Bonser event?" Ethan asked. "I've heard you mention it a few times."

Dallas grinned. "It's our annual, two-day tattoo convention. We have a stall and some chairs, and people can get tattoos done on the day as well as find out about and talk to us. Sometimes, meeting an artist in person and talking to them is the best way to help them relax about getting one. Last year, we tattooed…" He glanced at Finn. "How many was it?"

"Fifty-two," Finn said with a grin.

"Fifty-two people. We tattooed fifty-two people in twenty-four hours. That's over two an hour."

Ethan gaped. "How did you manage to do so many?" He glanced at Joey, who chuckled.

"We made sure they were smaller tattoos that didn't need as much work."

"Why do you do events like that, though? It's not like you need the clients."

Beck shrugged. "It's not about the client list. It's about exposure. If we keep ourselves in the light, people are more likely to keep track of us and follow us, and then our clients also benefit. It's a two-way street."

"When is it?"

"In two months. It takes a lot of organising, though," Ani said.

"I can imagine." Ethan shook his head. "I don't know how you do it."

Joey slid his arm around him. "You'll find out in two months." He winked and dropped a kiss on his lips. "Want to help me write my speech?" he whispered.

"I'm pretty sure we know he's not going to be helping you write it," Dallas said. "He'll be on his knees while you pray."

Ani slapped the back of his head. "That's none of your business, Dallas. We don't guess what you do when you've not got any appointments, do we?"

Dallas didn't look at all repentant. "I'm happy to tell you, but I don't have time."

Ani shook her head. "Yes, get the hell out and on your way."

Joey glanced at him. "Where are you going?"

"Perth to see Donovan."

"Nice," Joey said. "Enjoy the scenery." He turned to Finn. "Aren't you going out, too?"

"Yep. Southampton."

"Beck?"

Beck nodded, too. "I get Paris."

Joey chuckled. "Annabelle?"

"You got it."

The speed and familiarity they spoke of was something Ethan knew he would get used to, but the distance they were willing to travel was immense. "You do make a profit here, don't you?" he blurted.

Ani laughed. "My sweet boy. You still have a lot to learn. Yes, we make a profit, and when you learn more of the ropes, you'll see why and how much." She glanced at Joey. "Unless the boss man doesn't want you to know."

Joey rolled his eyes. "I have no secrets from him."

Dallas clapped and rubbed his hands together, grinning. "I'd love to test that theory."

"You have to leave," Ani said. "Now."

Dallas stuck his tongue out at her, waved and pounded up the stairs.

"I told you, babysitting, not managing," Ani said, winking at him.

Ethan chuckled. "I'm getting the idea."

Despite Joey's words to the contrary, he didn't want help with his speech. He sat at the table, head lowered, scribbling away on the paper while Ethan scrolled on his phone, alternately reading something and watching Joey work. He wasn't sure how long they both sat there with their respective tasks, but finally, Joey sighed and leaned back.

"I think I've finished. Could you read it for me? I'm not always very eloquent."

Ethan rose and slid a hand along Joey's shoulders. "Of course."

Joey handed him the sheet, which was around three-quarters full. Ethan settled beside him, but Joey stood. "I can't sit here and wait. I'll make something to eat." He pressed his lips to Ethan's head and disappeared into the kitchen.

Ethan focused on the words.

Elliott Kennedy was my best friend. Some of you may wonder why I haven't spoken out before now, and my answer is this. My grief is for me and Elliott alone. I do not have to share it with anyone if I don't want to. That being said, I would now like to offer you these words.

Elliott was an amazing person and friend that anyone would have been grateful to know. He was passionate about so many things in this world. So many charities he wished he could help. So many causes he tried to assist. But he was mainly passionate about his family and friends. They meant the world to him.

That bright light was taken from us far too soon. It's not something I will "get over" soon. It will stay with me—Elliott will stay with me until my last breath. Please give us this time to grieve properly because burying someone does not end the grieving period. If anything, it restarts it back at ground zero.

Depression and suicidal thoughts are not something to trivialise. They matter a lot. We need more light shed on such subjects. More help for those who need it. More support for those suffering. It's a dark world, and people need to realise it's not as easy as just "thinking happy thoughts."

Elliott Kennedy was a great person, and our loss is profound. Now, I just need to figure out how to continue without my best friend beside me.

Thank you for your time.

Ethan sniffed as he finished reading, wiping the tears from his eyes. He didn't try to find Joey, understanding just how much this must've taken from him to write it. It was perfect as far as Ethan was concerned. Joey made no apologies for taking the time he needed, and that was the right thing to do.

Joey finally came back in, carrying two plates of steaming food. He placed them at the table, laying cutlery beside them and sat back in his chair.

"What do you think?"

Ethan rested his hand over Joey's. "It's perfect."

Joey nodded and sighed. "It's not everything I wanted to say, but I'd be soaking for an hour if I did that. And even then, that might not be enough time."

"I didn't know Elliott, but from what I've heard from everyone, he would've loved it."

Joey chuckled. "He would've hated being so far in the limelight. Which makes me wonder about his relationship with Denny. How much was Denny wanting to keep it quiet, and how much was Ell wanting to stay far away from the spotlight?"

"It's nice to know that he'd found love, though," Ethan said. "Even if it would've been a tricky road ahead."

Joey smiled. "If he'd told me about his relationship, I don't think I would've believed him."

"Why not?"

Joey picked up his fork. "It's the kind of thing he would've joked about. He once said to me that if he ever said he was becoming an actor, I would know it was code for something's wrong." Joey swallowed hard, tears shimmering. "Why didn't he say anything?"

Ethan's heart ached. "I don't know. He possibly kept quiet about Grey and Robert to protect you, but something..." He didn't want to finish his sentence.

"Something...?" Joey prompted.

Ethan sighed. "Something pushed him to the edge that night. An edge he couldn't step back from. If I'm honest with you, Joey, I don't think we want to know what it was."

"Why?" Joey frowned. "I want to know why he chose to take his own life instead of talking to me about it."

"It can't be a pleasant reason. Would Elliott really want you to know why?"

"It doesn't matter. I want to know."

Ethan nodded, though he believed when Joey found out, he would want to take his words back. Although Ethan didn't know what had happened, he had a host of ideas about what it could be, and none of them were nice.

They descended into silence while they ate, Ethan swallowing the delicious food as if it were Lego bricks. He wouldn't take back what he'd said, and Joey would insist on finding out. Neither of them would be happy with the answer because it wouldn't change the fact that Elliott was no longer with them.

"When are you thinking of giving your statement?" he asked.

Joey exhaled. "I want Ani to read it through as well, and then if she agrees it's okay, I'll set something up for tomorrow afternoon or the next day."

"Sounds good."

Joey reached for his hand. "I'm sorry."

"For what? Knowing what you want?" Ethan smiled. "That's a good thing. I'm just worried, that's all. Once you know, there's no un-knowing, if you get my drift."

Joey didn't say anything for a minute, his dinner left to cool. "I feel left out, Ethan. I thought Ell and I told each other everything. I didn't think we had any secrets from each other. Since he died, I feel like he's left me out of the important parts of his life. As if he didn't want me there sharing the happiness or the burden with him. I know it's stupid, but I can't help but feel like he didn't trust me."

Ethan leaned forward, making eye contact with him. "Elliott loved you, Joey. He wouldn't have wanted you to miss out on anything. He would've told you about Denny if he thought there was anything more to the relationship. Denny loved him, but maybe Elliott wasn't there yet. If he loved Denny, he would've told you. I know that much."

Joey's eyes cleared a little, but he could tell he wasn't entirely convinced. It would take time for him to forgive himself and to forgive Elliott. Because no matter what anyone said, there was guilt on both sides of the coin. Unnecessary guilt, but guilt all the same.

An idea crossed his mind. "I want you to tattoo me."

Joey's head jerked up, and he stared at him. "Really?"

Ethan nodded, more determined with every minute. "Yes."

"What do you want and where?" Joey leaned forward.

"That's the thing. I want it on my back, but I want you to choose the design for me."

"You trust me with that? Usually, designs are meaningful in some way to the person getting it."

Ethan took his hand. "But it will be. Because you chose something for me. Something you believed was right for me. That makes it meaningful."

Joey's eyes glistened again. "I'd love to. When?"

"Soon."

Joey stared at him, shaking his head. "You're amazing. I don't know how I ever got so lucky for you to choose me in that bar."

Ethan smiled. "I had no choice. I was just about to leave when I saw you. Pure chance. And approaching you was the best decision of my life."

"Even with all this hassle?"

"Even with." Ethan stood and leaned over, cupping Joey's cheek. "I love you. I can't think of a single thing in this life or the next that could change that."

"I don't deserve you."

"Yes, you do. And I deserve you. We deserve each other because we're perfect for each other. Nothing can stop us from happening. Nothing." Ethan kissed him, pouring every ounce of love into that kiss, hoping to heal some of the cracks in his armour and replenish his battered soul. He refused to give up Joey without a fight. And anyone who was coming for them? Well, they better watch out. He had a snarky tongue, and he knew how to use it.

22

JOEY

J oey had been no use to anyone for the rest of the previous day. After getting the confirmation that Grey had been playing them all this time, he felt sick to his stomach about tattooing Elliott's name on his back. He couldn't think of a reason for Grey wanting it. Some sort of trophy, maybe?

He barely slept, tossing and turning and disturbing Ethan enough times that he got out of bed and sat on the sofa with the remote, flicking through the options. He chose nothing. Just kept scrolling through while his mind did a similar thing with images of Elliott, Grey, Ethan, and basically everyone he cared for. His mind was awash with information he couldn't sort through.

When Ethan roused at six o'clock that morning, he'd settled on the sofa beside him and held him. No words were spoken until Ethan asked him what he wanted for breakfast around an hour later.

Now, he was pacing his studio after receiving a call from the police asking to speak to him. Ethan sat in the tattoo chair.

A knock sounded, and Ethan opened the door, inviting Detectives Harmon and Keith inside.

"Thank you for agreeing to see us. This isn't something we wanted to discuss over the phone," Harmon said. "We arrested Grey Kennedy yesterday."

Joey stared at them. "For getting David involved?"

Harmon shared a look with Keith, and Keith took over. "Yes, but also for other things. Drug supplying, assault and..." He sighed. "Grievous bodily harm."

Joey frowned. "I can understand the drugs if he's involved with his father, but GBH? On who?"

"Elliott."

Joey's legs trembled and didn't want to hold him up again, and Ethan noticed, helping him to a chair. "I don't..." He paused, memories resurfacing. "We'd noticed bruises on him a few months ago. Grey told us Robert's men gave him a warning."

"It wasn't Robert's *men*. It was his right-hand man," Keith said.

Joey's stomach rolled. "And you said there were more bruises that were unaccounted for." Keith nodded. "What kind of bruises?"

Harmon shook his head. "You don't need to know the details—"

"What kind of bruises?" he said again, this time more forcefully.

Harmon sighed, looking down at the floor before meeting his gaze again. "Finger marks in various places on his body. Straight lines on his back."

Joey's vision clouded. "Finger marks where?" Harmon shook his head, and Joey stood. "FINGER MARKS WHERE?"

Ethan held him back, but Joey shrugged him off, moving closer to the detectives. He stared at them both, waiting for an answer. Keith crossed his arms.

"Jaw, neck, forearms, thighs, ankles and...buttocks," Keith finished.

Joey closed his eyes, knowing exactly what had been done to Elliott for him to drink enough to be trashed that night. To want to leave earlier than normal.

To not want to stay in the world any longer.

Joey swallowed repeatedly as he wandered the room. Heat built inside him, and he raked his fingers through his hair, scratching at his scalp. His throat closed as he tried to keep it all inside.

"What about Robert?" Ethan asked.

"We have no evidence of him taking part or being part of it," Harmon said.

"As usual," Keith added. "He keeps his hands clean, sending others to do his work, no doubt. We've had nothing we can actually pin on him."

"Please tell me you have enough evidence to convict and jail Grey?" Joey said, his voice straining through his wrecked throat.

"We do."

"Can I just ask one thing?" Ethan said, and Joey glanced at him. "What made you take another look at Elliott's death? I know you said the bruising had come to light. Why wasn't that noticed earlier?"

Harmon cleared his throat. "We were given a tip-off from an anonymous source that the autopsy report wasn't...complete." He fidgeted and sighed. "Basically, the coroner was remiss in detailing *everything* that he should've. When we found out, he provided the full report but refused to say who had paid him. It was only when Detective Hines connected the dots between David Thurl and Grey Kennedy that we took another look at the coroner, and he admitted it was Grey who had paid him. Another thing we're adding to his charges."

Joey shook his head, the fight gone out of him, leaving tiredness in its place. "Will you please see if Grey will answer one question for me?"

Keith narrowed his eyes. "We'll consider it."

Joey exhaled. "Ask him why he wanted Elliott's name on his back."

Keith nodded. "We'll see what we can do."

Joey barely noticed when they left, standing at the window and staring into the street but seeing nothing. He didn't jump when Ethan slid his arms around him.

"It's a stupid question, but how are you doing?"

Joey swallowed. "I feel like he's been taken from me all over again. But at least this time, I have someone else to blame rather than myself."

"It was never your fault. Elliott wouldn't have wanted you to know what happened to him. He was protecting you."

Joey leaned his forehead against the cool pane. "Maybe. But not knowing was worse than knowing what he went through. I want to kill Grey—with my bare hands—but I have a feeling he'll get his comeuppance. I doubt Daddy dearest will take too kindly to being arrested. After all, Robert has evaded the police for years. Grey obviously doesn't come with the same strength of genes." As he spoke, his body released the tension, and he twisted in Ethan's arms to face him. "Thank you for being here."

Ethan smiled, though it didn't sparkle in his eyes like it usually did. "I'll always be here."

"I'm going to call Polly and ask her to get in touch with her contacts about my statement."

Ethan nodded. "I'll be right beside you."

Five hours later, he stood outside his shop, Ethan by his side, and faced the gathered reporters. He'd changed some bits of the speech once they'd returned to the apartment, his newfound knowledge needing to be mentioned in passing, even if he couldn't directly.

"Thank you for being here." He glanced at everyone and exhaled. "Elliott Kennedy was my best friend. Some of you have been asking why I haven't spoken out before now, and my answer is this. My grief is for me and Elliott alone. I do not have to share it with anyone if I don't want to. That being said, I would now like to offer you these words.

"Elliott was an amazing person and friend. Anyone would have been grateful to know him. He was passionate about so many things in this world. So many charities he wished he could help. So many causes he tried to assist. But he was mainly passionate about his family and friends. They meant the world to him." Ethan's hand rested on his back, knowing what was coming.

"Family is a big word. It doesn't have to encompass just blood relatives. My best friend was part of *my* family. But you don't have to include relatives at all. I know Elliott had at least one person he would've now wished were not included in his family legacy." Those words caused a rumble through the crowd, but he ignored it.

"Elliott's bright light was taken from us far too soon. It's not something I will 'get over' quickly. It will stay with me—*Elliott* will stay with me until my last breath. As he will with those he meant a lot to.

"Please give us this time to grieve properly because burying someone does not end the grieving period. If anything, it restarts it back at ground zero. Along with random memories that crop up at inopportune moments." He swallowed, trying to push down some such memories so he could get through the rest of his words.

"Depression and suicidal thoughts are not something to trivialise. They matter a lot. We need more light shed on such subjects. More help for those who need it. More support for those suffering. It's a dark world, and people need to realise it's not as easy as just 'thinking happy thoughts.'

"Elliott Kennedy was a great person, and our loss is profound. I know I can continue living my life without my best friend beside me because he's here, in my heart, every day. I don't want to, but I will.

"Thank you for your time."

The crowd burst into questions, flashes of light and noise, but Joey turned and went back inside the shop, Ethan at his back. They closed and locked the door, the blinds having already been shut, and Joey settled into a chair. Ethan crouched in front of him.

"How are you holding up?"

Joey exhaled. "I'm okay, but I'm sure I'm in for hell when John and Melinda hear it." He shook his head. "They deserve everything they get. Playing with people's lives like they meant nothing. I would've backed them up with anything before we found out they knew about it all and did nothing."

After he'd recovered from the police's visit, he'd called Elliott's parents and told them the news. They hadn't seemed shocked, and when Joey had pressed further, they'd admitted to knowing Robert and Grey were targeting Elliott. At that moment, he had cut them free. He would never forgive them for abandoning their son.

"I'm sure the police will have words with them at some point if they haven't already," Ani said.

He'd wished his tattoo brothers had been there, too, but the needs of the shop came first. Elliott had been the first one to drum that into his head.

"We need to visit Italy," Ethan said suddenly.

Joey frowned at him as Ethan rose and rounded the counter. "Why?"

"Two reasons," he said, nudging Ani out of the way of the computer. "One, you need to tattoo Ginevra—she called for an appointment earlier. And two, you need to show me the sights if we're going to retire there." Ethan's mouth curved. "I better polish up my Italian."

"You speak Italian?" Ani asked him.

Ethan chuckled. "Not a chance. I'm really bad with languages." Ani laughed. "There we go. I've booked Ginevra in for Monday afternoon. That means," he wandered towards Joey, "we have to pack and book flights so we can spend Sunday evening lazing in a hotel." He frowned and glanced back at Ani. "Dallas will be back by then, won't he?"

Ani nodded, a smile playing on her lips. "He will."

Ethan smiled at Joey again. "See. We're going to Italy."

Joey found his smile. "So I've heard." He grabbed Ethan's hips, dragging him between his spread legs and staring up at him. "I'll take you anywhere you want to go."

Ethan leaned down and kissed him, and just when Joey suggested taking it upstairs, he pulled back. "I know."

"Are you sure you want to do this?" Ethan asked him.

Joey blew out a breath as the taxi pulled up to the curb. "Not really. But I want answers."

They climbed out of the car, and Joey glanced up at the barbed wire along the top of the fences surrounding the prison they were entering. He turned to the driver.

"You'll wait here until we return?"

"Yes, sir. I will be here."

"Thanks." He closed the door and exhaled again before taking Ethan's hand. "Please keep reminding me he's only doing this to annoy me."

Ethan nodded. "I will."

Detective Harmon had called Joey that morning to tell him that Grey refused to answer Joey's question unless they were face to face. Initially, Joey had thought to say no, but he really did want to know. So, Harmon had arranged for them to make a short visit to Grey, who had been remanded into custody until his court date. The courts had decided he was too much of a flight risk, amongst other things, like potentially interfering with witnesses to his case. Joey didn't blame them for not trusting him. He wished he hadn't in the beginning.

They went through security, handing over everything they had on them before being allowed into a room with several chairs facing a wall with windows. Harmon had told them they would not be allowed to be in the same room as Grey, as he was unpredictable. Joey stared at the window as Grey sat in the chair opposite it. Joey's anger pushed to the surface with Grey's smirk.

Grey cupped his hands around his ear and waved them forward, his smile never wavering. Why had Joey not seen the maniacal look in his eyes before?

He took the seat, Ethan standing behind him with his hand on his shoulders.

"I hear you have a question for me," Grey said. "Go ahead. Don't be shy."

Joey bit his lip, trying to contain an outburst that wouldn't help anyone. He swallowed it down. "Why did you want Elliott's name on your back?"

"That wasn't too hard now, was it?" Grey chuckled. "You gave me the idea for it, actually." He crossed his arms.

When he said nothing further, Joey gritted his jaw and played the game. "What idea was that?"

"A list of my conquests."

Joey frowned. "Conquests? How did you get that from me?"

"I heard you spouting off several times about the people who could've been involved with Elliott's death. It made me realise I could have a list of all those who I've...dealt with. Kind of like a tally."

Joey clenched his fists, and Ethan's hand tightened. "Why get me to do it?"

Grey laughed, a full belly of humour that echoed through the grate. "I wanted to see how far I could push you." He leaned forward and lowered his voice. "I was sure you were on to me.

So sure. But when you agreed to tattoo me, I second-guessed myself. Maybe you weren't so clever after all." He grinned. "It's the best feeling in the world." Joey couldn't say anything, but Grey was on a roll and didn't need any prompting. "Having my brother's name tattooed on me by his best friend. My brother—the man I helped destroy. And the first of many conquests I plan to claim."

Joey closed his eyes and battled with the heat rolling through him in waves. "Are you not planning on leaving this place, then?"

Grey's confidence faltered. "What do you mean?"

"If you plan to claim all these 'conquests,' as you put it, surely, you're advertising what you've done. If the police get wind of it…" Joey didn't finish. He didn't need to.

Grey shook his head. "No one will know."

Joey chuckled and shook his head. "How will they not know?"

"They're just names. Could be anyone."

"What did you want with Elliott?" Ethan asked.

Grey glared at Ethan. "Dad wanted him in the business, but when we realised he wouldn't be turned, we needed him gone. He knew too much."

Joey stood, finished with the guy once and for all. "Good luck then. I'm sure the police will love to wait and see who you 'claim' so they can charge you for it." He gripped Ethan's hand and walked away, stopping when Grey said his name.

"Elliott looked—"

Ethan shoved him through the door before he could hear what Grey was going to say, and as much as he wanted to hear it, he also didn't.

"Sorry. I had a feeling I knew what he was going to say, and it would've riled you up on purpose."

Joey hugged Ethan, taking strength from him to replenish his own. "Thank you. I probably would've listened and ended up in prison myself."

"Yeah, we don't need that." Ethan kissed him and led him back to security. "Let's go home. We need to pack."

Joey chuckled. "Yes, we do."

Despite wanting to know every titbit of information Grey could give about Elliott, just to shed some light on the parts of his best friend he hadn't known, he couldn't trust what the man said. But he could trust one person. Denny. After they visited Italy, he planned to sit down with the man and fill some gaps in his knowledge, and maybe he could share some things with Denny, too. Something that might ease the pain of Elliot's death. Nothing would ever take away the pain, but the memories would always be with him. And with Ethan at his side, he could weather even the most heartbreaking memories.

They settled into the back of the taxi, and Joey slid his arms around his boyfriend. He had plans for Italy. Plans Ethan didn't know about. He couldn't wait to see his face when they arrived.

23

ETHAN

The flight to Naples was late on Sunday afternoon, but it was only two and a half hours long. It took less time to fly to Italy than it did to drive from London to Whitby, which blew Ethan's mind.

They grabbed their bags from the carousel and headed towards the exit when Ethan noticed a sign with Joey's name on it. He nudged him.

"Is that for you?"

Joey glanced at it and grinned. "It is." He tugged Ethan over in the direction of the man wearing a black suit, white shirt and black hat. "This is us."

"Good evening, gentlemen. Signora Ginevra has sent a car for you to use throughout your stay in Italy." The man's English was tinted with an Italian accent, but perfect. "My name is Lorenzo. Whatever you need for your stay, please just ask."

"Thank you, Lorenzo. That means a lot."

"If you have everything you need, follow me," Lorenzo said.

Ethan just gaped at the exchange and moved when Joey guided him.

"Close your mouth, Ethan. You'll catch flies," Joey whispered.

Ethan backhanded his chest, and Joey laughed. "Shut up. I've never had a chauffeur before."

Joey slid his arm around Ethan's shoulders and kissed his temple. "You'll love this experience then."

And he did. There was champagne in the car, which they cracked open when Lorenzo took them through the streets to their destination. When the car stopped, Ethan frowned, not seeing the hotel he'd booked. Joey had kept him talking throughout the journey.

"Where are we? This isn't where I booked."

Joey grinned. "Where we're staying this week."

Ethan snapped his gaze to him. "Week?"

Joey nodded and smiled. "Come on. Let's go inside."

Lorenzo opened the doors for them, and Ethan said nothing while they took the bags into a large house. Ethan glanced around him at the open space. He could see for miles. It was stunning.

Arms came around him, and he smiled. "How did you manage to get this over on me?"

Joey chuckled. "I had help."

"Ani," they both said at once.

"It's beautiful. Thank you." He turned in Joey's arms and gripped his nape. "A week?" he asked. Joey nodded. "What about the shop?"

"Well... that's the other thing. Ani booked me a few more clients this week. Ginevra was more than happy to let people know I was here, so I thought it would be nice to extend our holiday. This place," he gestured to the house, "belongs to a tattoo artist friend of mine, Rocco. He's on holiday in Australia right now, but he let us use his house instead of a hotel. I even have free rein with his tattoo room and supplies."

Ethan chuckled at Joey's excitement. "That's why you didn't bring much with you."

Joey nodded. "No point when it's already here." He lowered his head. "I need to practise with his tools. How about we get your tattoo done?"

Ethan bit his lip. He wanted it done, but he was still nervous. "Yes."

Joey kissed him, exploring his mouth beneath the warmth of the sun, in full view of anyone who was passing, and Ethan couldn't care less. A week in Italy was just what they needed.

An hour later, Ethan entered Rocco's tattoo room. It was a lot bigger than Joey's, not that he was comparing.

"So, I've been thinking about the design, and this is what I've come up with." Joey placed a sheet of paper on the table, and Ethan stared down at it.

"That's the Claddagh symbol," he said.

Joey nodded. "Yes. With a few extra bits."

"Love, loyalty and friendship. It's perfect."

The heart was in the centre, with a crown resting on top of it and a pair of hands on either side. In the centre of the heart were two interlinked ovals, and arching over the design was an arch.

Joey pointed to the arch. "I'd been second-guessing this one. It's supposed to be the whale arch in Whitby, but I'm not sure if it's too much."

Ethan rested his hand on his mouth, not wanting to cry. "I love it," he murmured.

Joey hugged him. "I'm glad. Do you want anything changing?"

"No. It's perfect."

"Okay." Joey took Ethan's jaw in his tattooed hand and turned his face to him. Biting Ethan's lower lip, Joey said, "Now get undressed and straddle the chair."

Ethan's brain misfired, but not enough that he didn't frown and say, "Undressed?"

Joey tightened his hold. "Are you questioning me?"

And just like that, Ethan's blood ran hot. "No, Sir."

"Glad to hear it. Now, go."

Joey let go, and Ethan quickly undressed. He was a little uneasy being in an unfamiliar place, but Joey wouldn't let anything happen to him. He glanced over his shoulder when he heard the door lock, and Joey nodded once at him and then carried on preparing the tattoo equipment.

Naked, Ethan exhaled and climbed onto the chair, straddling it and facing towards the back. The leather was cold, to begin with, but quickly warmed up. The tattoo was going on his back, so Joey needed to be able to reach it. Ethan sat upright, waiting for more instructions. Despite wanting to, he didn't look around and see what Joey was doing, but he could hear every click, scrape and clink.

Joey wheeled a tray over beside him, and Ethan looked from the corner of his eye.

"Lean your chest against the chair," Joey said. Ethan scooted forward, his cock rubbing against the leather. "Good."

The chair rocked a bit, and Ethan couldn't stop himself from peering behind him. Joey had straddled it behind him. Made sense. It would be easier to tattoo from close up.

"Lift up a bit," Joey said, tapping Ethan's thighs.

He did and jumped when Joey's lubed fingers massaged his pucker.

"What...?" He inhaled when his fingers penetrated.

"I've fantasised about doing this to you, and I can't wait to see whether reality is as good."

Ethan licked his lips as heat bloomed through him. His dick pressed harder against the chair with Joey's ministrations, and it wouldn't be long until he messed it up with precome.

Joey took his time preparing him, and Ethan's thighs burnt with the strain of keeping himself up.

"That's it. Ready for more?"

"Yes, Sir." Although Ethan wasn't sure what more was. A plug? Nope.

Ethan gasped as Joey worked his cock inside. As huge as he was, Ethan felt it every single time Joey slid inside, and he wouldn't change it for the world. But as always, Joey took his time and helped Ethan stretch. When Joey was fully seated, Ethan breathed into the chair, adjusting as best he could. Joey stroked his hands up and down Ethan's spine, soothing him.

"That's it. I can feel you relaxing now."

Ethan wanted to move. He wanted to lift and lower until he brought them both to release, but it wasn't his call to make. Gritting his teeth, he fought past the need and stayed still.

"Well done, sweetheart. Now, stay still until I've done this tattoo, yeah?"

Ethan gasped, suddenly realising exactly what Joey had in mind. There was no way he'd be able to stay still while Joey tattooed him. No way at all.

"And this time, I give you permission to come whenever you need to—as long as you don't move. Warn me when you're close, though."

"Yes...Sir," Ethan panted.

Joey's legs bracketed his own, and the heat of his limbs and his cock warmed Ethan until sweat beaded on his skin, and that was before Joey had even started the design.

"Okay. All ready?" Ethan nodded. "Words."

"Yes, Sir." He trusted Joey with his life, and there was no way he would take the chance of messing up something as permanent as a tattoo, so he breathed out and rested his head against the chair, focusing on his breathing.

The buzz of the machine seemed extra loud in the otherwise silent room. He braced himself for the pain, and when it came, he exhaled. It wasn't as bad as he'd expected. Joey chuckled behind him, the vibration strumming Ethan's ass.

As Joey continued, tattooing, wiping, tattooing, wiping, Ethan got lost in the rhythm. His cock pulsed with every prick of the needle. His ass clenched with every movement Joey made. Then, at one point, fire licked down his spine when Joey hit a specific area. It seemed he might have a bit of a pain kink.

"Doing okay?"

"Yes, Sir."

The gun stopped, and Ethan's ears rang. Joey moved again, sending sparks through Ethan's groin and then reached around him to offer a drink. He held it for him while Ethan gripped the chair, and he drank deeply. Joey wiped the sweat from his face, chest and stomach, the towel rubbing against the head of his shaft.

"Fuck," Ethan whispered.

Joey put the towel down and gripped his hips. "I can't begin to describe how fucking sexy this is. You wrapped around my cock like it was made to be a cock warmer." He thrust, pushing a little deeper. Ethan's eyelids fluttered. "Roll your hips for me."

Ethan moaned as he was granted movement. Rolling in a circle, Joey's cock dragged against his prostate, and he groaned louder. He circled faster, feeling his release approaching. Joey had said he could come whenever he wanted, so he reached for it, his dick rubbing against the chair, which was wet with his precome.

"Oh, please, Sir," Ethan panted. "Please."

Joey tightened his hold on Ethan's hips, stilling his movements. Ethan whined as his climax halted. Joey lifted him slightly and slammed him down, and Ethan's orgasm washed over him. He rolled his head against the chair and writhed, dragging it out as long as he could.

Joey's head rested against Ethan's nape. "Fuck, Ethan. You test my restraint. I thought this was over before we got to the best bit." He exhaled and thrust once, and Ethan could feel his cock was still hard. "You've got at least one more in you."

Ethan wasn't sure. He was exhausted already.

The gun started again. "Stay still again now."

The prick of the needle started, and Ethan found himself already reacting to the sound and the pain. Was this Joey's plan?

To get him addicted to tattoos? Because it was working if this was what he got every time.

Fire began to build in his groin again, and his eyes widened at another release arriving so quickly after the first.

"Sir!"

The gun lifted from his skin, and Ethan erupted again. Not as fierce, but still just as pleasurable. When he came back from his release, the gun was already against his skin again. Yet again, he could feel fire bubbling inside him. Surely, he couldn't go again.

"Not much more to do."

Ethan had completely lost track of time. They could've been there for ten minutes or ten hours, and he would be none the wiser. He called out another quick warning as an unexpected rolling orgasm took him by surprise. That one was almost painful. He couldn't have any more left to give.

Finally, the machine stopped, and Joey set it down. "All done. Now, stay still." Joey reached beneath Ethan's spread legs and lifted him under his thighs. The feel of Joey's jeans against his bare skin was erotic. Ethan braced himself on the chair as Joey lifted and lowered, lifted and lowered, and Ethan panted as he crescendoed once more. He cried out, a dry orgasm taking over him, and Joey slammed him down once more and bit Ethan's neck as his release took him.

When Joey's body relaxed, Ethan slumped against the chair. He wanted to say something, but he had no words. He was completely wiped out. As Joey moved, Ethan whimpered, his ass complaining of the usage, but it wasn't emptiness that Ethan wanted. It was Joey in his arms.

And sleep.

Joey chuckled, and Ethan mumbled. He'd no doubt said that out loud again without meaning to.

"You did, yes." Joey lifted him, and Ethan hissed. "Next time, I'll add extra lube during the session."

Next time? Ethan couldn't keep his eyes open.

"Come on, sweetheart. Let's go to bed. I'll clean up in here tomorrow."

Ethan hummed but made no move to get up. Joey chuckled again and picked him up, carrying him from the room, if the cooler air was any sign. He rested his head against Joey's shoulder and allowed himself to float between sleep and awake. Cool fabric touched his skin, and he groaned, curling onto his side. From a distance, he felt something warm and wet wipe over his skin, but he fell asleep before he could inquire.

Sunlight streaming directly onto his face woke him, and he scrunched his nose and turned his head away.

"Good morning," Joey said.

Ethan blinked one eye open, seeing Joey sitting on the bed in just trousers and nothing else. "What time is it?"

"Eight o'clock local time. You've been asleep for hours. I was starting to get worried, but you were still breathing." Joey shrugged.

"You should've woken me."

"I would've if you had still been asleep when I needed to leave."

Ethan rolled to his back, a slight twinge from his tattoo, and rubbed his face with his hands. "We've got three hours."

"We do, but I have something for you first. You need to have breakfast, and then you can have your surprise."

"Surprise?" Ethan dragged himself upright. "You're spoiling me."

Joey leaned over and kissed him, uncaring of Ethan's cotton mouth. "You deserve it." He stood. "Go have a shower and get dressed. Come down to the kitchen when you're ready."

"Yes, Sir."

Joey grinned, grabbed a T-shirt and left the room, closing the door behind him. Why, Ethan didn't know. It wasn't like anyone was there with them.

The shower was divine, Rocco having spared no expense at the amazing overhead spray that fell like torrential rain. Ethan's ass smarted a little, but he didn't mind one bit. He couldn't remember a single time he'd managed to come three—or was it four times, one after the other? He'd never even realised it was possible. He dried himself, dressed in khaki shorts and a T-shirt and headed down the stairs to the kitchen. When he entered, he froze.

"Aren't you going to come and say hi?" Christi said from her perch at the breakfast bar.

"He needs coffee," Kole said from beside her.

Joey wandered over and handed him a mug, sliding his arm around his shoulders. "Surprise."

Ethan glanced at him and almost burst into tears. He put the mug down, ignored his best friends and threw his arms around Joey's neck, joining their lips in a kiss that would've heated the coldest of loins.

"Bloody hell. We gave you yesterday. Don't make us give you another day, too," Christi said. "We've come to explore, not watch you two snog all day."

Ethan smiled, breaking the kiss. "Thank you."

Joey grinned. "I thought it would be a nice break for them, and you would have someone to keep you company while I worked. It was the only flaw in Ani's plan of booking me more clients this week."

"You're bloody amazing, Joey Reynolds."

"I have my moments." Joey pecked his lips. "Now, drink your coffee. Someone is wanting to see where the shops are."

Ethan groaned. "I hope you've cut up your credit cards, Christi. I don't even want to hazard a guess at how much you would likely spend here."

"Hey! I can budget." Ethan raised his eyebrows at her as he drank. "Okay, I can *try* to budget."

Ethan chuckled and glanced at Kole. "We might just have to save her from herself."

Kole nodded solemnly. "We might."

Ethan turned to Joey when he handed him a plate of scrambled eggs. "Is Ani or anyone joining us this week?"

Joey shrugged. "It depends on their schedules. We don't usually leave the shop unattended and closed, but I'm happy to make an exception. It might be too short notice, though. We can arrange another holiday. Make it a bit further away, and I'll make sure everyone can make it if they can't this week."

"Sounds like a plan."

"Ooh!" Christi said. "Let me see your tattoo."

Ethan glanced at Joey, whose cheeks reddened. "I was excited and might've broken the news."

Ethan chuckled and put his plate down, sliding his T-shirt off and turning around.

"Oh, I love that," Kole said.

Joey explained the different parts of it, and when he got to the ovals in the middle, he said, "And these are the rings we will eventually exchange."

Ethan gasped and stared at him. "You never told me that!"

Joey bit his lip. "I didn't think you'd mind. Was I wrong?"

Ethan dropped his T-shirt to the floor and jumped up Joey's body, wrapping his legs around him and trusting that he'd catch him.

"I don't mind at all," he whispered. "I'd gladly be your husband...when you ask me."

Joey grinned and kissed him. "I'll keep that in mind."

"Can you have your wedding in Italy? It'll give us an excuse to come back," Christi said.

Ethan smiled and kissed Joey again. He didn't care where they got married as long as they did. It was too soon—far too soon—but he knew. He knew with no uncertainty that Joey was the one for him.

"Don't worry. Joey will do anything for me. I'm adorable, remember?"

24

JOEY

Six months later

C onflicting and busy schedules had not allowed them to book a holiday until six months after his and Ethan's visit to Italy. It had taken another couple of weeks to decide where everyone wanted to go, but they'd eventually decided on Lanzarote. According to Dallas, it was the perfect blend of relaxation and fun. Joey didn't care where they went as long as they were all together.

After thinking about it, he'd realised it had been a while since the four of them had been together for any length of time. They were always off gallivanting somewhere for work. Maybe that had been his fault for pushing them too hard, but he was going to change that.

Their holiday coincided with another event they were going to celebrate while they were there—Elliott's birthday. It had been a tough road he'd walked, but with the support of everyone around him, he'd come out the other side of therapy with a new awareness of himself and what he was capable of.

"Good afternoon. The plane will begin its descent into Arrecife in the next few minutes. Please ensure your seatbelts are secured, and all belongings are stored in the compartments. Thank you for flying with British Airways."

Joey inhaled and glanced at Ethan. "Are you ready for two weeks of chaos?"

Ethan grinned. "Can't wait."

"You may regret that later."

"I think I've spent enough time with them over the months to know how they are. I'm not naïve."

Joey raised his eyebrows. "You ain't seen nothing yet, sweetheart. This isn't real life. This is a holiday. All bets are off."

Ethan didn't look like he believed him, and Joey kept his smile to himself. As he'd said, all bets were off on holiday. He couldn't wait to see what Dallas got up to. Finn would probably stay by the pool or the beach for most of the time, and Beck... Well, he would probably find as many hookups as he could while he was there. It was something he didn't indulge in often when they were home, mainly because he wanted to find his person. His version of Ethan. But when he took a break, he went wild. Joey wondered what Kole would think about them all. Ever since his attack, he'd been more reserved around men in general, but maybe they could persuade him to take a chance on someone while they were here.

Ani, Christi and Di were planning to stay away from the guys and find their own fun. Joey didn't blame them. He planned to split his time between Ethan and his friends. After all, what was the point of them all going on holiday together if they never saw each other? He'd already told them that dinner together every night was mandatory.

By the time they'd worked their way through the airport, grabbed their bags and found the cars they'd rented, it was getting late.

"Right," Joey said when everyone had piled out of the car onto the driveway of the villa they had rented for their stay. "Get cleaned up and be back in this spot in an hour. Our first meal here is being spent at Amura!"

Everyone cheered, although he was sure they didn't care as long as they were fed. Their friends disappeared, and Joey pulled Ethan into his arms.

"You spoil them," Ethan said into his chest.

"They deserve it. We've all been through so much lately. It's my way of thanking them."

Ethan chuckled, pulling back to peer at him. "Paying for us all to come here was more than enough, I think."

Joey shrugged. He didn't see it as a waste of money. He saw it as a necessity, and he didn't mind footing the bill. He had enough money to last him a couple of lifetimes, so why not use it on his friends?

They entered the villa and got sidetracked several times by things they saw along the way to their suite.

"I don't know how I'm going to be able to leave here when the time is over."

Joey slid his arms around Ethan's waist and stared over his shoulder at the ocean view. "You'd like a villa to live in all the time?"

Ethan cocked his head. "Hmm. No, I probably wouldn't. I wouldn't want to take it for granted by being around it all the time."

"I doubt you would, but I understand what you're saying."

Ethan twisted in his arms to face him. "I'm happy in our apartment above the shop."

Joey dropped his head, joining their lips, and what started as a gentle kiss built to an inferno. Just like it always did when they kissed. Joey pulled back and rested their foreheads together.

"Let's take a shower to clean off the travelling grime."

Ethan smirked. "We're going to be late, aren't we?"

"Probably."

They were. The rest of them were waiting in the extensive lounge area with drinks and a resounding cheer when they entered.

Joey gave them the finger and tugged Ethan closer. "You'd be the same if you had what I do." He smacked a kiss on Ethan's cheek. "Come on then. Dinner awaits."

Joey had arranged for them to be driven to the restaurant so they could drink if they wanted to and not have to worry about having a designated driver between them. Amura was a sight to behold. A beachfront restaurant that served the freshest food straight from the ocean. The food was delicious, the drinks were divine, and the company was perfect.

But Joey had a plan, and only one other person knew about it. He met Ani's gaze and nodded slightly, and she smiled and excused herself to the bathroom. She wasn't going to the bathroom at all, but she was being his errand person. Five minutes later, she was back, settling into her seat again. She nodded back at him, and Joey's heart raced. He tried not to let his nerves show because he didn't want to ruin the surprise.

Half an hour later, when he was about to jump out of his skin, a special dish was delivered to the table and set in front of Ethan. The server lifted the lid and revealed an oyster shell.

"What's that?" Kole asked.

Ethan peered at it. "It's an oyster shell." He glanced at Joey. "Isn't it?"

Joey nodded, licked his lips and pushed his chair away. Taking a deep breath, he dropped to one knee beside Ethan, who covered his mouth with his hand.

"I wanted this to be special, and I remember the time you said that you would wait for me to ask. Well, I'm asking now. Ethan, will you marry me?" He had so much more he wanted to say, but the question was so much more important than him waffling on.

Ethan nodded, tears overflowing. "Yes! Of course, I will."

Cheers and clapping sounded all around.

Joey gestured to the oyster. "Open it."

Ethan wiped his eyes with his hands and opened the shell, revealing a gold band that was woven into a Celtic knot pattern. Over the past few months, they'd both figured out they loved those designs, and Joey had been drawing more and more for his wall. Ethan had already added another tattoo to his shoulder, a design Joey had created just for him again. Having a blank canvas to work on was addicting for Joey. He was sure he could find many new designs to fill his skin with.

Joey slipped the ring onto Ethan's finger and cupped his jaw. "I love you."

Ethan kissed him, tasting of salty tears. "I love you. Forever and always."

"Jeez. I'll never be able to top that," Beck said, rolling his eyes. "Couldn't you have made the bar a little lower?"

Joey chuckled and took his seat again, sliding his arm around Ethan's shoulder. "Only the best for Ethan. I'm sure when your time comes, you'll figure out the best thing for you both."

"Well, I was going to ask for dessert, but that was so sweet, I don't think I need any more," Christi said with a grin.

Ethan threw a napkin across the table at her. "Desserts are happening whether you eat it or not."

When they'd finished, Dallas said, "Who wants to visit the nightclub with me?"

Most of them raised their hands; the others groaned but didn't decline, so Joey paid the bill, and they headed down the street. Trust Dallas to have researched the best clubs on the island. Joey didn't mind because his plan was to find a dark corner for him and Ethan and drive him insane without doing anything they shouldn't.

While the music wasn't to his tastes, the vibe within the club was pumping. It reminded him of some of the events he'd been to for premieres. Well, it reminded him of the after-parties. That thought took him back to memories of Elliott. Thoughts of him didn't cause tearing pain any longer, but it still hurt that his best friend wasn't there to celebrate with him. But Elliott was at peace now, and nothing could hurt him anymore. That was the one solace he'd found within the memories.

Beck bought a round of drinks for everyone, and they found a couple of booths near each other to use as a base. Dallas disappeared as soon as he put down his drink, and Joey didn't expect to see him until it was time to go back to the villa. Finn settled into the far corner of the booth and pulled out his phone. Ani, Christi and Di had become fast friends over the past few months, and they headed off to the dance floor. Beck slid into the booth next to Kole and said something that made Kole laugh. Joey rested back, turning sideways so he could pull Ethan between his legs and have his back against Joey's chest. Ethan snuggled into him, and Joey exhaled. As they watched the goings-on and joined in with the conversations around them, he played with Ethan's ring, loving how it felt on him. He wasn't averse to wearing one himself, but he didn't want to presume that Ethan didn't want to choose his own design for him. If not, Joey would just get identical to Ethan's. He already had ideas for their wedding bands, but he would get Ethan's input before then. He didn't want a long engagement, but he'd be happy with whatever Ethan chose.

Joey palmed Ethan's cock with his free hand, and he felt him inhale.

"Don't make me come in here," Ethan said.

Joey tightened his grip. "Sorry?"

Ethan peered at him from the corner of his eye. "Whatever you wish, Sir."

"That's more like it."

He had no plans to make Ethan come in a club full of people, any of whom could be watching them at any time, but Ethan didn't have to know that. It would keep him on edge enough to explode when they got back.

"Hey, Joey. Look at this," Beck said, passing over a napkin.

Joey took it and glanced at it before taking a closer look, turning it more to the light. "What's this?" The drawing was an intricate tribal-style design but in different-sized circles, making a mandala effect.

"Kole just drew it. We were talking, and he was just doodling on the napkin, and this is what he created."

It was amazing. He stared at Kole. "I never knew you were an artist."

Kole shook his head. "I'm not. I like drawing, but I've never done anything with it."

"You should. This is amazing." Kole ducked his head. "I'm being serious. Would you consider doing some designs for the shop? We'll pay you for them."

Kole waved his hands out in front of him. "You don't have to pay. I'm happy to do it. Just tell me what you want, and I'll see what I can do."

"You do whatever you feel like doing and bring them in. I can guarantee, if they're as good as this one, we'll take them off your hands," Beck said.

Ethan leaned forward. "This is great, Kole. Why have you never told me?"

Kole shrugged. "It's not something I planned to do anything with. It's not even that good. You're biased."

Ethan chuckled. "No, I'm not. These guys are artists. Even if you don't believe me, believe the people who make a living from art."

Joey could see Kole didn't believe any of them, but he'd work on him. If nothing else, it would give Kole a second income in addition to his ghost tours. Maybe it might even entice him to move a little closer to Ethan because Ethan had mentioned that Kole had dropped a few hints about heading south to live. Whether it happened or not was another thing.

Elliott would've had no problem convincing Kole. He had been great at getting people to see his way of thinking and explaining why he thought it would work to their advantage. It was something even Denny had mentioned when they'd spoken once. Denny had told him that Elliott had convinced him to invest in something, and he'd not been wrong. To this day, the investment continued strong. Denny, on the other hand, hadn't been doing as well. His manager had dropped him, and his band were in talks to see if they could salvage their business or if they were letting Denny go and going it alone. It sucked for him, but Denny didn't care either way. He was already making a name for himself as a solo artist, so he didn't need them and their negativity.

Ethan pushed back into his arms, and Joey held tighter. "Everything feels so right," he said.

Joey knew what he meant. "It's because it is. Everything is as it should be. At least for now."

"For now?"

Joey nodded towards their friends. "They need to find their Ethan. Only then will I be settled."

"Agreed. We'll have to have a think and see if we can't help jig it along."

Joey chuckled. "Jig it along?"

Ethan snorted. "It just came out. No idea where it came from."

Joey nuzzled his neck. "I know exactly what I'm doing to you tonight."

"What's that?"

"Well, it involves ties and a cock cage."

Ethan shivered. "Sounds intriguing."

He thought it would, but that wasn't all he'd decided to use. It was a good job that they had the suites at the furthest edge of the property. Everyone would still be able to hear them, he was sure, but it would make Ethan feel better if he believed they couldn't.

Life was great.

Life wasn't permanent like ink was.

But someone could tell a whole host of stories from their lives through their ink.

Hence, he'd called his shop Life in Ink.

Even when life threw a scar or two, the stories remained. The memories remained. Forevermore.

Read on for a teaser of Beck, book 2.

Would you like to read my books before anyone else? You can sign up to Steamy Delights, a membership subscription service on Ream, and gain early access to chapters from my work-in-progresses, exclusive bonus content and more. I have four tiers available: Contemporary, Kink & Daddy, Taboo & Dark and Club Royal Bonus: https://elouiseeast.com/ream

And for a taste of the free short story you get if you sign up to my newsletter...

Protecting Jason

J ason doesn't have the strength to fight his stepfather for a happy life, so, to stop the man from turning his fists and words to his younger siblings, he takes the brunt of his anger himself. He vows to get those children away from him as soon as possible. Then, when there is one bruise too many for his best friend's eyes, they come up with a plan for a fake boyfriend for Jason—someone who's really a bodyguard.

Darius doesn't get asked to the royal family's domain often, but he doesn't say no when he is. Being asked to be a fake boyfriend is far from usual, but he's happy to do it if it means he gets to spend time—and protect—the man he can't stop staring at. When things don't quite go the way Jason hopes, Darius offers another option. One that might backfire. But with Darius at his side, Jason finds more strength than he ever thought possible.

And maybe, he might've found the one person who could give him his happily ever after.

This is an MM bodyguard romance that spans both the Club Royal and Guarding Royalty series.

Get this book FREE here: https://elouiseeast.com/newsletter

Beck Teaser

While Joey, Beck, Dallas and Finn finished up on their last clients, Ethan and Ani closed up their table, and Kole tidied away his designs. Whether they saw the light of day again was something he'd decide later.

"What was the final figure for today?" Joey asked Ani.

Ani shared a smile with Ethan. "Twenty-nine."

Dallas threw his hands in the air, Joey and Beck hugged, and Finn stood with a grin on his face, the most expressive Kole had ever seen him outside of the shop.

"We're over halfway, baby!" Joey said, lifting Ethan and spinning him around.

"Put me down, you big oaf!" Ethan said, laughing, belying his words by wrapping his legs around his boyfriend's waist.

Kole chuckled at their antics. Their need to break last year's record was cute. He hoped they hit the mark the next day. Kole might need to ice his hand that night if he was to draw for twelve hours the following day. He also needed some sleep. He stood.

"Congrats. I'm glad you're on track. I'm heading back to the hotel." He gestured over his shoulder. "Same time tomorrow?"

Joey held out his hand despite still holding onto Ethan. "You were amazing, man. I appreciate you helping us out so much."

"It's not a problem at all. I've had fun." He smiled. "I'll see you all in the morning."

Kole waved and headed out, torn between wanting to celebrate with them and wanting to crawl into bed and sleep for hours. As soon as the frigid January air hit his lungs, he could breathe a little easier. Why, though, he wasn't sure. It hadn't been stifling when he'd been working, but as soon as they'd stopped, the walls had closed in on him.

He wandered slowly down the street, lit only by streetlights, and the now-regular feeling of someone watching washed over him. He quickened his pace, his pulse pounding in his ears until he started a jog. Only a few steps away from the hotel, a hand grabbed his arm.

"Kole!"

Kole yanked his arm away, held his hands in front of him and backed into the wall.

"Kole?"

He blinked a few times, trying to understand what else the person said, but still only catching his name.

"Kole." Indistinguishable mutterings. "Kole. Beck."

The new piece of information slipped in, and his gaze darted over the face swimming in front of him. The dark hair, the beard, the full lips, the blue eyes staring at him with something Kole couldn't name in them.

"Kole. It's Beck. Breathe for me, okay? Just breathe."

His hearing cleared, and he sank into a crouch as his surroundings came into focus. Nausea swam around in his stomach like a tsunami, his head pounded, and his entire body shook.

"It's okay. I'm here, Kole. I'm here."

Kole glanced up at Beck through watery eyes and launched himself forward. Beck caught him with a grunt but tightened his hold around him.

"I'm so sorry I scared you. I'm so sorry. So sorry," Beck repeated, brushing his hand against his hair, soothing him.

Kole, being the coward that he was, hid his face in Beck's neck, tears streaming down his face. His legs wouldn't be able to hold him until the panic faded, so he didn't try. When would it be over? When would he get his life back? A one-night stand, someone he never thought he'd ever see again, had attacked him, unprovoked, while he was telling his ghost stories on one of his tours. Someone he hadn't thought about once they'd parted ways. Someone who would never be forgotten again.

How could one small thing have such a profound effect on the way he lived his life?

"I've got you. I'm so sorry," Beck continued to say.

Kole heard him whisper something else and other voices, but he couldn't get the energy to rise and run away from whoever it was. Beck had said he'd got him, and for once, Kole was going to hold someone to those words. He didn't plan on moving for a little while, despite how cold he was getting.

"It's okay. Take your time, Kole. I've got you."

If only he could lean on someone for more than a few moments. He needed the respite, but he didn't have a choice. He would not bother Ethan with his burden. He didn't know the artists well enough to ask for help. Christi was busy with Di and their new business venture. His family had told him to get over it by going to therapy. He had no one.

But for these few minutes, he had Beck, and he'd remember the feel of his arms around him, his strength, whenever he needed a reminder that one day, just maybe, he might be able to have that for himself.

Books by Elouise East

Life in Ink
Joey
Beck
Dallas
Finn

Guarding Royalty
Protecting his Past
Protecting his Heart
Protecting his Secrets
Protecting his Life

Club Royal
Royal Firsts
Rogue Royal
Secretive Royal
Grieving Royal
Disowned Royal
Trained Royal
Awakened Royal
Commanding Royal

Illuminate Matchmaking
Ignite

ELOUISE EAST

Blaze
Kindle
Scorch

Boys, Daddies, Snuggles & More
Need Him
Trust Him

Daddy
Love Me, Daddy
Soothe Me, Daddy
Spoil Me, Daddy
The Complete Daddy Series

Love in Flames
Fight Fire with Fire
Out of the Frying Pan
Smokescreen
Breathing Fire
Love in Flames Collection

Crush
Love Conquers
Instant Desire
Primary Seduction
Deep Down
A Crush for Christmas
Life Support
Covert Strength
Love Scene
Lawful Attraction
Crush Collection Volume 1
Crush Collection Volume 2

JOEY

Crush Collection Volume 3

Just A Little Crush
First Kiss
He's Behind You
A Special Love

Standalone
Treehouse Whispers
Star-Crossed
Protecting the Thief
Sizzling Chauffeur
A Home for Barney
Mattie

<u>Elouise R East (taboo)</u>
Dark & Divergent
Forbidden Temptation
Too Many Secrets: A Life of Secrets
Too Many Secrets: The Lake House
Secrets in his Eyes

Collide
When Fantasies Collide
When Dreams Collide
When Pleasures Collide
When Cravings Collide
When Hungers Collide

Dark
Defying Sanity
Stronger Together

About Elouise East

E louise East writes sweet and steamy connections in gay romance. She also touches on taboo stories under the name Elouise R East.

Books that tell the stories where friendship and family are the focal point - be it blood family or chosen - are very important to her. That's why she includes a variety of personalities, talents, ages, situations and abilities as she believes a story or character needs. She wants her characters to be real, to be relatable, to be free to have whatever views they tell her they have. And trust her, most of the time, she does not have *any* say in the matter!

Her characters come to life on the page for her as well as her readers. Their stories unfold in front of her as she writes, and she has very little input into how they want to be shown. Just like real life, the lives of her characters change with every choice, every interaction and every conversation. And she wouldn't have it any other way.

She writes books that are emotionally realistic, even if liberties are taken with other aspects of the stories. She doesn't know any other way to write. It comes from deep inside.

Who is she? A single parent to two children living in the UK. An avid reader who still tries to devour every book she can get her hands on. A student of learning about any subject that takes her fancy. An author of books she would read herself. And a romantic at heart who loves anything cheesy.

Who's joining her on her journey?

Stalk her here... ;-)
Website : https://elouiseeast.com
Newsletter : https://elouiseeast.com/newsletter
All links : https://elouiseeast.com/links